HOT ON HIS TRAIL

HOT ON HIS TRAIL

ZAVO

alyson books
NEW YORK

This trade paperback original is published by
ALYSON BOOKS
P.O. BOX 1253
OLD CHELSEA STATION
NEW YORK, NEW YORK 10113-1251

Distribution in the United Kingdom by
TURNAROUND PUBLISHER SERVICES LTD.
UNIT 3, OLYMPIA TRADING ESTATE
COBURG ROAD, WOOD GREEN
LONDON N22 6TZ ENGLAND

ISBN-13: 978-1-55583-975-8

BOOK DESIGN BY VICTOR MINGOVITS.

Thanks, Kiwi, for all your hard work.
And thanks, Doobie, for your unconditional support.
Both of you made this possible.

CHAPTER ONE

I'd been riding after Ben Masters for three weeks. When I left Abilene he already had a two-day head start on me. I'd lost his trail a few times when rain had washed it away or the tracks of animal, usually horses or cattle, had obliterated it. My persistence finally paid off when I caught up with Ben this morning, shortly after sunrise. Deadwood was the first town I'd come to after capturing him. I decided to stay the night, and head out refreshed first thing in the morning. Several of the townsfolk eyed me in sullen silence as I led my horses down the dusty street of the nondescript town. The late-afternoon sun penetrated my thin, cotton shirt, warming the skin underneath. I'd been in several small cow towns in my day, but Deadwood was by far the smallest. I was sure, however, that the townsfolk were staring at more than my dusty, dirty, trail-worn appearance. Their sidelong glances were most likely for the man, even dirtier than myself, slung face down across the saddle of my packhorse.

As I walked, I recalled the events of the morning. I was rounding a bend in the trail I'd been riding on since early yesterday, when I heard the unmistakable sound of a galloping horse approaching from the direction I was headed. I immediately rode off the trail, leading my packhorse, and sought concealment in a large stand of sagebrush. I quickly dismounted and placed a hand over the muzzle of each horse. Shortly thereafter a riderless horse sped wildly past me, disappearing down the trail. I'd never laid eyes on Ben's horse, but my gut feeling told me that this was it. I'd been in this godforsaken territory for more than a week now, and during that time I'd met no other riders, nor seen any telltale signs of any. If it was Ben's horse, he had somehow become separated from it. Maybe the horse had been spooked by some animal, like a coyote or a rattler, and had thrown Ben. Or perhaps there was another rider in the vicinity whose tracks I'd missed, one who had chanced upon Ben and inadvertently finished my job for me. I remounted the Black and moved back onto the trail. I rode cautiously, my eyes and ears alert for the slightest movement or the smallest sound.

I'd gone about a mile when my horse suddenly shied. I heard the telltale rattling and spotted a big snake in the trail a few feet in front of me. I slid my rifle slowly from its scabbard near my right foot as I tried to calm my shaking horse with my free hand. The rattler was in the dead center of the trail; there was no way around it. His forked tongue darted in and out of his mouth as he picked up my scent. At first I was reluctant to shoot him because the noise would alert anyone in the vicinity to my presence. The decision was made for me, though, because the big fella had risen up and was prepared to strike. I sighted in his head and squeezed off a shot a split second before the snake launched itself at my horse. He fell to the ground, inches from my horse's right front foot. I reined the Black sideways and leaned over in the saddle to make sure the rattler was dead. As I did so, a shot rang out, raising a plume of dust off the ground next to the rattler. A second shot immediately followed, landing close to the first one. I put heels to the Black and bolted off the trail straight into a stand of scrub, pulling the packhorse with me. The thorny, dried brush tore at my clothing and scratched my left cheek. I halted, dismounted, and looped the reins of both horses over a branch.

I crouched down, my heart beating wildly in my chest. I knew the shots had come from in front of me, but I was uncertain if I faced one or more assailants. I had no way of knowing, either, if the shooter was indeed Ben, or some other ornery outlaw who'd spotted the silver star on my shirt. A strong masculine voice suddenly called out to me.

"Good mornin', stranger. I was pretty sure someone was fol-lowin' me fer the past few weeks. Ya sure are persistent, an' I'm bettin' my last dollar you're the law."

I didn't reply, hoping the stranger would continue to talk, thereby helping me to pinpoint his location.

"I wouldn't be holed up right now, on foot, if'n that rattler hadn't spooked my horse. The good-fer-nothin' animal tossed me an' lit out. I didn' shoot the bastard though, because I wanted to save him fer you."

The man then began to rant, cursing his bad luck, me, my mother, and all my ancestors several generations back. It wasn't long before I had a good idea of where the stranger was hiding. But I still wasn't sure if it was Ben Masters. It took me more than an hour of maneuvering and hard climbing to circle around behind where I thought the man was. He squeezed off a few shots whenever I kicked a stone loose, or started a small slide, but luckily none of them found its mark. What with the echoes from the surrounding rocks, it was hard to tell exactly where any sounds originated. I crawled to the edge of a rock prom-ontory, and finally spotted the stranger. He was laying on his stomach on a ledge a few feet below me. His position gave him a perfect view of the trail I'd been riding on. I slowly cocked my Colt, hoping to take him by surprise. But he must have heard the click, for he whirled around quickly, firing off a shot as he did so. I felt the bullet whiz past my left ear. The stranger raised his hands when he found himself staring into the blue-gray muzzle of my Colt.

"Howdy. My name's Jake Slater. Would you by any chance be Ben Masters?"

I already knew the answer to my question, though, because this man fit the description the rangers in Abilene had given me of Ben. The man eyed me sullenly.

"An' if'n I am?"

I smiled as I held my gun on him, knowing I'd found my man.

"I'm a Texas Ranger, Masters, an' I'm takin' ya back to Abilene with me."

I marched Ben at gunpoint back to my horses. I mounted the Black but forced Ben to walk beside me when we headed out. I had tied his hands together, then looped the end of the rope around the pommel of the Black's saddle. Ben spewed a steady stream of curses and protestations of innocence as the miles fell away behind us. When spoken by the tall, handsome figure that Ben cut, those curse words, on more than one occasion, produced an unexpected twitching in my cock. We'd covered several miles when I was forced to join him on foot after the Black threw his right-front shoe. As morning turned into afternoon and the heat increased, along with the number of black flies that tormented us, Ben became even more irritable. Finally, having grown tired of listening to his ravings, I quickly stepped in front of him and brought my Colt up sharp and hard against the side of his head. Ben dropped in his tracks. I bent down, picked him up, and heaved his massive frame over the saddle of my packhorse. I unwound the rope from the Black's pommel and looped it around the pommel of the packhorse. I tied his feet together as well. The overpowering smell of Ben's sweat and manliness almost made me giddy. He didn't regain consciousness until we reached the outskirts of this tiny town. Then his curses started in anew, so I gagged him with a dirty bandana.

My mind quickly came back to the present, as I stumbled down the dusty main street leading the Black and the packhorse. I scanned the fronts of the wooden buildings that lined the street, looking for the law in this sleepy town. At the end of the street I finally spotted a silver star. It was painted on a white board hanging from a post in front of an unpainted, wooden building. I headed over to the dilapidated structure, tied the reins of both horses to the hitching rail, and climbed the rickety wooden steps. I crossed the boardwalk, opened the weathered door, and stepped inside. The heat in the office was the same as that outside. I closed the door softly behind me and paused to let my eyes adjust to the dim light. I took in the layout of the room in a single glance. To my immediate left stood a pot-bellied stove. Pots and pans covered its surface. To my right stood a scarred, wooden desk. WANTED fliers, empty whiskey bottles, tin plates, forks and knives, and the remains of numerous past meals littered the top of the desk. Fliers were also plastered on the wall to the left of it. A worn gun rack stood in the back corner, filled with Winchesters, shotguns, and assorted Colts. A large ring of keys hung on a wooden peg on the back wall.

Amidst the clutter on the desk rested a pair of legs. They were attached to one of the most disreputable looking men I'd ever seen. His large, ham-like hands were resting on his gunbelt. The backs of them were covered in thick brown hair. Remnants of his noon meal, and probably his breakfast as well, were scattered across the front of his worn, brown-leather vest and dark-blue homespun shirt. Pinned to the left breast of his vest was a silver star, dull and chipped. His faded black hat was pulled down over his face, hiding his eyes. Loud, deep snores reverberated from his huge frame.

I studied the man for several moments, then stepped to the desk and kicked one of its front legs. He came to with a start, swinging his legs off the desk as he did so. As he sat upright in his chair, I found myself staring into hostile, dark-brown eyes. Several days' worth of dark-brown stubble covered his cheeks, chin, and throat. I noted, though, that despite my initial judgment of his appearance the man was, indeed, quite handsome. I processed all this in the few seconds it took for his hand to automatically reach for the holstered pistol on his right hip. My own Colt appeared as if by magic in my hand, and the man quickly raised his hands in the air.

"I take it you're the law in this town?"

My voice was low and mean as I pointed the muzzle of my Colt at his forehead. The question was an obvious insult, for his silver star was clearly visible.

The man finally found his voice.

"Yes. I'm Sheriff Rawlins."

I held the gun on him for a few seconds more, then slowly lowered it.

"Ya can put down yer hands now, Sheriff. My name's Jake Slater. I'm a Texas Ranger."

I pointed to the silver star on my own left-front shirt pocket. The sheriff eyed it with suspicion.

"I guarantee ya, Sheriff Rawlins, it's the real thing."

His gaze shifted from the badge to my eyes. The open hostility was still evident in his eyes.

"I don't know how things are done where you're from, Ranger, but here 'bouts lawmen don't go 'round pointin' guns at one another."

"Beggin' yer pardon, Sheriff, but you were ready to draw on me. And with ya slumped over like that, sleepin', I wasn't sure who ya were."

The jibe was not lost on the sheriff.

"What can I do fer ya, Slater?"

"I've captured a desperado by the name of Ben Masters. He killed a Texas Ranger in Abilene three weeks ago. I've been trailin' him ever since. Right now he's tied to my packhorse out front. I'm takin' him back to Abilene fer hangin'. It's been a long, hard ride, an' this is the first town I've come across since I caught up with him early this mornin'. I'm goin' to be stayin' in town fer the night. I need to rest my horses, an' myself, before I start fer Abilene in the mornin'. I also need a bath, provisions, an' a new right-front shoe fer my horse. I'd like to lock Ben in one of yer cells fer the night."

Rawlins stared at me for several seconds, his face expressionless. Then he spoke, matter-of-factly.

"Ya passed the blacksmith on yer way here. It's in the livery stable. The dry goods store is next to it and the saloon's next to the dry goods store. You can rent a cheap room there, an' supper's thrown in fer free. I'll house yer pris'ner overnight, but this ain't no damn hotel here. My deputy's away fer a few days, leavin' only myself to look after things."

"No problem, Sheriff. I can see that ya definitely have yer hands full 'round here. Like I said, I'll be headin' out of town first thing in the mornin.'"

I glanced meaningfully at the empty whiskey bottles, turned and, without saying another word, walked out, slamming the door behind me. I was greeted with a fresh stream of curses from Ben. While I'd been visiting with the sheriff, he'd managed to loosen the bandana covering his mouth.

"Ya rotten son of a bitch. Ya dirty no 'count ranger. When I git my hands on ya I'm gonna cut yer balls off an' feed 'em to ya. Then I'm gonna . . ."

The rest of what Ben was going to do to me once he was loose was abruptly cut off as my fist crashed against his skull, sending him back into the darkness he'd recently arisen from. I untied his feet and unwound from the pommel the rope that looped around his hands. I let Ben fall to the ground, as if he was a sack of feed. I left his hands tied in case he got any fool notions in his head to try to strike me if he suddenly regained consciousness. I bent down, wrapped my arm around his legs, grabbed his right arm, swung him over my right shoulder, and carried him into the sheriff's office. This was no small feat, either. Ben stood well over 6 feet tall, and must've weighed close to 220 pounds.

Rawlins had not been idle while I was outside fetching Ben. A fresh bottle of whiskey stood uncorked on his desk. He didn't get up when I carried Ben in. Ignoring the sheriff completely, I grabbed the large ring of keys from the peg on the wall and carried Ben down a short hallway to the cells. There were two of them, each one as dark and dirty as the rest of the jail. In the first cell something huddled in the far corner. Upon closer inspection I could see it was a man. I opened the door of the second cell, the smell of unwashed bodies and rotting food making me gag. I deposited Ben on the dirty cot against the back wall.

He moaned and stirred slightly as I spread him full length on the cot. As I stood next to him, I realized that I'd never taken a really good look at Ben. If you washed away the trail dirt and grime, and after the cuts, scrapes, and bruises had healed, I wondered what that red hair and those green eyes would look like waking up next to me each morning. I felt the familiar stirring in my loins. I shook my head as if to clear my thoughts, closed the cell door, and locked it behind me.

I returned to the office, irritated, but not surprised, to find that Sheriff Rawlins was sound asleep again. I kicked the side of the desk as hard as I could, waking him for the second time that afternoon.

"I'm goin' to git me a good meal an' a nice hot bath. I'll be back later this evenin' to check on my pris'ner. An' fellow lawman or not, sheriff, if'n anythin' happens to him while he's locked in that cell, I'll break yer neck."

Rawlins glared at me but didn't say a word. As I turned and went out the door, I could feel his eyes boring into my back.

I stood outside the sheriff's office for a moment, taking in the layout of the town. The sheriff had said that I'd passed the dry goods store, saloon, and livery on the way to his office. I went down the steps and untied my horses' reins from the hitching post. Both horses were caked with mud and dotted with burdock from the long hours on Ben's trail. I led them down the dusty street to the blacksmith and livery. No one I passed spoke to me. As I neared the livery I could hear the clang of the blacksmith's anvil and smell the pungent odor of horse shit. The smell almost completely smothered the sweet scent of the hay. A nice-looking young man greeted me as I entered. He promptly informed me that he was the liveryman as well as the blacksmith's apprentice. He went on to say that the blacksmith was out at one of the local ranches, tending to some horses. He would be gone for a few days. I told the young man that the Black had thrown his right-front shoe, that both horses needed to be fed, watered, and groomed, and that I was leaving town first thing in the morning. The young man assured me they would be ready to travel.

I retrieved my saddlebags and Winchester from the pack-horse and left the livery stable. I stepped onto the boardwalk and headed for the dry goods store. A sign above the door identi-fied it as Smith's Mercantile. A sign farther down the boardwalk proclaimed the next building to be the Last Chance Saloon. I opened the door and stepped inside. The interior was stuffy and dim. My nostrils were immediately assailed by the odors of cof-fee, leather, gunpowder, and cigar smoke. No customers were in the store, and there was no proprietor behind the counter. I walked over and rang the worn silver bell for service. A nonde-script man stepped through a small doorway in the back wall and slowly approached the counter. He eyed me suspiciously, which I had begun to feel was normal in this town.

"Can I help ya," he asked, in a none-too-friendly tone.

I ignored his searching, weasel eyes and quickly ran through my list of purchases. They included a Bowie knife, coffee, flour, hardtack, extra shells for my Winchester and Colts, two cans of beans, a sack of sugar, a blanket, a bag of oats (as a special treat for the horses), and a packet of saddle grease (to protect my sad-dle and my skin from the sun's harsh rays). As an afterthought I added a package of cheroots, a packet of rolling tobacco with papers, and a half-dozen bottles of whiskey. It had been a long, hard ride in pursuit of Ben, and all my bad habits were suddenly rising to the surface. I paid for my purchases with two gold coins, which caused the proprietor's eyes to open wide. I distributed my purchases in my saddlebags, bid the storeowner a good day, which wasn't returned, and walked next door to the saloon.

I pushed through the batwing doors and stepped inside. The large, dimly lit room was overflowing with tables and chairs. A few dusty cowboys were sitting around one of these tables, nursing drinks and playing cards. A battered piano stood in the far corner, with no one playing it. The bar was to my immediate right, and ran the entire length of that wall. The cowboys eyed me intently as I walked to the bar; I ignored them. Leaning against the bar was a tall man dressed entirely in black, his back to me. I stood beside him and dropped my saddlebags on the floor at my feet. I leaned my Winchester against the front of the bar and ordered a whiskey. I could see the stranger eyeing the silver star on my shirt in the large mirror behind the bar. I turned toward him to give him a full view of my front. Emboldened by my move, he tipped his hat back and turned to face me. I found myself looking into the deepest blue eyes I'd ever seen. They scrutinized me from underneath thick, bushy eyebrows, as black as night. A thick moustache hid his upper lip; his bottom one was full and sensual. His cheeks, chin, and neck were covered with at least a week's worth of black stubble. He smiled as he watched me look him over. His teeth were large, even, and white. His hat, shirt, leather vest, denim pants, and pointed boots were all black, albeit a dusty, faded black. His hands were large, the backs of them covered in dense, black fur, and his fingers were long and thick. Several tufts of black hair poked above the top button of his cotton shirt. Two shiny Colts rested at each hip. The handles were inlaid with ivory.

"Afternoon, stranger. My name's Jake Slater."

I held out my hand. He studied it for a moment, spit a large wad of tobacco juice expertly into the spittoon at our feet, and clasped my hand in his own. His grip was strong and firm, his hand rough and callused. I briefly imagined what it would feel like to have that hand wrapped around my cock, or those fingers pinching my nipples.

"My name's Travis."

That brilliant smile lit up his face once more.

"Can I buy ya a whiskey, Travis?"

"That'd be nice, Jake."

I ordered two whiskeys from the barkeep. As he poured them I inquired about a room, a meal, and a hot bath.

"Rooms go fer two bits a night, paid in advance," he replied. "The first one on the right at the top of the stairs is unoccupied. The bath will run ya five cents. My son will bring the washtub to yer room an' fill it with water whenever you're ready. He'll also leave ya towels an' a bar of soap. The missus is fixin' supper in the kitchen right now. It ain't nothin' fancy, but it's free, an' it'll fill ya up. We also serve breakfast fer no additional charge."

"That's ev'rythin' I need. Thanks, mister."

I turned to face Travis.

"Would ya like to join me fer supper?"

"Sure."

I paid for the room and the bath and we drank our whiskeys. Travis ordered two more, then suggested we move to one of the tables. I grabbed my Winchester and my saddlebags and, once we were seated, told Travis of my pursuit and capture of Ben. He asked a few polite questions concerning Ben, then our talk turned to local events—the weather, the price of beef, the recent Indian trouble. When the food arrived, we ate in silence. The meal was passable. The thick steak was a little on the tough side, but the potatoes and biscuits were palatable. When we'd finished eating, I excused myself to go to the sheriff's office and check on Ben. Travis said he would wait at the table until I returned.

I made my way to the jail and found both the sheriff and Ben sound asleep.

When I returned to the saloon, Travis was still seated at the table as he'd promised. I got a deck of cards from the barkeep, told him I'd be ready for my bath in about an hour, and rejoined Travis for a friendly game of poker. After playing several hands, most of them won by Travis, my eyes began to droop with weariness.

"I think it's time fer that bath, Travis, an' then some shuteye. It's been a long, hard day. It sure was nice meetin' ya."

"Perhaps we'll meet again, Jake. I'm stayin' in town fer the night, an' I have the room right next to yers. Wake me in the mornin' an' I'll join ya fer breakfast before ya ride out."

As he finished speaking, the smile appeared again.

I tipped my hat to him, thanked him for the whiskey and his company, grabbed my Winchester and saddlebags, and climbed the stairs to my room. When I opened the door, I saw a boy of about fourteen pouring a bucket of water into a large, wooden washtub. When he was done, the tub was half full. Two more buckets stood on the floor beside the washtub. He turned to me and smiled.

"That 'bout does it, mister. I left a couple of extra buckets fer ya fer when the water turns cold."

I thanked him as he walked past me and shut the door behind him. The room was small, clean, and simply furnished. It contained a bed, a chair, a wooden bucket in the corner for relieving my bodily functions, and the washtub. French-style doors opened onto a small balcony. I stepped out onto it, surveying the town spread out below me in the dusk. As I stood there, I noticed that all the rooms on this side of the saloon had small balconies, similar to mine. I went back inside and began undressing, leaving the doors open to let the cool evening breeze in. I placed my holster on the floor by the washtub next to the towels, large homemade sponge, and bar of dark lye soap that the barkeep's son had left there. I tested the temperature of the water with my hand, then stepped into it and sat down. The water was hot and soothing on my tired, aching muscles. I lay back and let over three weeks' worth of trail grime soak from my body.

I'd been sitting quietly for only a short time when a furtive movement outside on the balcony caught my eye. When I saw a shape on the balcony, I quickly reached for one of my Colts. I hid my surprise when Travis stepped into my room, a bottle of whiskey in his right hand.

"Hi, Jake. I hope ya don't mind me droppin' in like this. Our balconies almost touch, an' I saw ya out on yers a while ago. I've been likin' what I saw watchin' ya from the balcony, so I decided to come inside fer a closer look."

I sat up in the washtub as Travis walked over to it. He set the bottle of whiskey on the floor and stood looking down at me, his eyes scanning my face and then my hairy, muscular chest.

"Ya know, Jake, I've known a few Texas Rangers in my day, but not one of 'em was as handsome as you. How's 'bout I scrub yer back fer ya?"

In reply, I grabbed the sponge and handed it to him. I slid forward in the washtub, baring my back to him. Travis grabbed the bar of soap, rubbed it across the sponge, and stepped around the tub so he was facing my back. I smelled whiskey on his breath as he knelt next to the tub. I closed my eyes when I felt the sponge touch my back. Travis's strokes were short but firm. After the first few, my dick was as hard as a rock. As he scrubbed, Travis didn't miss a single spot on my back, and the skin there was soon tingling. Suddenly, I felt his hot, whiskey-filled breath in my right ear.

"Now fer the front, handsome ranger."

He gripped me by both armpits and pulled me back against the washtub. I felt the massive strength in his hands and arms. He leaned over my right shoulder and began vigorously scrubbing my chest. The stubble on his face rasped against my own.

"I do like a hairy man, Jake."

Travis sponged my tits, then continued down to my stomach. I gasped when he suddenly stuck the tip of his tongue into my right ear and swirled it around. Pulling his tongue from my ear, he gently nipped on the lobe. I moaned softly and pushed back against him. From my stomach he worked his way down to my crotch. Travis wrapped the sponge around my cock and stroked it a few times, then washed my ball sac. When he was done, he sponged my stomach and chest again, then dropped the sponge into the tub. He rubbed my chest and stomach with his hands, then pulled and pinched my nipples until they resembled brown pebbles. He playfully curled the dark-brown hairs on my chest around the tips of his fingers. Then, grabbing each arm, he lifted them and eased them back, exposing my sweaty, hair-filled underarms. Leaning over me, Travis sniffed then tongued each pit. When both areas had been thoroughly licked, he leaned over farther and, as I turned to him, pressed his lips to mine. I tasted whiskey and tobacco on his lips, as well as my own salty sweat. I felt the bulge in his crotch pressing insistently against my right shoulder. Travis kissed me deeply, his mustache tickling my own. His tongue pushed past my lips and into my mouth, where it eagerly twined around my own. After sucking my tongue briefly, he released it and shifted on his knees around to my right side.

Travis undid the buttons of his shirt, revealing the white undershirt beneath. He undid these buttons as well, took both shirts off as one, and tossed them on the floor by the tub. His chest and stomach were muscular, and covered in thick black fur. His large, dark-brown nipples were almost hidden by the mass of hair. His navel was small and deeply cut.

Travis stood up and began unhooking the buttons on his pants. When he had undone the last one, he bent down, tugged his faded black boots off, peeled his denim pants down over his legs, and kicked them off his feet. He stood beside the tub, in just his socks and drawers; the latter covering him from waist to ankles. A short row of buttons barred entrance to his manhood. He stepped to the washtub and pressed his knees against it. I reached up and rubbed the thick mound that was inches from my face, feeling the heat through his cotton drawers. The smell of his crotch was strong.

I undid the buttons on his drawers with the fingers of my

right hand. His dick squirmed and swelled beneath them. I sat up in the washtub, grabbed the waistband of his drawers in both hands, and pulled them down to his ankles. His fat cock sprang free, slapping hard against my cheek and leaving a tiny smear of his fluid.

"Nice cock, Travis," I murmured.

He replied with a "thanks" as he stepped out of his drawers and, bending down, peeled off his socks. He was now completely naked. I drank in the sight as a thirsty desert traveler partakes from a watering hole. The dark hairs on his stomach blended into the equally dark hairs that covered his crotch and continued down his massive thighs and beefy legs. His cock was long and thick and fully hard, the fat head completely free of its protective covering. Several tiny blue veins snaked along the length of the shaft. His balls were enormous and hung low in their sac.

I grabbed his dick in my right hand. It was heavy and hot to the touch. My fingers barely met around it. I grabbed his ball sac with my free hand and gently squeezed the fat globes through their thin layer of skin, which was sprinkled with black hair, before letting them flop back between his legs. I let go of Travis's shaft, spit into my right hand, and spread the saliva around until my whole hand was coated with it. I grabbed his stiffer once more and began sliding my thumb and forefinger up and down it. He started slowly pumping his hips to match my strokes, his balls swaying with each thrust.

"Stroke it, Jake," he moaned softly.

I leaned into him and licked the large, blood-engorged cock head. Clear fluid was leaking from the tiny slit like water flowing from a cracked well pump. I inserted the tip of my tongue into the cleft and lapped up his juice. The smells of sweat, piss, and man spunk emanating from his crotch overloaded my senses.

I engulfed the swollen, purple knob and sucked on it noisily. I then ran my tongue over it in small, lazy circles before slowly sinking down on Travis's hawg. It tasted salty with the slight flavor of piss added in. He entwined his fingers in my hair and pressed against the back of my head. The head of his cock hit the back of my throat and stopped. He continued to push with an urgency I also felt.

"Take it all, Jake," he whispered.

I relaxed my throat, allowing the rest of his dick to slide home. His bristly crotch hair poked into my nostrils.

"Ya sure got a nice, deep throat, Jake."

In reply I slowly slid my mouth up Travis's dick until just the head was still ringed by my lips. I released the knob and began running my tongue up and down the thick shaft. I paused again when I reached the head, ran my tongue over it once more, then engulfed his cock again.

Travis began pumping his hips, forcing his thick pole down my throat on each of his thrusts. He slid his hand to the top of my head and began drilling my throat with lusty abandon. His hefty ball sac slapped against my chin. The floor around the washtub was soon soaked with water.

I grabbed Travis's ball sac and squeezed it once more, then trailed a finger from beneath it to the moist, hairy crack of his ass. He spread his legs, granting me entrance to his secret spot. I explored his crevice with my finger, then began tracing circles over and around the tiny opening nestled there. Withdrawing my finger, I stuck it in my mouth alongside Travis's cock to wet it, then again stroked the taut opening between his ass cheeks, trying to force the stubborn ring of muscle to relax. It finally did, and I slid my finger in up to the second knuckle. Travis bucked forward when my finger hit the muscle hidden inside his ass. I began strumming it slowly.

"Yeah, Jake, use yer finger on me."

He let out a series of small cries on his next powerful thrust, and a drop of warm fluid hit the back of my throat.

"Shit, Jake, here it comes."

Travis immediately slid half of his cock out of my mouth, leaving just the head inside as he spurted again and again. I swallowed his thick load as fast as I could, but there was too much of it; some ran out the corners of my mouth and dribbled down my chin. Travis shuddered one last time, then pulled his still-dripping member from my mouth and rubbed the swollen head across my lips, coating them with his spunk. I licked it from my lips, then swallowed his hawg once more and sucked a few last drops from it.

"That was right pleasurable, Jake."

I held his cock in my mouth as it grew soft. When he was completely limp, Travis withdrew his dick. I caught and held the fat head briefly with my lips, then released it. He stepped away from the washtub and walked to the wooden bucket on the floor in the corner. Shortly thereafter a thick stream of bright-yellow piss flowed into the bucket. Its acrid smell carried to the washtub. When he was done, he shook his dick a few times, then came back to the washtub, his large member flopping from side to side as he walked. When he reached the tub, Travis grabbed one of the buckets of water on the floor and emptied it into the washtub.

He stood looking down at me, a smile playing about the corners of his mouth.

"It's been a while since I've been serviced that good, pardner. Now, it's yer turn."

I started to get up out of the washtub, but Travis bent down and placed his hand firmly on my chest, pushing me back down into the warm water.

"You'll be fine right there, Jake."

I lay back against the washtub as Travis knelt beside it once more. My rod was still hard from the excitement of our recent encounter. I pressed my knees against the sides of the tub, then raised my pelvis until my equipment was above the surface of the water. Travis rubbed soap into his hands and leaned over the tub. Grabbing my swollen shaft around its thick base, he began sliding his hand slowly up and down its length. The soap felt good against the sensitive skin of my tool. I closed my eyes and concentrated only on the feel of his rough hand on my cock. He slid his hand up the shaft once more, then released it. I opened my eyes to find him easing his upper body farther over the rim of the washtub until he was leaning into it from the waist up, his face directly over my crotch. I felt his hot breath on the head of my dick. Travis rinsed my cock thoroughly, then his tongue darted out and trailed over the swollen knob. I reached over and pulled one of his nipples, twisting it between my thumb and forefinger until the little nub was rock hard and straining through the hair that surrounded it. I did the same to the other nipple, then ran my fingers through the thick hair on his chest.

Travis engulfed the large head of my cock, then swallowed the shaft inch by inch. I moaned as the warmth and wetness of his mouth completely surrounded my pole. Soon his lips were sucking greedily at the thick base. He began sawing slowly up and down on my stiffer, his lips forming a perfect ring of suction around it, while his hand stroked the shaft.

"Suck that dick, Travis," I cried as I began thrusting my pelvis toward him.

Travis squeezed my sac with his other hand, then released it and slid a finger along the crack of my ass, searching for the tender hole hidden between my ass cheeks. He found the opening and began rubbing it with the tip of his finger. He pushed against the opening with his fingertip until the ring loosened and his finger slid in deep. A good amount of warm water accompanied it, flooding my hole. He began sliding the large digit in and out, and I bucked my hips to match his thrusts.

The combination of Travis's mouth on my dick and his finger working in and out of my asshole quickly brought me to the boiling point.

"I'm gonna blow, Travis," I gasped.

As his finger thrust inside me once more, the first drop of cream exploded from my dick. As more spunk spewed forth, Travis held my stiffer in his mouth and swallowed every drop. He continued to suck on my cock even after I was spent. He then inserted the tip of his tongue into the sensitive, swollen piss slit in the head, prompting several more small spasms of pleasure to sweep through my upper torso. He held my hawg in his mouth until it was completely soft, then released it.

Travis leaned into me once more, his lips again seeking mine. We kissed deeply, our tongues twining, our juices mingling. I tasted my spunk on his tongue. Finally, he withdrew his tongue and stood up. He walked to the bed, bent down, grabbed his shirt, and pulled two cheroots and a couple of wooden matches from the right-front pocket. He bit the ends off both cheroots, struck a match on the barrel of one of my Colts, and soon had both cheroots smoking steadily. He picked up the bottle of whiskey from the floor and returned to the washtub. He stepped into it and sat down at the other end, facing me. Travis handed me a cheroot and the bottle of whiskey, and placed his feet on the rim of the washtub on either side of my head. I placed mine on either side of his head; we were both good-sized men, and it was a tight fit. I took a long pull from the bottle before passing it back to him.

We sat in the tub smoking our cheroots and drinking whiskey until the water cooled. I was the first to rise. Stepping out of the washtub, I grabbed one of the rough, homespun cotton towels and began drying off.

"Here Jake, let me do that fer ya."

Travis got out of the washtub, grabbed the towel, and began vigorously drying me. He started with my chest, then moved down to my legs, both front and back, skipping my crotch entirely. I turned around and he dried my back, then ran the towel between the cheeks of my ass several times, rubbing across my hole with each swipe. The rough fabric of the towel

on my wrinkled opening made the hairs on my arms and legs
stand up straight. I turned back around and Travis began drying
my crotch. Wrapping the towel around my cock, he squeezed
it hard, several times. He released it, scrubbed my thatch of
crotch hair, then pushed my basket up against my shaft to dry
the hard-to-reach area below it.

When Travis finished drying me, my cock was completely
hard.

"I guess it's true that ya can't keep a good man down, Jake,"
he said, laughing as he slapped my stiffer playfully. I grabbed
the second towel and began to dry him off, giving him the
same treatment I'd received. By the time I was finished, Travis's
member had swelled to its full proportions as well. He pulled
me to him, his lips seeking mine. Our cocks pressed together.
Grabbing the cheeks of my ass in his hands, he kneaded them
roughly. Travis continued to kiss me as he maneuvered me to
the bed. The edge of it suddenly struck the back of my knees
and I sat down heavily upon it. I swung my legs up onto it and
lay full length on the bedspread.

Travis stood by the bed, his gaze roving over my body from
head to toe.

"Ya sure are a good-lookin' man, Jake."

He climbed onto the bed and crawled on top of me. The
rough hairs of his chest scraped against my own, making my
nipples immediately harden. Once more his mouth sought mine
and he kissed me hungrily. Pressing his tongue firmly against
my lips, he parted them, and explored the inside of my mouth.
Grabbing my tongue gently with his teeth, he pulled it into his
mouth and sucked on it as if it was a tiny dick. Finally releasing my tongue, Travis licked over my chin and down my neck.
He stopped his swabbing once he reached my nipples. Pulling
the sensitive brown points into his mouth, he bit and sucked
on them none too gently, eliciting small moans and cries from
deep within me. When Travis was done working my nipples, he

grabbed my arms and pushed them up and back until they lay flat on the bedspread on either side of my head. He nuzzled each armpit, then swathed each hairy underarm thoroughly with his tongue. I moaned softly and squirmed on the bed. Pulling his face out of my right armpit, Travis returned his attentions to my chest, licking a path through the dark-brown fur that covered it and my stomach, and continuing down to the forest of hair at my crotch. He slurped the hair there like a dog drinking water. When he'd tongued the entire thatch, I felt his lips graze my turgid cock. He licked up and down the shaft several times, briefly sucked the blood-engorged knob, then tongued his way to my balls. He took the entire sac into his mouth and softly sucked on it before releasing it and licking a path to my shit hole.

Travis spread my legs, swabbed my inner thighs thoroughly, then parted the cheeks of my ass. I felt his warm breath against the tiny opening nestled there and jumped when his tongue began probing it. After several passes, he licked along the crack of my ass, then returned to my secret opening. He swirled his tongue around it then forced the tip into my hole as far as possible, causing my ass to rise off the bed.

"Lick that hole, Travis. Use yer tongue like ya mean it."

My words spurred him to greater efforts and I was soon thrashing on the bed and moaning repeatedly. Clear fluid bubbled continuously from the small cleft in the head of my dick.

When Travis stopped tonguing my hole, I had to place my forefinger on the underside of my cock, just below the large knob, and press firmly to control my rapidly approaching eruption. I wasn't ready yet to shoot my seed. I heard him spit and I felt his saliva running down the crack of my ass. He spread the fluid over and around my corn hole, then pushed against it with a finger. I pushed back against his finger and gasped when it slid inside me. Travis pushed the digit in deep, held it there for a moment, then began plunging it in and out of my chute. After a few strokes I began pumping my hips to match his strokes. Suddenly, he withdrew, grabbed me beneath each knee, and pushed my legs up and back over me until my toes were touching my shoulders.

Travis rose up onto his knees and shuffled between my legs; I felt the fat head of his cock push against my opening. He gripped me by the back of each thigh and pushed determinedly against my bung hole, demanding entrance for the large knob. When the ring of muscle relaxed, the head of his dick popped through. The old familiar pain coursed through my asshole, and I gritted my teeth to stifle a cry. Travis paused with his cock head just inside me, allowing my asshole to adjust to the intrusion, then slid the rest of his massive pole deep inside. The head hit the special muscle hidden inside my ass, igniting small fires of lust throughout my body.

Travis held his cock deep inside my channel, allowing the walls of my asshole to conform to its size, then slowly pulled out until just the knob remained inside. He slid into me once more and began pumping slow and easy. I squeezed Travis's hawg with the muscles in my asshole as it entered and exited on each of his plunges. Soon he increased the power of his thrusts, plowing into me determinedly. I could feel and hear his heavy nuts slapping against my ass cheeks. His grunts and moans came nonstop, and the smell of our coupling was heavy about me.

I spit into my left hand, grabbed my cock, and began jerking it as Travis continued to hammer my ass. Balanced above me with a hand on each side of my waist, he slammed his fat dick into me repeatedly. I lifted my ass off the bed to meet his thrusts. His eyes were squeezed shut and his mouth was slightly open; his tongue protruded from the right corner. Sweat covered his chest and stomach. The strong smell of it and his armpits was almost overwhelming. I ran my fingers through the damp hairs on Travis's chest and stomach, then held my fingers to my nose, inhaling his musky odor. I locked my feet against his ass and pulled him fiercely into me on each of his thrusts, wanting him inside me as deeply as possible. Wrapping my arms around his midsection, I hugged him tight and covered his cheeks and forehead with kisses. Travis was moaning continuously, and his thrusts were becoming even more powerful.

"Here it comes, ranger. I'm gonna fill yer ass," he cried, as he sank his cock into me to the hilt.

His body began convulsing and I felt his hot spunk flooding my back door. He collapsed on top of me and bit my shoulder as he continued to fill me with his cream.

I was very close to my own explosion when Travis pulled out. The head of his stiffer made a plopping noise as it slipped out of me. He slid down my torso and began licking the head of my dick as I stroked it.

"Open yer mouth wide," I growled as my eruption began. The first blob squirted from the head and landed in Travis's mustache. He took the knob into his mouth and swallowed the rest of my load. When I was done shooting, Travis released the head of my cock and licked his lips. He then sprawled on top of me again, the hairs of our chests sticking to each other. We lay quietly, the scent of our sweat mingling with the odor of man sex.

After a while, Travis rolled off me, climbed off the bed, and walked over to the piss bucket. I watched as once again a bright yellow stream of piss arced into the bucket. I got up and joined him, my own stream mixing with his. The smell of our combined piss was strong. We went to the washtub, rinsed off in the cold water, and dried ourselves once more with the towels. Travis took me in his arms and kissed me deeply, then we returned to the bed and lay side by side on top of it, my back to his front. He wrapped his strong, hairy, brawny arms around me, and I drifted off to sleep.

CHAPTER TWO

I woke at first light to find Travis gone. I dressed quickly, grabbed my saddlebags and Winchester, and went downstairs to see about breakfast. The saloonkeeper informed me that Travis had left before dawn. Breakfast consisted of bacon, eggs, biscuits, beans, and coffee, and I ate hurriedly, anxious to get to the sheriff's office, collect Ben, and start out for Abilene. I thanked the owner for the meals and his hospitality, then pushed through the saloon doors and stepped onto the board-walk. The same sleepy town from the day before greeted me. I went down the street and climbed the steps to the sheriff's office. When I opened the door, Sheriff Rawlins wasn't sitting (or sleeping, I thought to myself) at his desk as I'd expected he would be. I called out to him but received no reply. My ranger's intuition immediately warned me that something was wrong. I set down my saddlebags and Winchester and drew one of my Colts. I crossed the room in two long strides and headed down the hall leading to the cells. I stopped dead in my tracks when I saw that the door to Ben's cell was wide open. When I heard a small noise, I moved cautiously toward the open door.

What I found almost made me chuckle except for the fact that Ben was not on the cot, nor in the cell. The cot, however, was occupied. Sheriff Rawlins was laying on it on his side, fac-ing me, trussed up as nice as you please. His pants were down around his ankles, a bandana was tied across his mouth, and his hands and feet were tied to the wood frame of the cot. The one eye in his limp dick peered at me from beneath the forest of his brown crotch hair. The noise I'd heard was the sheriff's cries, muffled by the bandana. He followed me with his eyes as I walked into the cell and over to the cot. I had a sudden hunch and, turning him unceremoniously over on his stomach, I spread the cheeks of his ass. The small hole between those cheeks was coated with a brown substance. I ran the tip of a finger through the substance and held it to my nose. Saddle grease. I smiled as I finished piecing together in my mind what had happened. Sheriff Rawlins must have decided to help himself to a piece of Ben while it was so easily available. Ben had managed somehow to turn the tables on the sheriff, tie him to the cot, and tear off a quick piece of his own before making good his escape.

My first thought was to leave the sheriff trussed up on the cot to make him suffer added embarrassment when his deputy returned and found him. My need to know how long ago Ben had escaped, though, compelled me to remove the bandana from Rawlins's mouth. Also, I had to find out what, if anything, Ben might have said to the sheriff that could give me a clue as to where the outlaw was headed. As soon as his mouth was free, the sheriff began cursing.

"That no 'count pris'ner of yers jumped me when I was bringin' him supper," Rawlins spluttered. "He grabbed my gun, tied me up, an' high-tailed it outta here. Untie my goddamned hands, ranger, an' I'll help ya track down that son of a bitch."

Fellow lawman or not, Sheriff Rawlins had been surly, uncooperative, and downright rude since I'd first stepped into his office yesterday afternoon. I made up my mind right then and there to let his deputy discover him tied to the cot. He needed a lesson in manners.

"Not just yet, sheriff. I have a few more questions fer ya. You're positive that's how Ben escaped? If'n he was in such a hurry to leave town, why would he take the time to sample yer wares?"

Rawlins glared at me with murder in his eyes.

"I don't know what you're talkin' 'bout, ranger. I was bringin' his supper to him, like I said. An' if'n ya don't untie me this minute, you'll live to regret it."

I made no move to untie Rawlins.

"It sounds to me, sheriff, like you was tryin' to help yerself to a little bit of 'supper' as well. What time did Ben escape?"

"Shortly after midnight."

"That's awfully late to be servin' supper, don't ya think, Sheriff?"

Rawlins didn't answer me, but if looks could kill, I would have been six feet under. I mulled over what the sheriff had told me. If Ben had escaped around midnight, that meant he had a good six hours head start on me.

"One more question before I untie ya, Rawlins. Did Ben say anythin' while he was, uh, escapin', that would give ya any idea of where he was headed?"

"As a matter of fact, the blame fool did. Claimed he was innocent of the murder charge you was bringin' him back to Abilene fer. Said he was headed to Silverton to find the man that could help him prove it. He didn' say the man's name. I can rustle up a posse to ride with ya if'n you'd like, ranger. I'll even lead it myself."

"No thanks, Rawlins. You've helped enough already."

Sheriff Rawlins didn't miss the sarcasm in my voice. Without another word I left the cell and walked back down the hall into the office, leaving the sheriff tied to the cot.

"Untie me, ranger, ya son of a bitch."

Rawlins's angry words carried down the hall to where I stood.

I ignored the sheriff's pleas and threats and walked over to the gun rack on the back wall. There were several empty slots. Too many for the deputy to have taken them with him, which meant that Ben was probably armed, and I already knew he was capable of murder. As I stood looking at the gun rack, a sudden thought struck me: the horses!

I bolted from the sheriff's office and ran down the street to the livery stable. When I entered, I found the liveryman gagged and tied to one of the loft's support posts. His eyes pleaded with me to untie him, but I ignored him for the moment as I quickly searched the stable. I discovered what I thought I would: the Black and my packhorse were gone. I returned to the apprentice, untied the gag from his mouth, and undid the ropes that bound him. He rubbed his chafed wrists to get the blood flowing once more and gasped out a plea for water. On a corner shelf I found a water bucket with a large wooden dipper. I carried the bucket to the young man, filled the dipper, and held it up to his lips. He drank it down and I filled the dipper a second time. When the young man finally had his fill, I prodded him to tell me what had happened.

He began speaking, slowly at first, then more assuredly as he fully regained his senses.

He had fed, watered, and groomed my horses, but he'd been so busy with his other charges due to the blacksmith's absence that he hadn't gotten around to replacing the Black's shoe until almost midnight. He'd just finished nailing the new shoe in place, but hadn't filed off the rough edges, when a man burst in. When the apprentice described the man, I knew it had been Ben. He'd held a gun on the young man, demanding he get both horses ready to travel immediately. Fearing for his life, the apprentice did as he'd been ordered. When the horses were bridled and saddled, the man had bound and gagged the apprentice and ridden away. I asked if he had any horses for hire and he nodded his head yes. I helped him to his feet and followed him out the back door to a small corral. I quickly chose a sturdy-looking gelding and mare.

I paid for the horses, quickly equipped them with saddles and bridles, and led them down the street to the sheriff's office. I would need to buy a new scabbard for my Winchester. On second thought, maybe I'd find one in the sheriff's office. I opened

the door and stepped inside. Sheriff Rawlins must have heard
the door, because his pleas started in once more.

"Who's there? Is that you, ranger? Please untie me, I'm beggin' ya. I swear I'll help ya go after yer pris'ner, even if'n we have
to ride all the way to Silverton."

His tone was now soft and cajoling. I ignored him and
quickly gathered my saddlebags and Winchester. In the corner
by the stove I spotted a rifle scabbard. I grabbed it as well and
headed toward the door. As soon as I opened the door, Rawlins
realized I wasn't going to untie him, and his words once more
became threatening.

"I'll git ya fer this, ranger. I swear. I'll track ya down, you an'
that rotten pris'ner of yers, an' take care of both of ya. Mark my
words. I'll . . . ."

The rest of what Sheriff Rawlins had to say was cut off as
I closed the door behind me. I placed my saddlebags on the
mare and tied the leather scabbard on the gelding so that it
would hang parallel to my leg. I slid the rifle home, mounted
the gelding, and paused to collect my thoughts and form a
plan of action. If Ben was indeed headed to Silverton, there
was only one direction out of town he could have headed. And
he wouldn't be hard to track with the Black having an unfiled
right-front shoe. Finding that particular hoofprint among the
numerous prints made by the folks coming in and out of this
town, however, could take some time. And time was something
I had precious little of.

During the portion of our ride into Deadwood for which Ben
had been conscious, he'd gone on and on about his innocence,
and how he was willing to help me find the man who'd actually shot the Texas Ranger in Abilene. I hadn't believed a word
he'd said, for what guilty man doesn't proclaim his innocence
once he's been caught? And after listening to his ranting for so
many miles, I'd finally turned a deaf ear to it. Before leaving the
sheriff's office, though, Ben had also told Rawlins that he was

innocent of the shooting, and that he was headed to Silverton to find the man who could back up his claim. But Ben hadn't mentioned the man's name. Suddenly, my ranger's intuition was telling me that somewhere in Ben's ramblings of that morning there was an important fact I was overlooking. Had Ben also told me his destination was Silverton and I had paid no heed? Had he mentioned the name of the man who could prove his innocence? All at once a thread of Ben's diatribe popped into my head, and I knew I had my answer. Ben had indeed told me that he was headed to Silverton to find a man named Bart Jensen. Bart had shot the ranger, not Ben, and was hiding out in Silverton, or so Ben attested.

After an exhaustive search I finally found the Black's prints. They'd been partially obliterated by the wheels of a wagon. The majority of hoofprints and wheel marks were on the main trail that headed off in a northerly direction. But the next set of prints I found indicated that Ben was striking out to the west, taking a circuitous route to Silverton. He was headed for the Badlands, where water was scarce, and the terrain was populated by scorpions, rattlesnakes, and coyotes. Also, the Chiricahua Apache, as well as several outlaw bands, were rumored to roam these hills. I rode to the dry goods store, bought two additional canteens, then returned to the livery stable to fill them. The blacksmith's apprentice was nowhere in sight. I tied the canteens together and hung them across the saddle in front of me. I retrieved the cheroots, tobacco, and rolling papers from my saddlebags, filled my shirt pockets with them, and rode out after Ben.

The sun was high overhead when I reached the low, sandy, rock-strewn hills that marked the beginning of the Badlands. I halted and fished a cheroot from my pocket, lit it, then rode on. I followed Ben's tracks the rest of the day, across miles of endless sand dunes, rocks, cactus, and sagebrush. I lost them several times when the swirling sand covered them, but I always managed to find them again. Most likely Ben was in such a hurry to hightail it out of Deadwood that he wasn't bothering to hide his trail. As I rode, I ate several pieces of hardtack, washing it down with gulps from one of the canteens. When it got too dark to see Ben's trail, I halted for the night. I made camp below a weathered rock overhang and ate more hardtack for supper. I desperately wanted a cup of coffee but was afraid that the glow of a fire would be seen in the darkness. I had no desire to attract unwanted visitors. I unsaddled the horses, grabbed my Winchester and saddlebags, and gave each horse a couple handfuls of oats. Then I deftly hobbled them, which enabled them to move around to crop the sparse, dry grass, but prevented them from running away. I spread out my blanket, lay my Winchester down beside me, and, using my saddle as a pillow, drifted off to sleep.

I rose at first light, deciding to risk a fire because I couldn't stomach another meal of hardtack. And I would not start my day without coffee. I quickly gathered an armload of small branches and dry grass. I was hoping that no one would see the flames without me seeing them first. I would have to risk what little smoke the fire would create. I grabbed the sack of flour, the frying pan, and the coffeepot from my saddlebags and made biscuits and coffee, using as little of the precious canteen water as possible. I rolled several smokes for the trail while the biscuits cooked. They weren't perfect, but they'd fill the hole in my stomach. I opened a can of beans with my Bowie knife and ate them cold. When the biscuits were done I ate four of them, and stowed the rest in one of the saddlebags. I could eat them in the saddle when I got hungry without losing valuable time by stopping to eat. I finished my mug of coffee, then stood up and pissed on the fire to douse it. I unhobbled the horses, saddled them, and headed out once more.

The day passed much the same as the previous one had. I drank sparingly from the canteens, stopping to refill them and water the horses at every small stream I came to, which weren't many. I knew from past excursions into these Badlands that the distance between watering holes would become greater, the watering holes themselves fewer. The sun beat down upon me mercilessly, and the wind occasionally blew sand in my face. Shortly after the sun had reached its zenith, I found an old campfire in a small stand of sagebrush. I dug up the coals, crushed them, added water to them, and rubbed the mixture underneath my eyes to protect them from the sun's glare. Close to sundown I chanced upon a large rattlesnake, lazily sunning himself on a rock. Not wanting to risk a gunshot that would undoubtedly echo in these hills, I killed it with a lucky shot to its head with a large rock. I ate the meat raw. I made camp shortly after darkness set in. I spread my blanket and quickly drifted off to sleep.

I was on foot and something was chasing me through the desert. I was tired and thirsty. I hadn't yet caught a glimpse of whatever was after me, but I knew it was behind me, and I knew it was plain bad. I tripped over a rock and was sent sprawling. Something with a pair of monstrous, hairy feet stepped in front of me. I jerked myself awake to find the muzzle of a Winchester pointed at my nose. The sun was just poking above the horizon. As my eyes adjusted to the shadows surrounding me, I could see it was Ben Masters at the other end of the rifle. I felt for the Winchester that had been beside me when I went to sleep; it wasn't there.

"Mornin', Mr. Ranger. Don't bother lookin' fer yer rifle. I moved it so's ya wouldn't hurt yerself while ya was sleepin'. I didn' figure ya as bein' this persistent, Slater. I should've known better though, knowin' what they say 'bout Texas Rangers. Now, slide yer pistols an' knife over to me, nice an' easy like."

I did as Ben ordered, certain he wouldn't hesitate to shoot me if I made any sudden moves. He picked up the pistols and knife and threw them into the scrub brush. I silently cursed myself for behaving like a greenhorn and letting Ben get the drop on me.

"Stand up, Slater, an' no funny business either. I have no intention of goin' back to Abilene with ya. If'n I have to, I'll kill ya right here. I told ya after ya first captured me that I didn' shoot that ranger. I'm headin' to Silverton to find Bart Jensen, my ex-partner. We owned a ranch together back in Abilene. He's the one that did the killin', an' he's goin' to help me clear my name. He hightailed it out of Abilene the night of the shootin', bound for Silverton. I was followin' him when ya caught up with me outside of Deadwood. Since you're hell-bent on followin' me, I'm goin' to take ya with me to Silverton. When I find Bart and he confesses to the killin', you can take him back to Abilene. Or, ya can hang him on the spot if'n ya like. Either way, you an' I can part company fer good."

I stared at the good-looking bandit standing above me but made no move to rise.

"Holdin' a gun on a ranger is no way to prove yer innocence, Masters. Also, what makes ya think this Bart Jensen character will confess to the shootin' if, an' when, we do find him in Silverton?"

"Don't worry yer pretty head 'bout that, Slater, 'cuz I'll git a confession out of him, one way or the other. He an' I were real close at one time. That is until he decided to let me take the blame fer the killin'."

"What makes ya so sure he's headed to Silverton, Masters?"

"Because he told me that's where he was headin', an' I believe him. Also, he an' I first met in Silverton several years ago, before we moved to Abilene. Now, let's leave it at that. Okay, Ranger. Now, fer the last time, git up, nice an' easy."

Ben kept me covered with his rifle as I stood up. He sidestepped the few feet to my saddle and grabbed the coil of rope looped around the pommel, never taking his eyes from me.

"Turn 'round, Slater, an' put yer hands behind yer back. An' no funny business neither."

I turned and faced away from Ben, again cursing my stu-

pidity at being caught so easily. The rope was looped around
my wrists and drawn up tight. I winced slightly as it dug into
my skin. Ben spun me around and, without warning, swung
his right hand up, catching me square on the chin with his fist.
There was a moment of pain, I felt myself falling, then darkness
enveloped me.

When I came to, my first sensation was the throbbing in my
jaw from the blow Ben had struck. When I opened my eyes,
I found myself staring at horse hooves churning up sand. As
I slowly regained my senses, I realized I was slung face down
across the saddle of the gelding. My hands were tied together
behind me, and when I tried to move my feet I discovered that
they were tied together as well. The merciless sun beat down
on me, and the dust thrown up by the horses caked my mouth
and nose. The swaying of the gelding, the position I was in, and
the ache in my jaw—an ache that was slowly spreading through
my entire head—were making me sick to my stomach. I closed
my eyes and tried to doze, hoping sleep would quell my rising gorge. I came to several times, each time unable to gauge
how long we'd been traveling because I was unable to see the
sun's position overhead. What little of the ground I could see
was clear of any telltale shadows. After what felt to my aching
body like days of riding, I noticed that shadows were gathering
around the base of the rocks, cactuses and sagebrush that we
passed; the sun had started its descent.

Ben turned off the trail we were following onto a much
smaller one that zigzagged through a stand of large cactuses.
Suddenly, we halted, and Ben's boots appeared in my line of
vision. He stood by the gelding for a moment without speaking;
I could hear his shallow breathing. Then, without a word, he
unceremoniously yanked me off the gelding and let me fall to
the ground. I landed on my back with a thud, the wind driven
from my lungs. He left me tied where I'd fallen.

Eventually, I struggled to a sitting position and saw that Ben was busy making camp. I surveyed the small clearing he had chosen. Water trickled from a crack in the base of a rocky ledge, forming a small pool of inviting, clear water. Cactuses and sagebrush grew in profusion around the small pool, vying for the precious moisture. We were hidden from anyone riding past on the outer trail by the height of the cactuses, and the rock ledge partially hid us from any prying eyes above. Our right flank was open, but I was too tired and sore from the day's journey and too angry over my predicament to share my concerns for our safety.

Ben unloaded my saddlebags from the mare and stowed them under the rock overhang. The Black and my packhorse were standing quietly by the gelding and mare. He unsaddled each horse, rubbed them down, and led them in turn to the pool to drink. He fed each of them a measure of oats, then took a length of rope and picketed all four next to the pool. There they could pull at the short, lush grass growing around its edge.

When he was finished tending to the horses, Ben walked over to me. He bent down, grabbed me around the waist, picked me up, and carried me over to the rock wall. He set me down with my back against its rough surface, next to the saddlebags. He stood looking down at me, his green eyes never wavering from mine, then retrieved another coil of rope from my saddlebags. He looped it around my ankles several times, then around my wrists, and finally tied it underneath my knees. Straightening up, Ben surveyed his handiwork. Seemingly satisfied, he set about gathering grass and twigs for a fire. Soon he had a large pile a few feet from me. He stopped after a few more armloads, grabbed one of the saddles, and carried it over to me. He placed it behind me, then grabbed a second saddle for himself and dropped it by the pile of grass and twigs. He stood in front of me once more, surveying me.

"I'm goin' to see if'n I can hunt us up some fresh meat fer supper before it gits too dark," Ben said, scratching the dark-red stubble of his chin as he spoke. His voice had lost the hard edge it had held when he first captured me. "I don't expect you'll be wanderin' off while I'm gone." I don't think he expected a response to his remark, and I didn't disappoint him.

He turned from me and headed back down the trail we'd ridden in on. I found myself admiring his long, powerfully-built legs, his well-rounded ass, and his broad back. Was I crazy, thinking about this outlaw as if he were some horny cowboy I'd met at a Saturday night barn dance? I shook my head to clear my thoughts. As soon as Ben disappeared around a bend in the trail, I tested the ropes on my wrists and ankles. They didn't yield to my efforts.

Ben had been gone for only a short time when I heard several gunshots from the direction in which he'd headed. He returned shortly thereafter, carrying two large jackrabbits by their ears. Skinning them quickly and expertly, he cut the meat into strips. He built a small fire, knelt beside it, and began roasting the strips of rabbit on a stick over the flames.

"Shootin' those jackrabbits an' buildin' a fire to cook 'em wasn't very smart, Masters. Anyone travelin' within a mile of us surely heard those shots. An' the smoke from the fire an' the smell of that roastin' meat will carry a long way on this wind. If someone did hear those shots an' decides to investigate, they won't have much trouble findin' us. You're just askin' fer trouble in a place that's famous fer brewin' it."

Ben glared at me across the fire. The sheepish look on his face let me know that what I'd just mentioned hadn't occurred to him.

"I'm hungry," he shot back at me.

I made no reply.

When the rabbit was done to his satisfaction, Ben ate his fill, then brought several strips to me, along with a canteen. He squatted down, untied the rope beneath my knees, and loosened it from around my wrists. This allowed me to move my hands enough so I could eat. Returning to the fire, he knelt down again and cooked the rest of the rabbit. When he was done, he thrust the stick into the ground next to the fire.

I devoured the rabbit, not realizing how hungry I was. I licked the grease off my fingers and wiped my hands on my pants as best I could. I was unable to hold the canteen to my lips to take a drink. When it fell from my grasp, Ben walked over and held it to my lips for me. Once I'd drunk my fill, he took his place by the fire again. I licked the moisture from my lips as I stared across the fire at Ben. He sat quietly, gazing vacantly into the flames, stirring the coals with a stick. Suddenly, he looked directly at me.

"Why don't ya believe I'm innocent, Slater?"

Ben's unexpected question surprised me; he continued before I had a chance to reply.

"I swear I'm tellin' ya the truth. I didn' kill that ranger in Abilene. I was in the saloon when he was shot, but I didn' do the shootin'. It was Bart that done it, then he lit out durin' the commotion that followed an' rode back to our ranch. I left the saloon myself, an' ran into Bart back at the ranch house. He rode out that night fer Silverton, leavin' me to take the blame."

I mulled over what Ben said before answering him.

"I've been in this profession fer a good many years, Masters. I've arrested men who swore to me on their sweet momma's grave they was innocent, even when eyewitnesses had seen 'em commit their crimes. Why should I believe you're any diff'rent from the rest of 'em? Runnin' from Abilene the way ya did didn' help yer case none, neither."

"I was scairt, Slater, an' angry at Bart fer leavin' me like he done after all we'd been through together."

He stared at the fire again, lost in his own thoughts, seeming to forget I was even there. Then he lifted his head and looked at me once more.

"I'm innocent, Slater, an' I'm gonna prove it to ya. That's how

I'm diff'rent from the rest of the riffraff you've tracked down."

My remarks seemed to have honestly stunned him, and I was momentarily swayed by the sincerity in his voice. When you've been a lawman for as many years as I have, you learn to recognize the truth when you hear it. My gut was suddenly telling me that Ben was speaking the truth, though my head fought it. He sat back against the saddle and pulled the cork from a bottle of whiskey he'd taken from my saddlebags. As he sat drinking in silence, I gave him the once over.

Other than the cursory glance back in the jail cell, I'd never taken a really good look at Ben. The flames from the fire illuminated his large frame. Beneath the mixture of sweat and trail dust that coated his face, his features were strong and chiseled. His cheeks and throat were covered with dark, reddish-brown stubble. His mustache was full and thick, completely hiding his upper lip.

As I scrutinized him, Ben removed his hat. His tousled hair appeared even redder in the firelight. His shirt and denim pants fit him well, accentuating his musculature. My eyes were drawn involuntarily to the large swell at the crotch of his pants; it definitely added to his overall masculinity. As I continued examining his body, I felt the familiar stirring in my loins. This is crazy, I thought to myself for the second time that evening. This man is a wanted murderer that I was sworn to bring in.

"Can I have a taste of that whiskey, Masters?" The words were out of my mouth before I even knew that my brain had formed them.

"Not a chance, Slater," he replied evenly.

Noticing the tobacco pouch protruding from my shirt pocket, he stood up, walked over to me, and pulled it, the rolling papers, and my cheroots free. He then hunkered down on the ground beside me and rolled a smoke. When he was finished, he stuffed everything in his shirt pocket and rose and stepped to the fire. Picking up a small stick, he held it in the fire until it caught, then lit the smoke. When the tip was glowing, he returned and sat beside me. As he sat and smoked in silence, I could feel his raw sexuality beating against my body. Nervous but excited, I finally broke the silence.

"How'd ya manage to git the drop on that good-fer-nothin' sheriff, Masters?"

He blew out a thick cloud of smoke before answering.

"Rawlins came sneakin' into my cell, must've been 'round midnight or so. He thought I was asleep, I guess. I knew he was up to no good, so I pretended I was. He thought he was goin' to have a nice little slice of Ben pie. I waited until he had untied my feet, then I kicked him in the balls as hard as I could. He doubled over an' I whacked him on the head with my fists, knockin' him out. While he was unconscious, I found a knife in the outer office. Holdin' it between my teeth, I cut the ropes that bound my hands. When I went back to the cell to tie him up, he was just comin' to, but he was no match fer me. I trussed him up nice an' tight, then gave him a big piece of Ben he wasn't expectin'. He's lucky that I used the saddle grease on him that I found in his desk. He deserved no such consideration, but without it my size might've hurt him real bad. I took a big chance stayin' fer some pleasurin', but it'd been a good while since I'd had me a piece of man. It's too bad I couldn't have stayed with him a while longer. He was pretty good, if'n ya know what I mean."

I knew exactly what he meant, and the picture I'd formed in my mind of him and Sheriff Rawlins already had my dick leaking fluid.

When Ben finished speaking, he tossed the stub of his smoke into the fire and stared directly into my eyes. His eyes held mine as if a kind of strange magic was at work between us.

"I'm sure you'd feel a whole lot nicer, though, Slater."

Ben moved closer to me and placed his hand on my thigh. Even through the coarse denim of my pants I could feel the heat from his hand. He squeezed my thigh roughly, sending shivers of excitement straight to my crotch. He then ran his fingers lightly up and down my leg. I squirmed as my cock stirred in my pants. My heart was pounding in my chest, and I didn't pull away from him.

"I don't aim to untie ya, Slater, cuz I don't trust ya one bit. Don't matter anyway, seeins' how I don't plan on usin' either yer hands or yer feet."

Ben slid his hand up to my crotch and squeezed my manhood through the fabric of my pants. It hardened completely, its thickness visible to the left of my crotch. Rising up on his knees slightly, Ben reached for the buttons on my shirt and slowly undid them. He pushed my shirt back off my shoulders and down my arms until it bunched at the rope that bound my wrists. Next he unbuttoned my cotton undershirt and pushed it down to join my shirt. A cool, gentle breeze blew across my naked chest, stirring the dark-brown hair that covered it and causing my nipples to harden immediately.

Ben removed my hat and placed it on the saddle behind me, then laid his hand on my chest. He ran his fingers in small circles over my chest and then my stomach, curling the hair that covered both around his fingertips. Leaning into me, he licked my left nipple. The feel of his tongue on the sensitive flesh caused my dick to throb inside its denim prison. Taking the small brown nub into his mouth, he sucked and licked and bit it gently. I moaned softly and pushed against him as he did the same to the other nipple. He swabbed down through the hair on my chest and stomach, pausing briefly to flick the tip of his tongue inside my navel several times, then continued licking down my torso to my belt buckle. He undid the buckle and slid the belt out through the loops in my pants. To my surprise, he then looped the belt around my neck and drew it tight. His fingers moved to the buttons on my pants, and he undid each one, as well as the buttons on my cotton drawers. Pulling the flaps of my pants apart, he pressed his palm against my stiffness.

He then slid his hand inside my drawers, grabbed my dick, and squeezed it several times. He squeezed my stiffer a final time, then withdrew his hand. Ben grabbed my pants, along with my drawers, by each leg and pulled them down around my ankles, bunching them against the ropes that bound my feet. The proximity of the fire and Ben's hands upon me caused my body to break out in sweat from head to toe.

Ben stood up and began to undress, his eyes never leaving mine. Pulling his shirt off and then his undershirt, he threw them across the saddle behind me. The flames from the fire highlighted his burly chest and stomach. Both were covered in thick, reddish-brown fur. His nipples were dark brown. He bent down, pulled off his boots and socks, undid his belt, let it fall to the ground, unbuttoned his pants and drawers, and slid them down to his ankles. He stepped out of them and stood before me, completely naked. His cock was hard and stuck straight out from his crotch. It was long and fat, the head completely free of its protective covering of skin. Reddish-brown hair grew in profusion above the thick base. His large balls hung low in their sac. His legs were long and well-built, and also covered in reddish-brown fur.

Ben swung his left foot over my leg and stood above me with a foot planted on each side of my waist. From my position, his dick looked enormous. A small drop of clear fluid oozed from the tiny crack in the fat head. I watched as it slowly fell and landed amidst the hairs above my navel. From there it slid down into the tiny indentation. Ben squatted down until the cheeks of his ass were grazing my stomach. He paused, the hairs on his ass cheeks tickling the hairs on my stomach, then slowly settled his weight on me. His thick cock flopped onto my midsection, the head still oozing fluid. I could feel the heat and weight of it on my skin.

Leaning forward, Ben brushed his lips across mine. I could taste whiskey and tobacco on them. His mustache tickled mine.

My mouth opened of its own accord, and his tongue slid in eagerly. It quickly found my tongue and entwined around it like two lovers dancing. Ben's spit tasted of whiskey and tobacco. Withdrawing his tongue, he grabbed my tongue gently with his teeth, pulled it out between my lips, and began sucking on it eagerly. He sucked it for a while, then suddenly released it. Without warning, he scooted his ass up my torso until his large cock was staring me in the face. The hairs on his ass scratched my nipples, making them burn. He grabbed the end of the belt and pulled my head toward his crotch until his large cock head was pressed against my lips. He wiped the thick knob across my lips, coating them with his sticky fluid. His weight was heavy on my chest, but at that moment I wouldn't have asked him to move for the world. Nor, I'm sure, would he have if I did.

"Open up nice an' wide, Slater. Ben's goin' to feed ya dessert. An' don't even think 'bout bitin' it either, cuz I'll kill ya on the spot if'n ya do."

I could tell by the tone of Ben's voice that he meant what he'd said. I had no intention of chewing off his hawg, but I wasn't about to let him know that. The sight of this hairy man squatting on my chest, naked, the head of his dick scant inches from my mouth, had quickly started my juices flowing. I knew that I wouldn't be satisfied until Ben's pole was in my mouth or buried deep in my ass, flooding either hole with his thick cream. I opened my mouth wide, bobbed my head forward, and engulfed the big knob. I sucked on it gently and ran my tongue over its soft, almost silky surface. I could taste the salt from his recent piss. Ben moaned loudly and shoved his thick shaft into my mouth. The head hit the back of my throat and lodged there momentarily, before sliding down, inch by inch, until his crotch hairs were poking up my nostrils. He shifted his body farther up my chest and rested his knees on my shoulders, effectively pinning me to the saddle behind me.

"Yer mouth feels damn good on my pole, Slater."

Our eyes locked briefly as Ben slowly slid his dick back out of my mouth until just the fat head was inside. I sucked on it greedily, again running my tongue over the knob. I teased the slit with the tip of my tongue until he suddenly rammed his thick member back down my throat. He held it deep while I sucked on it lustily, my lips forming a perfect o around the thick base. As I sucked his meat, Ben grabbed my ears and began slowly pumping his hips, using my mouth like he would a saloon whore. With each downward lunge penetrating my throat, I tongued every inch of his cock I was able to before he withdrew it. Each time his meaty ball sac struck the wetness on my chin, it produced a small slapping noise.

Ben was grunting loudly and moaning uncontrollably. When he began to pump his hips even faster, I was sure he was getting close to shooting his load. Sweat was streaming down his chest and stomach, soaking the fur that covered both and pooling in the hairs of his crotch. The smell quickly overpowered my senses. Sure enough, after his next plunge, Ben quickly slid his pole back out of my throat. I managed to catch the fat head between my lips.

"Here's the dessert I promised ya, ranger," he panted.

I felt the large knob swell. Ben groaned long and loud as the first drop of spunk hit the back of my throat. More gobs of the warm fluid quickly followed suit. As the intensity, but not the amount, of his release lessened, the rest of his spunk landed on my tongue. I swallowed as fast as I could, but was unable to keep up with the heavy flow. Some of the fluid ran out the corners of my mouth and dribbled down my chin.

When Ben was finally spent, he pulled his dick out of my mouth and held it poised just in front of it. I stuck the tip of my tongue directly into the swollen slit in the head, and his body jerked forward, his thighs quivering. He stroked his stiffer a few times, then squeezed the head, coaxing out one last drop of his seed. I lapped it up with my tongue, then sucked softly on the head of his cock as the blood began to leave it and the shaft, and both returned to their normal size.

Ben climbed off my chest, undid the belt from around my neck, and collapsed beside me. He eyed me in silence. His dick lay limp across his thigh, its size still impressive. I licked my lips, savoring the combined tastes of Ben's cock and spunk.

"Ya sure do know how to take care of a man's needs, Slater. It's too bad we didn' meet under diff'rent circumstances. I think we would have had a hell of a good time together."

Ben grabbed the bottle of whiskey beside him and took a long swig of it. He rolled another smoke, then rose and stepped to the fire to light it. I admired his strong back and muscular butt and legs. When he had lit the smoke he returned to sit beside me. As he smoked, he stared at my still-rigid cock.

"From the looks of yer stiffer, Slater, you could use a little servicin' yerself."

Ben stood up and walked a few feet from me to take a piss. When he was finished, he again threw the stub of his smoke in the fire then began rummaging in my saddlebags. When he returned to my side once more, he held out his right hand, palm up. With his left he unfolded the small, leather packet of saddle grease. He scooped off a generous portion with his fingers, leaned over my crotch, and applied the grease to my stiffer. The unguent was warm on the sensitive skin of my dick. When it was completely coated, he grabbed my shaft with his right hand and began slowly stroking it. With his left hand he grabbed my nuts and began working the large ovals of flesh with his fingers.

Ben leaned into me and began biting and sucking on my nipples. Releasing the left one, he buried his face in my left armpit. He sniffed loudly, tongued the hair-filled region, then gently pulled a few of the hairs with his teeth. At the same time, he released my basket, slid his hand below it, and began strumming the puckered opening nestled there with his fingertips. I spread my legs and leaned back as far as the ropes would allow, forcing my ass cheeks farther apart and giving Ben greater access to my hidden treasure. He withdrew his hand, scooped up more of the grease, and spread it along the crack of my ass, making sure my asshole was generously covered. He pressed firmly against the tiny opening with a finger. I pushed back against his finger and gasped when the ring of muscle gave way and the large digit slipped inside. Ben probed deeply, coating the walls of my ass channel with the saddle grease, then began pumping his finger steadily in and out of my chute. As he increased the speed of his strokes on my dick to match his pumping finger, he began working my nipples with his lips and teeth once more.

"Work that bung hole, Ben," I moaned softly, surprising myself with my words.

I felt my balls roll up snug to the base of my cock as my release was triggered.

"Here comes my spunk," I gasped.

The first blob of white seed shot from the slit in my cock and plopped onto Ben's chest. As the thick drops continued to spew forth, Ben pulled his finger none too gently from my asshole and cupped his hand beneath the head of my dick, catching the white stuff on his palm. It quickly formed a small puddle. When I was done shooting, Ben continued stroking my hawg until it grew soft, then released it and raised his other hand to his mouth. He sniffed the white pile of spunk, then licked the entire mess from his hand, staring into my eyes as he did so. When his hand was clean, Ben shifted closer to me, his lips only inches from mine. A shadow suddenly fell across us, and a rough voice broke the stillness of the night.

"If we're takin' turns, fellas, I'm next."

I looked up and saw a tall stranger standing on the other side of the fire.

CHAPTER THREE

Ben instantly sprang away from me and reached for the Winchester. A shot rang out, and a small plume of dust rose from the ground, inches from his hand.

"Don't try it, Mister. I'd just as soon kill ya as look at ya. Git back over there by yer boyfriend."

Ben stared for a moment at the tall man who'd spoken; I was certain that in his mind he was still weighing his chances of reaching the rifle.

The stranger also seemed to sense what Ben was thinking.

"If'n yer faster than me, cowboy," he drawled, "an' do manage to shoot me, there's five more men behind me that will fill ya full of lead. Now, git back over with yer boyfriend. I ain't gonna tell ya again."

The man stepped around the fire and approached Ben. He pointed his rifle directly at Ben's bare midsection. Ben eyed him defiantly, then reluctantly crawled to my side. The stranger's command, "git back over there by yer boyfriend," was reverberating inside my head. Before I had time to think about it, five men joined the tall stranger, forming a small semicircle in front of us. They were as desperate a band as I'd ever laid eyes on, and in my profession I'd seen some pretty desperate men. All six were dirty, unshaven, and unkempt. Their combined smell—a mixture of sweat, dirt, and something unidentifiable—carried to Ben and me. In this hard land, age was difficult to judge by appearance only, but I guessed the men facing us ranged in age from early twenties, maybe even late teens, to early thirties. The baby-faced blond had probably just recently seen his eighteenth birthday. All six of them were armed to the teeth as well.

Upon closer scrutiny, however, I saw that beneath the trail dust, facial hair, and dirty, ragged clothing, they were all fine-looking, solidly built men. The one who'd spoken and then shot at Ben appeared to be the leader of the group. He was the tallest and heaviest of the bunch, but by no means was he fat. He was also the meanest-looking, which said a lot based on the caliber of men on each side of him. A bandana covered his left eye; his right was hidden in shadow. By the light of the fire I could see a long, jagged white scar that ran from underneath the bandana and down his left cheek, ending just below his jawline.

"The smoke from yer fire led us right to yer camp," the leader said. "Me an' the boys couldn't imagine what blame fools would build a fire at night in these parts, but now we see. Good-lookin' as hell, but plumb ignorant. I won't ask as to why one of you is hog-tied, an' you're both naked. I know it gits lonely in these parts, an' I can see ya was just givin' each other some good old-fashioned comfortin'."

I shot a quick, accusatory look at Ben. He held my angry stare for a moment, then looked away.

"Johnny," the tall man barked, "you, Shorty an' Charlie go an' git the horses. We're campin' here fer the night with our new friends. Slim, as soon as the boys git here with the horses, grab the lantern an' light it. Keep it low an' back against the rocks. We need to see what we're doin', but no one needs to see us. Then, douse that fire before we have the Chiricahua breathin' down our necks. When you're done, see if'n there's any of that meat left they was roastin'. I've been smellin' it fer the last half-mile or so, an' I'm damn near starved."

Three of the men headed back down the trail, disappearing into the darkness. The young blond named Billy, the tall leader, and Slim eyed us in silence, their rifles never wavering from Ben's and my midsections. The three that had left returned shortly with a string of horses as dirty as they were. I counted a mount for each man, plus five packhorses, laden with gear.

The three outlaws picketed the horses on the far side of the fire, unsaddled them, and unloaded the packhorses. They carried the saddles and supplies over near the fire, making several trips, then rejoined Billy, Slim, and the tall leader.

Slim went to the gear and began rummaging through it, finally producing a lantern. He lit it and set it on the ground at the base of the rock wall next to Ben. He then went to the fire and began shoveling sand onto it with his hands. When it was completely out, Slim grabbed the stick with the remaining pieces of cooked rabbit, rejoined the semicircle of men, and distributed the meat among them. The lantern gave off enough light to illuminate our small group, but did not travel above the top of the wall of rock behind us. The tall man continued to eye Ben and me as he ate the strips of rabbit, taking in our nakedness with a smile on his face.

"Johnny, git some rope an' tie the hands an' feet of the one that's loose, then tie 'em together, good an' tight. If either one of 'em makes any sudden moves, shoot 'em both."

"Should I lets 'em git dressed, Chet?" Johnny stammered.

"Nah, leave 'em naked. When you're done tyin' 'em, cut the clothin' off'n the one that's already tied. If by some slim chance they do git loose, they won't go far buck-naked. Also, they sure are nice to look at."

Johnny walked over to the pile of supplies, returning with several coils of rope. He quickly cut away the shirt and undershirt bunched at my wrists, and the pants and drawers at my ankles. He took the rolling papers, cheroots, and tobacco from Ben's shirt pocket when he was done. Chet, the leader, and Billy moved closer to Ben and me and continued to cover us with their Winchesters while Johnny tied Ben's hands and feet. Johnny then pushed Ben roughly against me so we faced each other, took a second rope, looped it several times around our legs, then tied it off. He ran another rope around our upper torsos, pinning our arms to our sides and making us one big, neat bundle.

"Now gag 'em too, Johnny. I don't want 'em talkin' to each other, plottin' somethin' durin' the night. Don't make any sudden moves, either, boys. I'd hate to put any extra holes in those nice bodies."

Johnny pulled two bandanas from his shirt pocket and gagged us. The bandanas were filthy, and smelled heavily of spunk. Johnny checked the strength of the individual knots on our wrists and ankles, then tested the knots in the ropes binding us together. Seemingly satisfied that they were secure, he stepped back and stood beside Chet and the rest of the men.

"Billy," Chet bellowed. "You take the first watch of our new friends. Wake Shorty 'round midnight an' he'll take the watch till sunup."

Chet turned without another word and walked over to the pile of saddles and supplies. He grabbed a saddle and a bedroll and carried them closer to the fire. The rest of the outlaws, except for Billy, followed his lead. Billy sat down by the lantern, his back against the rock outcrop, his rifle cradled in his arms. The bandits spread their bedrolls around the extinguished fire, using their saddles as pillows. Johnny and Slim began rummaging through my saddlebags while the rest of the outlaws sat on their blankets and watched. When Johnny came across the bottles of whiskey, he and Slim abandoned their search and rejoined the rest of the men. Johnny doled out the cheroots he'd taken from Ben's shirt pocket, and the men passed two of the bottles of whiskey back and forth between them as they each puffed a cheroot. I caught bits and pieces of their conversations, but nothing that shed any light on their plans for us. When the bottles of whiskey were empty, they tossed them into the sagebrush at the edge of the camp, uncorked two more, and proceeded to empty them as well.

Billy sat and watched Ben and me in silence. The light from the lantern highlighted his young face. His eyes were pale, and set a little too close together. His face was hairless, his lips full and inviting. I returned his gaze boldly, but he didn't seem to mind. When the last empty whiskey bottle had been tossed into the brush, the men turned in. Their conversations soon died out altogether, and snores began to carry to Ben and me. I pressed against Ben for warmth. The hairs on his chest scraped my nipples, causing my dick to instantly harden. I was amazed that even in this predicament, Ben could still have that effect on me. I started slowly grinding my cock against his.

I saw movement out of the corner of my eye, and raised up slightly beside Ben. Billy had risen and was standing watching us, his face expressionless. He laid his rifle on the ground and stepped over next to Ben. The light from the lantern threw his outline into shadow. Ben was facing me and hadn't yet realized that Billy was standing behind him. When I nudged Ben, he gave me a questioning look. I inclined my head in Billy's direction. Ben finally turned his head and saw the young desperado. Billy stood silently a moment longer, then turned sideways so the light from the lantern illuminated the front of him. He unbuttoned his pants and drawers, and pulled out his cock. Even soft it was incredibly long and fat, and as it quickly hardened to its full proportions, it got even longer. Billy shuffled closer until his boots were almost touching Ben. He spit into his hand, coated his hawg, and began stroking it. As his hand moved along the thick shaft, Billy pulled his ball sac free with his other hand and let it rest on the crotch of his denims.

The spit coating his dick glistened in the lantern light. His hand began to move faster as he continued to stare silently at Ben and me, his eyes glazed with his lust. After a few more strokes, he cried out softly and thrust his groin toward Ben. The first white drop shot out and landed on Ben's cheek. More of the man's spunk erupted, splashing onto Ben's nose, cheeks, and forehead. When Billy had finished shooting, he calmly tucked his nut sac and hawg back into his pants, retrieved his rifle, and returned in silence to his seat by the lantern.

I could see the startled look in Ben's eyes, but was there also something else? Amusement perhaps? Leaning toward him, I wiped Billy's spunk from his face with the bandana covering my mouth. As we settled next to each other, I again became aware of Ben's stiffer pressing against mine. He began to grind it slowly against my rigid pole, and I did likewise. We moved against each other as urgently as the ropes permitted. All too soon our bodies were jerking and we were both crying out, the sounds muffled by our bandanas. I shot my seed onto Ben's stomach and his spunk splashed onto mine. Ben kissed my forehead with his bandana-covered mouth. I moved closer to him, my thoughts churning, and soon drifted off to sleep.

I awoke as dawn was unfolding around us. Ben was already awake, struggling feebly at the ropes that bound us together. I could feel the heat of his skin against my own; the smell of our individual sweat and spunk from the night before was heavy between us. The hairs on my stomach were matted together with Ben's dried seed. Our morning stiffers poked against each other, as if to say hello and commiserate over the trouble their respective owners were in. I stared into Ben's light-green eyes and saw anger and a slight humiliation in them. But there was also concern. Was it concern for me? Was my brigand (or innocent bystander, according to him) developing feelings for me? Or was he concerned merely with his own welfare? Despite our circumstances, I again found myself wondering what it would be like to wake up each morning next to this man. I forced myself to remember the reason I'd been chasing him. At the same time, I chided myself for my foolish, schoolboy fantasies.

Shorty was fast asleep against the rock wall, having relieved Billy sometime during the night. I wondered briefly if Billy had related his late-night adventure to his comrade. As the rising sun gradually dispelled the shadows around us, the bandits began to stir from their bedrolls. Chet was the first to rise and immediately spotted Shorty sound asleep. Striding angrily over to him, Chet woke the man with a short, vicious kick in his ribs. Shorty grabbed his side, made a loud yowling sound, and fell over into the dirt.

"Shorty," Chet bellowed. "If'n I ever catch ya sleepin' like that again, I'll kill ya."

Chet turned and stomped over to Ben and me. He bent down and inspected the ropes that held us together. When he was done, he paused suddenly and sniffed the air like a wild animal. He then examined our torsos carefully. His eyes narrowed to slits when he spotted the matted patches of hair on our stomachs. Chet ran a finger across my stomach and held it to his nose. He stared at me intently, seeming to want to ask for an explanation, but already knowing what it would be. It was then that he spotted the packet of saddle grease that Ben had used on me. I could tell by the look on his face that he knew what it had been used for. He then turned his attention to Shorty once more, who still lay on his side, gasping.

"Shorty, ya bastard," he hollered. "Get these two up an' on their horses, an' let's hightail it outta here. I smell trouble comin.'"

Shorty struggled to stand upright, then strode over and stood beside Chet. He was holding his side where Chet had kicked him. A second outlaw joined them.

"Should I let 'em git dressed now, Chet," Shorty stammered. "This sun will bake the skin right off'n 'em before we git back to the cabin."

Chet turned to face the two brigands beside him. He handed the saddle grease to Shorty.

"No, Shorty. Just give 'em their hats to protect their heads. You an' Charlie can rub 'em down with this saddle grease. It'll keep the sun from blisterin' their skin too bad. Slim, you keep 'em covered until Shorty an' Charlie are finished."

Chet's suggestion was met with leering smiles from Shorty and Charlie. Chet turned and walked back to join the rest of the bandits, who were gathering up their gear. Slim approached us and trained his Winchester on us. Chet announced that he, Johnny, and Billy were going to scout the area briefly before the group rode out. When the three men had departed, Shorty divided the contents of the packet and gave half to Charlie. Shorty untied the ropes that bound Ben and me together, leaving our hands and feet tied. With Charlie's aid, he hauled us to our feet.

Shorty stepped in front of me and quickly applied the grease to my face and neck, while Charlie did the same to Ben. Shorty then began applying it to my chest. The grease clumped in my chest hair as Shorty spread it around. He suddenly grabbed each nipple between a thumb and forefinger and began tweaking and pulling them. They had minds of their own and soon hardened to resemble small, brown pebbles. Shorty leaned into me and began nipping the twin points with his teeth as he rubbed the grease onto my stomach. I looked over at Ben and saw that Charlie was following Shorty's lead. Shorty's teeth working on my tits soon had my meat hard and begging for attention from this dirty outlaw.

Shorty looked down at my throbbing tool, a grin splitting his face from ear to ear. He stepped around behind me and began rubbing the grease onto my back, eventually working his way down to my ass. He greased my ass cheeks, then roughly bent me over as far as the ropes would allow and coated the crack of my ass with the substance. I half expected what came next, but I still gasped loudly as Shorty stuck a finger up my bung hole. He drove the digit deep, then withdrew his finger and began working it in and out steadily. After several thrusts, he pulled his finger out of my corn hole, producing a loud sucking noise as he did so. He stepped back in front of me and applied the grease to my dick, then knelt down and began stroking my shaft. Beside me Ben was receiving the same treatment from Charlie. Ben's head was thrown back and his mouth was slightly open. Charlie's hand moved faster on Ben's huge member.

I closed my eyes and started pumping my hips to match Shorty's stroking hand. The familiar tingling had just begun at the base of my cock when, to my surprise, Shorty slumped to the ground at my feet. I opened my eyes and found myself face to face with Chet, his features contorted with rage. He had returned from his brief scouting trip and apparently was not pleased to find Charlie and Shorty working over Ben's and my hawgs. He'd stolen up behind Shorty and cuffed him on the side of the head. Charlie was slowly rising from the dirt as well.

"Goddamn you two," Chet bellowed. "We don't have time fer this right now. I'm tellin' ya trouble's comin'. I can feel an' smell it. Now, untie their feet, git 'em on their goddamned horses an' let's git."

Chet stepped closer to me and, with no warning, whacked my stiffer as hard as he could. It went soft as quickly as a turtle retreating into its shell. He then turned to Ben, but apparently one demonstration was enough, for Ben's cock immediately returned to a state of softness.

Shorty and Charlie saddled the Black and the gelding and led them to us while Chet and Billy kept us covered with their rifles. Shorty bent down to untie my feet; Charlie untied Ben's. They left our hands tied. I briefly thought about making a run for it, but I was outnumbered six to one. Also, I was buck naked and unarmed. I couldn't speak for Ben, but I was in no shape to put up much of a fight. My entire body ached from laying in the same position all night in the chill air of the desert. My ankles and wrists were rubbed raw from trying to work loose the ropes that bound them. One look at Ben's miserable face confirmed he was probably in the same condition I was. But the thing that surprised me the most was that the idea of bolting and leaving Ben alone with these desperados didn't sit well with me. Was it the lawman in me causing me to think this way, refusing to give up my prisoner? Or was it a growing desire on my part for Ben as a man? I tried to push these thoughts from my mind and concentrate on the situation at hand.

"Slim," Chet yelled, "help Shorty an' Charlie put these nice gentlemen on their horses."

Slim stepped to Ben and helped Charlie hoist him up into the Black's saddle. Slim quickly looped another length of rope around Ben's wrists, wound it around the pommel several times, ran it around each foot, then tied Ben's feet together beneath the Black's belly. While Charlie guarded Ben, Slim and Shorty hoisted me onto the back of the gelding and tied me the same as Ben. When Shorty was finished, he placed his hand on my thigh and roughly squeezed it.

"Don't worry, I'll have plenty of time to finish with ya later."

He then joined the rest of the outlaws, who were loading gear onto the packhorses, including Ben's and mine. When everything was loaded and the men had mounted, we set out in single file. Chet took the lead; Charlie was next, leading my horse; and Shorty was behind me, leading Ben on the Black. The remaining bandits and the packhorses were strung out behind us. After riding for several miles, we came across a small spring. We rested briefly, watered the horses, and refilled all the canteens. Shorty checked our ropes to make sure they were still tight. Satisfied, he swung up behind me and, reaching around me, held a canteen to my lips. As I drank the warm water, Shorty played with my tits. When I'd had my fill, he climbed up behind Ben and gave him a drink as well. I ran my tongue over my dry, cracked lips, to moisten them.

When the horses had drunk their fill and the desperados had slaked their own thirst, we made a quick meal of the ubiquitous hardtack. I mechanically chewed and swallowed the flavorless, dried meat Shorty fed to me, then we headed out once more. We rode in silence. The only noises marking our travel were the occasional clink of a horseshoe striking a rock or a soft snort from one of the horses. Chet repeatedly scanned the terrain ahead of and behind us; I presumed he was looking for signs of

the Chiricahua he had alluded to the night before. His concern
had infected the rest of his men, for they were beginning to act
a little spooked as well. Every few miles, Chet would send Billy
and Johnny along our back trail to scout for any signs of pursuit. The sun beat down upon my exposed flesh. I didn't want
to think about what my skin would look like without the coating of saddle grease Shorty had applied. My eyes were irritated
from the swirling trail dust and were constantly watering from
the sunlight reflecting off the sand. Despite the circumstances,
I chuckled to myself as I thought of what a sight we would be
if we chanced upon any other travelers: two naked men tied to
their horses, wearing only cowboy hats, being led through the
desert by a half-dozen men. They would think Ben and I were
peyote-sodden, or touched in the head.

  Close to sundown the trail started to climb, soon winding
between high, sandstone cliffs. I tried to memorize our route,
but with all the twists and turns the trail took, I soon gave up
on the idea. Every rock, clump of sagebrush, and cactus began
to look the same to me. As the sun started its descent, I noted
a dark gap in the cliff face we were approaching. As we drew
nearer, I could see that the gap was actually a narrow passage.
We entered the passage, our stirrups almost brushing the sides
of it, and followed it for several miles. Suddenly we emerged into
a large canyon. Our party halted when two men appeared from
out of nowhere on the rocks high above us, one on each side of
the pass. My initial alarm quickly faded when Chet raised his
hand in the air and the men disappeared back into the rocks as
suddenly as they'd appeared.

  We rode down a gentle slope and came to a meadow that
stretched to the far end of the canyon. There were no other
openings in the cliffs that formed the canyon other than the
passage we had just ridden through. We fought the horses during the ride across the meadow as they tried to stop and graze
on the luscious, green grass. As we neared the far end of the

meadow, I spotted a dilapidated cabin—built within a small stand of ancient pines—set back against the wall of the canyon. The roof of the cabin had caved in, and the two front windows were without coverings. They resembled two giant, black, staring eyes. To the right of it stood an equally shabby, two-story barn. The tall pines shielded both buildings from anyone looking down from the south rim of the canyon; the men guarding the passage would prevent any parties from approaching from the north. A large stream flowed parallel to the cabin and the barn, between them and a small, makeshift corral.

We rode to the corral, and the brigands dismounted. While Johnny and Chet kept Ben and me covered with their rifles, Charlie and Billy began unloading the packhorses and carrying gear and supplies into the cabin. The rest of the men unsaddled and unbridled their horses, the packhorses, and Charlie's and Billy's mounts, and led them into the corral. They laid the saddles and bridles over the split rails of the corral. Shorty and Slim disappeared into the barn, reappearing shortly at the loft door. They threw down several armloads of hay, which the horses ran to and began eagerly munching. On their last trip, Charlie and Billy stayed inside the cabin. Through the open door and windows, I could see them moving about. Shorty and Slim climbed down from the loft and stood beside Chet.

"Shorty an' Slim, untie our prizes," Chet said, rather sharply. He pointed his rifle at Ben and me. "An' no funny stuff neither."

Chet and Johnny continued to train their rifles on us as Slim ambled to the side of my gelding and Shorty strode purposefully to the Black. Slim first untied the rope that bound my feet, then unwound it from the pommel and my hands, then undid the rope that bound my hands. When my hands were free I rubbed my chafed and swollen wrists. They began to tingle as their normal flow of blood was restored. In spite of the saddle grease, my skin had turned a pinkish-red from the sun. Slim ordered me to get down from my horse. My legs were wobbly from riding all day, and I would have fallen if the outlaw hadn't caught my arm. Shorty had finished untying Ben, and the look Ben gave me was full of a new determination. As he climbed down from the Black, my eyes scanned his broad, muscular back, his firm, hairy ass, and his thick, hairy legs. The bandits appeared to have noticed as well. All eyes were on Ben and no one spoke as he stretched and flexed his tired, cramped muscles.

Chet was the first to speak, his words breaking the spell that Ben had cast over us.

"Slim, you an' Shorty scout the area behind the cabin, in case someone made it past our men in the pass an' are hidin' in the pines. While you're at it, see if'n ya can rustle up some meat fer supper."

Even in this canyon stronghold, Chet was still nervous about being followed. I watched Slim and Shorty as they headed toward the stand of pine trees.

Chet turned to face Ben and me.

"Okay, you two. Walk slowly into the cabin in front of Johnny an' me. An' don't try anythin' stupid either or you'll both regret it."

Ben and I walked side by side to the cabin with Chet and Johnny behind and a little to our right. I hoped Ben wouldn't try to make a run for it and, to my relief, he didn't. We stepped onto the porch and entered the cabin.

The interior was a shambles. The caved-in roof had spilled dirt, grass, and several logs, now rotted, in one corner. If it ever rained hard, the cabin would be flooded. Broken furniture was strewn about, along with pottery shards and rusty cooking utensils and cans. The only furniture still intact was a rough log table and two sizable beds set against the back wall, to the left of a large, fieldstone fireplace. A pile of wood was stacked to the right of it. The hearth was carpeted in ash. A large black-ened kettle hung on a metal rod, which allowed the kettle to be swung over the flames for cooking. To our right, a doorway led to either another room or the outside. The cabin smelled of rotten food, dead animals, and decay.

Chet ordered Charlie and Billy to tie Ben and me to separate beds.

"When are ya goin' to let us put our clothes back on, Chet," Ben asked in a none-too-friendly voice. "Our skin's turnin' red from the sun. Another day of this an' we'll be covered in blisters."

Chet swung around and faced Ben, his anger plain to read on his face.

"When I'm damn good an' ready, an' not a moment sooner. Ya best shut yer big mouth, before I shut it fer ya, permanently."

Ben took a step toward Chet, his own anger masking his face. The big man's hand went immediately to the Colt resting on his hip.

"Don't even try it," Chet snarled. "I'd hate to be layin' that pretty body of yers out fer the coyotes to pick over."

Ben made no further move, and Chet took his hand away from his pistol.

Charlie and Billy, prodding us with the barrel-end of their Colts, herded us toward the beds. I was pushed onto the one farthest from the fireplace. We were ordered to lay down on our backs, spread-eagle, and our hands and feet were tied securely to the rough wooden bedposts. As Charlie and Billy rejoined Chet, Slim and Shorty returned from their scouting trip.

"It's all clear, Chet. We found no footprints between the cabin an' the wall of the canyon, nor any other sign that anyone's been nosin' 'round. An' we managed to bag us a couple of nice plump jackrabbits fer supper."

Chet grunted an unintelligible reply, shot a last nasty look in our direction, then sat down at the table and began cleaning his Winchester. Slim laid the rabbits on the table, skinned them, and cut their meat into several chunks. Shorty started a fire in the fireplace. Soon he and Slim were cooking the meat as well as some flour tortillas that Shorty had made, probably with flour they'd stolen from my saddlebags. Slim also made a pot of coffee.

While the two men prepared supper, the rest of the outlaws unpacked their bedrolls and staked out clean areas on the floor on which to sleep. The aromas of roasting rabbit, tortillas, and strong coffee soon filled the cabin. When the meat was done to Shorty and Slim's satisfaction, they wrapped chunks of it in the tortillas and served it, along with cups of coffee, to their comrades. My mouth was watering, and I thought that Ben and I were going to be ignored. But, when Shorty had eaten his fill, he brought Ben and I each a tortilla filled with chunks of rabbit. He fed me first, then Ben. The meat was burnt, but delicious. We washed it down with cups of strong, black coffee, held to our sunburned lips by Shorty.

Darkness had almost set in when the bandits finished eating. Johnny grabbed the last two bottles of whiskey from my saddlebags, pulled the cork on one with his teeth, took a long swallow, and passed it to Chet. Slim found a battered lantern in a far corner and lit it, along with the one he'd used in our camp last night. The combined light from the lanterns filled the cabin with a soft glow. The group of men sat Indian-style in a circle on the floor between the beds, the only area in the cabin clear of debris and the men's bedrolls and supplies. They busied themselves with various mundane tasks: rifles and pistols were polished, their firing mechanisms checked, their chambers refilled with bullets and their barrels cleaned; ammunition was counted; deadly-looking knives with foot-long blades were sharpened; and the rest of my tobacco was rolled into smokes. When the first bottle of whiskey was empty, Johnny uncorked the second one and passed it around. Slim had removed his pants and was mending a tear in the crotch. Shorty was stitching his ripped cartridge belt. When the men had finished their chores, Chet produced a deck of cards and a small cloth bag from one of the saddlebags. The rest of the outlaws also went to individual saddlebags, returning with similar bags that turned out to be filled with coins. Chet shuffled the worn deck quickly and expertly, and dealt cards to each man.

"Five card stud, two bits to open. The usual rules apply."

As each man bid, the small pile of coins on the floor steadily grew. In the first hand, Johnny's full house beat Chet's pair, and everyone groaned as Johnny slid the coins in front of him.

"Let's have 'em, boys," he said, childlike glee filling his voice. "An' don't fergit that boots count as one item."

My mouth fell open in amazement when each of them shed an article of clothing and tossed it beside Johnny, forming a small pile. I glanced over at Ben; he smiled at me and shrugged his shoulders. Johnny dealt the next hand, and was the winner once again. More clothing was added to the pile beside him. As the game progressed, it was clear that Johnny was a consummate card player. Four of the men were soon down to their socks and drawers. Slim, who'd started the game minus the pants he'd been mending, was wearing just his drawers. Johnny was still fully clothed.

I was becoming more and more aroused as the outlaws' bodies were gradually revealed to me. When the next hand had played out, all socks came off, except for Slim's; he was forced to remove his drawers. He did it unselfconsciously, even standing up in the process, apparently to give the rest of the men a better view. He slid the cotton material down over his beefy, hairy thighs and muscular legs, until they bunched around his ankles. He stepped out of them, caught the waistband with his big toe, and flung his drawers into Johnny's face. The other men roared with laughter. Unfazed, Johnny grabbed the drawers, held them to his nose, and inhaled deeply. Slim watched, his lust plainly visible on his face, as his drawers were passed around the circle and each man took a whiff of his odor.

Despite the circumstances, I couldn't help but admire Slim's body. His chest was muscular and covered with thick black hair; his tits were capped by large, dark-brown, prominent nipples. His stomach was hairless. Hair began again just below his navel, and grew in a line that eventually merged into the thick patch of his crotch hair, which was black like the rest. His arms were thickly muscled, his forearms covered in the same dense, black fur. Even soft, his dick was long and thick, resting atop his large ball sac.

Slim stepped in front of Johnny and thrust his cock into his face.

"I've got somethin' fer ya, Johnny," he said, his voice thick with lust.

Johnny grabbed Slim's hawg and began stroking it lightly with his thumb and forefinger. As the thick piece of flesh quickly filled with blood, the large head emerged from the foreskin. When fully hard, Slim's member was sizable indeed. Chet leaned over to Billy and whispered in the young man's ear. Billy jumped up and practically ran to the pile of supplies, returning with a worn blanket. He spread it on the floor in the center of the circle of men. Slim stepped back onto the blanket, then lay down on his back facing Johnny, and Ben and me as well, his legs spread wide. The invitation was not lost on any of us.

The rest of the bandits, except for Johnny, shifted closer to Slim until they were almost touching him. Johnny stood up and began undressing, his eyes only for the naked man sprawled at his feet. As he shed the last garment, he revealed a body that was just as impressive as Slim's. The two men were equally matched in musculature, but Johnny outdid Slim when it came to body hair and poundage. His chest and stomach were completely covered by a thick, red pelt. His arms and legs were similarly furred. His cock was already completely hard and resembled a good-sized club protruding from his crotch. Johnny gave a few quick tugs on his dick, then knelt between Slim's outstretched legs. Grabbing Slim behind each knee, he pushed Slim's legs up and back over his upper torso. Slim grunted slightly as he tucked his toes over his shoulders.

The rest of the desperados sat dead still as they watched the scene unfold almost on top of them. Johnny placed a hand on each of Slim's ass cheeks and spread them wide, exposing the tiny treasure spot hidden between them. He bent down until his face was scant inches from the crack of Slim's ass, then ran his tongue up and down it, swirling it several times over Slim's brown hole. Slim moaned and wriggled his ass toward Johnny. Soon Johnny resembled a rooting pig as he continued to tongue Slim's bung hole. Suddenly, he withdrew his tongue, spit twice onto Slim's shit hole, and then once into his own hand. Spreading the saliva along his thick shaft, Johnny shifted forward slightly and placed the fat head of his cock against Slim's opening. Slim gritted his teeth as Johnny pushed against his corn hole with the large knob. When the slick opening finally yielded, the entire length of Johnny's meat slid inside Slim in one single, swift motion. Slim grunted and lifted his ass off the blanket as he took all that Johnny had to offer.

Johnny rested his weight on Slim, and Slim wrapped his legs around Johnny's waist, locking his heels against the man's hairy ass. He probed Johnny's ears with the tip of his tongue. Johnny moaned softly as he withdrew from Slim's asshole, leaving just the fat head inside. He locked eyes with Slim as he drove deep into him once more. Johnny then began hammering Slim's ass for all he was worth, his strokes long, deep, and rabbit-like, each thrust rocking Slim on the blanket. The only sounds in the cabin were the two men's moans and cries, and the heavy sound of Johnny's thighs slapping against the cheeks of Slim's ass. The smell of their coupling drifted up to me.

"Give it to me, Johnny," Slim moaned repeatedly.

By now, my arousal had reached a fever pitch, and my own asshole began to twitch as I watched the pounding Slim's was receiving. Clear fluid was dripping from the slit in the head of my cock. My nipples were hard, aching nubs; my chest was rising and falling rapidly, and glistening with sweat. I turned my attention momentarily to Ben. He was watching Johnny and Slim raptly, his hawg sticking straight up from his crotch. The rest of the brigands were also intently watching the heaving bodies in front of them. Four hands rubbed cocks through the cotton fabric of drawers; however, no dicks were pulled free. There appeared to be a set of rules to this sex ritual, and I knew intuitively that it'd been performed many times before. Johnny made one last deep plunge, then withdrew from Slim's hole. He quickly straddled Slim's chest and began stroking his own cock furiously.

"Open yer mouth, Slim," Johnny growled.

Slim opened his mouth wide and held out his tongue beneath Johnny's swollen cock head. On Johnny's next stroke he tilted his head back and yelled loudly as his eruption began. The first drop of cream shot from the slit in the engorged head and landed on Slim's tongue. His discharge continued to spew forth, coating Slim's entire tongue. When Johnny had wrung the last bit of spunk from his dick, Slim swallowed it all.

Johnny slid backward down Slim's stomach to his crotch. He grabbed Slim's swollen member in a big, meaty fist, and began pumping it furiously.

"Stroke me, Johnny," Slim moaned, as he thrust his hips frantically. "Make me shoot my seed."

On the next stroke, Slim cried out as his juice erupted from his cock. It quickly formed a white puddle on his stomach. When Slim was spent, Johnny bent down and licked Slim's stomach clean. Then he kissed Slim deeply, pushed up off him, grabbed Slim's hand, and pulled him to his feet. The other desperados remained silent as Johnny and Slim resumed their positions in the circle, however, the game continued without them. When Chet won the next hand, Billy, Charlie, and Shorty stood up, and three pairs of drawers were unbuttoned simultaneously, slid down massive, hairy thighs, and tossed aside.

Chet stood up as well. It was impossible to miss the massive bulge beneath the row of buttons in his drawers. He undid them slowly, one by one, teasing his fellow outlaws, then slid them down his legs to his ankles. Stepping out of them, he stood before us in all his naked glory. Ornery outlaw or not, he was an impressive man. His chest was covered in light-blond hair and thickly muscled. His tits were topped by large, pinkish-brown nipples. His dick was long, thick, and fully erect. A forest of blond crotch hair grew above it. Chet's balls matched the rest of his equipment, hanging low beneath his manhood.

My dick throbbed as I scrutinized the semicircle of naked men standing beside me. Ben was likewise staring at the group, his cock still standing at attention. They certainly were an impressive-looking bunch. Not one of them had an ounce of fat on his body, and all were heavily muscled in the chest, stomach, arms, and legs. Each chest was covered in a different color of fur, except Billy's, which was hairless. His nipples were light brown, and hard from the cool night air. All six were also well hung. Billy had the biggest dick in the group, and I was betting he had the boyish exuberance to go with it.

Johnny stepped to Billy and tweaked his left nipple. Billy tilted his head back and moaned softly as Johnny continued to pinch the hard little nub between his thumb and forefinger. Releasing the nipple, Johnny placed his hands on Billy's shoulders and pushed the young outlaw down on his knees. Placing his right hand on the back of Billy's head, Johnny pushed Billy's face into his crotch. Billy began swabbing the thick patch of reddish-brown hair above Johnny's manhood, then switched to the fat shaft. His tongue traced the tiny blue veins, then swirled over the large, purplish knob. Billy licked the crown a final time, engulfed Johnny's pole, and began eagerly sawing up and down on it. All of us watched as the young man gratified Johnny, making loud sucking noises as he did so.

"That a boy, Billy," Johnny said as the youth increased his efforts on Johnny's member.

"Since I'm the winner, boys," Chet exclaimed, "I git first dibs on the dark-haired one."

As he finished speaking, he stepped to the edge of my bed, making it clear to everyone that I, not one of his fellow hombres, was the dark-haired one he was speaking of. When he saw my rock hard, leaking cock, he smiled.

"An' by the looks of him, he's all primed an' ready to go. Johnny, you can have first crack at the red-head."

"It would be a pleasure, Chet," the outlaw replied.

Johnny grabbed a handful of Billy's hair, pulled his hawg out of Billy's mouth, and moved to the side of Ben's bed. He crawled onto the bed and knelt between Ben's outstretched legs. Billy quickly joined him, and resumed his bobbing on Johnny's thick pole.

Placing his hand on my thigh, Chet began lightly stroking it. His touch turned the skin on my leg to gooseflesh. I lay spread-eagle on the bed without speaking, staring up at the large, muscular, hairy naked man beside me.

"I'm not goin' to hurt ya none, pardner," Chet said. "In fact, I'm gonna make both of us feel real good."

Chet crawled onto the bed and grabbed my stiffer in his right hand. His balls hung low in their sac, resting on the blanket that covered the bed. Chet whistled softly to himself as if in admiration as he held my throbbing meat. He spit into his hand and began slowly pumping my hawg. After a couple strokes I started thrusting my hips to match the rhythm of his hand.

Tearing my gaze from Chet's hairy chest, I turned to see what was happening on Ben's bed. One of the bandits was on his hands and knees, his face over Ben's crotch, the dark crack of his hairy butt facing me. Through the v formed by the man's leg and his substantial equipment, I could see that it was Slim sucking on Ben's tool. Through the v formed by Slim's other leg

I could see Johnny, his face at the crack of Ben's ass, his huge thumbs spreading Ben's hairy ass cheeks wide, exposing his brown spot. His tongue darted between the twin mounds of flesh and he licked the tender hole. Meanwhile, Billy was still sawing up and down on Johnny's dick.

I turned back to Chet.

"Ya sure got a big one there, pardner," he said, as he slid the loose skin back over the sensitive head of my cock then bent down and stuck the tip of his tongue inside the hood. He licked the crown, then worked the tip of his tongue into the slit in the head, causing my ass to rise up off the bed. Waves of bliss flowed from my crotch through my upper torso as Chet repeatedly licked the tiny crack. My nipples ached. The skin of my chest and arms had also broken out in gooseflesh. Chet swirled his tongue over the head once more, let the excess skin slide back into place along the shaft, then took the swollen knob into his mouth. He sucked on it softly while he dragged his upper teeth gently across it. Chet's expert mouth and the tangle of gasping, writhing men on the bed next to me were quickly bringing me to the breaking point.

I closed my eyes and concentrated only on the feel of Chet's hot, wet mouth as he swallowed my cock to its thick base. He paused there, exhaling loudly through his nose because my stiffer completely filled his mouth and throat, making it difficult for him to breath. I jumped slightly when a warm, wet tongue began lapping my basket. I opened my eyes and saw Charlie kneeling on the floor on the right side of the bed, his upper torso flung across it. Taking each of the large globes into his mouth in turn, he rolled them around and flicked his tongue over their silky surface, all the while sucking on them avidly. After working both balls, he pulled the whole sac into his mouth and sucked it fiercely. Meanwhile, Chet sawed back up my pole until he reached the head, his lips applying incredible suction to the shaft as he did so. He swirled his tongue over the swollen knob several times, then swallowed my stiffer once more, trailing his tongue along the shaft until he reached the base.

Charlie suddenly let my nut sac drop from his mouth and began bathing my crotch with his tongue, working around Chet's bobbing head. He swathed my thick patch of crotch hair and lingered at the sensitive areas where my legs attached to my groin. From there he worked his way to the root of my cock, where he proceeded to run his tongue around the base each time Chet's lips relinquished it. The two of them were driving me crazy, one with his mouth, the other his tongue. From the base of my dick, Charlie licked down to the crack of my ass. Chet moved slightly to the right to give his comrade room. Once there, Charlie began nuzzling the hairy crevice. I spread my legs and raised my ass off the bed as far as the ropes binding me would allow, giving him greater access to the hole he was seeking. Charlie willingly accepted the invitation, and spread the cheeks of my ass wide, allowing the cool night air to hit the tiny exposed opening. The cool air was immediately replaced by Charlie's hot breath. He licked up and down my moist, hairy crack, then worked the area around my hole without touching the puckered flesh. He teased it repeatedly before hitting it dead center with the tip of his tongue. I yelped like a bitch coyote in heat and bucked against Charlie as he continued to probe my spot, alternating between short licks and full-length swaths of his tongue. Charlie suddenly withdrew his tongue and hawked spit several times. The warm liquid hit my opening and ran down the crack of my ass. After spreading the fluid around with his finger, Charlie poked tentatively at the furrowed opening. With just a little prodding, my hole yielded to his efforts and his finger slid in.

I glanced over once more to see what Ben and the men servicing him were up to. Johnny had finished eating Ben's corn hole and was straddling his chest, a knee firmly planted on each side of him. He was stuffing his substantial dick down

Ben's throat. I could hear his balls slapping against Ben's chin on each thrust. Ben's cheeks were sunken from the suction he was exerting on Johnny's cock, and his eyes were squeezed shut. Meanwhile, Billy had traded places with Slim, and was busily sucking Ben's fat pole. Slim had apparently untied Ben's legs from the bedposts, because Ben's feet were locked together in the small of Slim's back while Slim furiously plowed his ass. Billy released Ben's cock, licked Slim's hawg several times as it slid in and out of Ben's back door, then began switching back and forth between the two dicks.

As I was studying the four men coupling on the bed next to me, a crotch suddenly appeared in my line of vision. It was Shorty's. He crawled onto the bed and knelt, facing me, his crotch inches from my face. He shifted closer, laid his fat pole across my lips, and began sliding it back and forth. His balls smacked against my cheek as he did so, and his clear spunk soon coated my lips.

Charlie had two fingers inside my asshole now. With his other hand he squeezed my swollen nuts. Shorty slid his dick across my lips once more, then sat back and began pumping his stiffer with long, sure strokes. Chet rose up on my unit one last time and let the fat knob pop out of his mouth.

"Finish him off, Charlie," Chet said to the heaving outlaw beside him.

Charlie grabbed my hawg in his meaty fist and began vigorously pumping it. Chet took the fat crown into his mouth once more and began sucking on it, working it with his tongue as Charlie's hand moved faster on my thick shaft. The two men worked well together. Shorty was moaning beside me, his strokes coming faster and faster, his hairy chest rising and falling from his efforts. He suddenly gasped loudly and then cried out as the first white glob spurted from the tiny slit in the head of his hawg and landed on my cheek. I quickly turned my head to face Shorty and opened my mouth wide. He shoved his crotch forward and placed the head of his dick inside my mouth. More drops of the sticky white stuff spewed forth. The next couple splashed against the back of my throat; the rest landed on my tongue. Shorty gave one last jerk and deposited a final drop of spunk, then pulled his still-hard cock from my mouth. As I swallowed his copious ooze he wiped the head of his hawg on my cheek.

Charlie's next pull on my pole finished me off.

"I'm gonna shoot!" I cried, as I furiously pumped my hips.

Thick white cream began spewing from the swollen slit in the fat crown. Chet swallowed the first spurt, then quickly released the head and shifted on the bed to face Charlie. As I continued to shoot my load, the two of them took turns catching the flying white globs on their tongues and swallowing them eagerly. When I was spent, the two men licked my stiffer clean. When they had finished, they eyed each other above my still-swollen dick. Chet leaned toward Charlie and kissed him full on the mouth. His tongue parted Charlie's lips and slid inside his mouth. Chet then withdrew his tongue and kissed Charlie repeatedly. Shorty watched them in silence as he squeezed a stray drop of fluid from his cock, caught it with the tip of a finger, and sucked the finger clean. I seemed to be temporarily forgotten.

The three hombres on my bed turned their attention to their comrades and Ben. I did as well. Johnny was still slamming his meat in and out of Ben's mouth. He gave one last lunge and moaned loudly as his body went rigid, his eyes squeezed tightly shut. I could see Ben's throat spasming as he swallowed Johnny's spunk. When Ben had taken all that Johnny had to offer, Johnny pulled his hawg from Ben's mouth and wiped the leaking head across Ben's lips. As Johnny was climbing off Ben's chest, Billy's skillful mouth finally triggered Ben's explosion. Ben gave a strangled cry and thrashed on the bed, his hips bucking furiously. Billy released Ben's dick right as the first blob of spunk erupted, landing on Ben's stomach. Johnny swung quickly around and joined Billy at Ben's crotch. He and Billy watched in rapt silence as Ben spewed forth his seed, forming a small puddle in the hairs on his stomach. Billy grabbed Ben's rod and milked the last few drops from it, which he caught on his thumb and quickly sucked off. When Ben was completely spent, Billy and Johnny took turns licking up Ben's cream.

Meanwhile, Slim was still plowing Ben's ass. He gave two more quick lunges, then pulled his dick from Ben's asshole. Slim hollered "Billy!" and the young bandit moved forward and immediately engulfed the head of Slim's cock. Slim grabbed a handful of Billy's hair and held him on his fat pole as he squirted his seed into Billy's mouth. Billy took it all, then let the knob pop from his mouth and licked the outlaw's stiffer clean. Chet rose from my bed and took two steps toward Ben's. The first sign of trouble came when an arrow suddenly pierced the back of Chet's neck.

CHAPTER FOUR

Chet crumpled forward onto Ben's bed; the arrow-head barely missed puncturing Ben's thigh. All-too-familiar cries pierced the stillness of the night, and the room was suddenly filled with flying arrows. Johnny struggled frantically to untangle himself from the heap of bodies on Ben's bed. As he stood up and turned toward the cabin door, an arrow took him in the throat. He clutched feebly at the feathered shaft with his right hand as he fell onto the bed across Slim. Slim pushed Johnny off him, and he and Billy made a frantic dash for their guns which lay on the table. As if by magic, arrows suddenly protruded from each of their backs, and they fell face first onto the floor. Charlie climbed off the bed and stood next to it for a moment, his indecision written plainly on his face. That moment cost him his life. An arrow pierced his heart, and he dropped to the floor, dead.

The whiskey-sodden Shorty died instantly when an arrow pierced his heart as well. He slumped next to me on the bed. The melee was over as quickly as it'd begun. An eerie silence descended on the cabin. All of the desperados were sprawled dead, either on a bed or on the floor. Miraculously, neither Ben nor I had been hit by an arrow. I lay on the bed, still bound to it hand and foot, expecting an arrow to pierce my body at any moment. I looked over at Ben. Somehow he had managed to free his right hand, and was quickly undoing the rope that bound his left.

"Are ya okay?" he stammered, as he quickly freed his hand.

I was surprised by the concern in his voice, and further astonished when he came to my bed and began to undo the ropes that bound my wrists to the bedposts. His own wrists were raw and bleeding from rubbing against the ropes that had bound them.

"I wasn't hit, Masters, but I can't believe they missed us by accident."

"I have a bad feelin' that we were missed fer a reason, ranger. Let's not wait 'round to find out what that reason is."

My left hand was quickly freed, and Ben had just finished untying my right when I saw movement out of the corner of my eye. I turned my head and saw someone standing in the cabin doorway. At first I couldn't make out any specific details because of the deep shadows, but then the figure stepped into the cabin, and my heart sank in my chest. It was an Indian, and a good-sized one at that. White and red stripes ran horizontally down his bare chest and on both cheeks. In his left hand he carried a rifle. A bow and a quiver of arrows were slung over his right shoulder. Based on my knowledge of the Indian tribes of this area, I knew that the warrior facing me was a Chiricahua Apache. Close on his heels trod five more warriors, also armed with rifles and bows and arrows. The last one had two fresh scalps dangling at his waist. That explained why the two sentries at the entrance to the canyon hadn't sounded any warning shots. In the few seconds it took for me to digest all this information, the Apaches had converged by my bed.

Neither Ben nor I had time to react. Ben stood momentarily frozen in place, unsure of the warriors' intent. Two of them immediately covered Ben and me with army-issue carbines; a third motioned to Ben with his hand, indicating that he wanted Ben to join me on the bed. Ben climbed up next to me, moving so close he was practically on top of me.

The tall Indian stood at the edge of the bed, eyeing us in silence. His long, blue-black hair was shoulder length. It was held out of his eyes by a thin strip of red cloth wound around his head. Four feathers stuck up behind it. His chest was broad and thickly muscled. Large, dark-brown nipples capped the swells of his tits. His stomach, legs, and arms were also heavily muscled. Wide bands of leather encircled his muscular arms, just above his elbows. A single feather protruded from each band. A leather breechclout covered his groin, and leather moccasins covered his lower legs from his feet to his knees. Except for the flowing black hair on his head, his body was entirely hairless. I briefly wondered if hair grew above his manhood, but quickly cast the thought aside as the tall warrior loomed over me. A long, wicked-looking knife rested in a leather sheath on his right hip.

The remaining Apaches formed a semicircle at the foot of the bed. All five warriors matched the tall Indian in their muscu-lature, but lacked his height. Their headbands were white, with only two feathers protruding from the backs. No stripes adorned their broad, brown chests. Only their faces were painted, lead-ing me to believe that perhaps the one with four feathers was a young war chief, and thus the leader of this group.

"Don't make any sudden moves, Slater," Ben whispered. "I'm sure they wouldn't hesitate to kill us."

My gut feeling told me that these warriors had no intention of killing us for the moment, because they had a more sinister purpose in mind: perhaps slow torture, or captivity. The same two warriors kept us covered with their rifles, while the one I'd deemed a war chief and the three others moved among the slain outlaws, quickly relieving them of their scalps. When they were finished they searched the cabin. They piled Ben's and my supplies, along with those of the bandits, on the floor at the foot of my bed, then proceeded to sort through the pile, setting aside food, weapons and ammunition, and blankets and per-sonal items. They had no interest in the outlaws' clothing. One of the warriors voiced a loud cry and held aloft a half-finished bottle of whiskey. The chief uttered one short, sharp word, and the man reluctantly tossed the bottle back onto the pile.

The chief spoke again, and two of the warriors ran swiftly out the cabin door. They hadn't been gone very long when I heard rapid hoof beats, which abruptly stopped, then the soft nickers of horses. Through the open door I could see several horses milling in front of the cabin. Shortly thereafter, the two warriors reentered the cabin and rejoined the rest of the war party. The Apaches began gathering their spoils and carrying them out to the horses. They tossed the outlaws' clothing in the still-smoldering fire.

Meanwhile, the young chief was still standing beside the bed, his dark-brown, almost black eyes studying me quizzically. I tried to return his stare as calmly as I could, but my fear prevented me. His skin reflected the firelight, and a sheen of sweat covered it. My eyes went of their own accord to the substantial lump in his breechclout. I found myself wanting to see his shaft. The direction of my gaze didn't go unnoticed by the rugged Apache.

The war chief laid his weapons on the floor by the bed, and knelt beside them. His eyes scanned my naked body from head to toe several times. He leaned against the bed, placed a hand on my chest, then ran it lightly over my chest and stomach. He played with the hair covering both, curling it around the tips of his fingers and tugging on it gently. When it seemed his curiosity had been satisfied, he slid his hand down to my crotch. Grabbing my flaccid and leaking dick, he scooped up the clear fluid with the tip of a finger, held it to his nose, then put the finger in his mouth and sucked on it. His face remained expressionless as he grabbed my cock and began slowly pumping it. My rod quickly swelled to its full proportions, the head emerging from beneath its skin covering. The two warriors covering us with rifles placed the muzzles against Ben's chest, clearly indicating that he was not to interfere with the chief's actions.

Bending at the waist with his upper torso now on the bed, the young chief swirled his tongue over the large head of my hawg. After several more licks he took the knob into his mouth, sucked on it noisily, then slowly swallowed my tool until his nose was buried in my crotch hair. He held my entire stiffer in his warm, wet mouth, sucking on it softly, then began sliding his mouth up and down it. Before long I felt my explosion building. On the chief's next saw, I released into his eager mouth. He swallowed it all without hesitation. When I was spent, he relinquished my cock and licked his lips in evident satisfaction.

The war chief stood up, slid off the bed, eyed me for a moment, his expression unreadable, then moved around toward Ben. The warriors covering Ben made way for the chief, then pointed the muzzles of their rifles at me. Apparently the chief was going to service Ben as well. He knelt at Ben's side of the bed, and his face began moving inexorably toward Ben's crotch.

Just as the chief was about to take the head of Ben's cock into his mouth, Ben brought his left knee up swiftly, catching the warrior on the jaw and knocking him backward onto the floor. The two warriors guarding me instantly burst into action, one moving to the fallen war chief, the other whipping out his knife and placing the blade against Ben's throat. I watched, horrified, certain that Ben was going to die in front of me. The warrior holding the knife to Ben's throat looked to the fallen chief, as if awaiting the signal to end Ben's life. The young chief spoke as he picked himself up off the floor, and the Apache withdrew his blade. The handsome chief stepped to the side of the bed and dealt Ben a blow across the face with his clenched fist that rocked Ben's head on the pillow. A small trickle of blood appeared at Ben's right nostril and ran down past the corner of his mouth. He glared defiantly at the chief.

"If'n we want to make it through this alive, Masters," I whispered, "then ya better let the chief have his way with ya. Besides, he's pretty good at it."

Ben turned to me, his green eyes holding my own. It was several moments before he spoke.

"I guess you're right, Slater."

Ben faced the young chief once more and spread his legs wide. The invitation was not lost on the Apache. He knelt once more, swallowed Ben's hawg, and began bobbing up and down on it steadily. Without quite knowing why, I placed my arm behind Ben's head for support. I felt small spasms coursing through his body as the chief pleasured him. Soon Ben was moaning, gasping, and writhing against me. The chief wet his middle finger and deftly inserted it into Ben's asshole. A few strokes quickly brought him to the point of explosion. I held him as he emptied his seed in to the chief's mouth. The chief swallowed every drop that Ben fed him, then released his fat pole and licked it clean.

Ben turned to me and smiled.

"You were right, Slater. He ain't half bad."

During Ben's encounter with the chief, the warriors had finished removing their booty from the cabin. Besides the chief, only one Apache remained. The warrior retrieved the bottle of whiskey his comrade had found and emptied its contents onto the wooden table. Grabbing a flaming piece of clothing from the fireplace, he flung the cloth onto the table. The old, dry wood was soon burning fiercely. The same warrior came to my side of the bed, cut the ropes that bound my ankles, tied my hands together, and Ben's as well, then motioned with his hands for us to get up. Once we were on our feet, he herded us from the cabin. The chief was right behind us. Outside, Ben and I were hoisted onto separate horses. Our feet were tied together beneath our mounts' stomachs, and the rope reins were looped around our hands. The Black and my original packhorse, as well as the gelding and the mare, were loaded down with the Apaches' loot. We sat and watched the flames engulf the outer walls of the cabin, lighting up the night sky with an orange glow. There was a loud crash when the remainder of the roof caved in. The young chief gave a loud, sharp cry, put heels to his horse, and we headed out across the meadow. The bandits' horses were strung out behind us, joined by a single rope. They carried neither rider nor baggage.

Soon my head dropped onto my chest and I was fast asleep. The motion of the horse eventually brought me back from the depths of slumber. Dawn was slowly unfolding across the sand dunes, rock formations, and scrub brush around me. As my senses returned, I noticed that I was on a different horse. Also, warm flesh was pressed tightly against my back, and a strong hand gripped my waist.

I glanced over my left shoulder, fully expecting to see Ben. Instead, I met the cold stare of the war chief. Sometime during the night I'd been transferred to his horse. I'd been so exhausted that I'd never even woken up. I was perched in front of him, one hand holding me securely on the colorful blanket he used as a saddle, the other holding the rope he used as reins. The substantial lump of his manhood pressed firmly against my backside beneath the soft leather of his breechclout. My hands were tied in front of me, resting on the horse's mane. My feet were tied beneath the horse's stomach. My equipment flopped about with the movements of the horse. I couldn't see any of the other Apaches. They must've been strung out single file behind us. I wondered if Ben was on a new mount as well.

The sun was high overhead when we stopped at a small, muddy stream that was all but evaporating in the desert heat. A sizable outcrop of sandstone offered the only nearby shade. The chief was given first rights to the water. He dismounted and led his horse to it, and it drank thirstily. Kneeling beside the horse's head, the young Apache drank from the stream as well. When he had slaked his thirst, he united my hands and feet and pulled me from his horse. I knelt at the edge of the stream and forced the warm, muddy stuff down my throat, trying hard not to gag on its milky quality. When I could drink no more, the chief hoisted me onto his horse and retied my hands and feet.

This appeared to be the signal for the other warriors to drink, because they now led their horses to the stream.

As the warriors formed a line on each side of the stream, I saw Ben for the first time. He was mounted in front of a sinewy warrior, his hands and feet tied the same as mine. There was a large black and purple bruise on his left cheek. He must have put up a fight when switching mounts during the night. The Apaches let their horses drink first, then quenched their own thirst. Ben's warrior unbound his hands and feet and hauled him to the ground. He drank briefly, then was mounted on the warrior's horse once more.

Once again I was aware of the war chief's muscular torso pressed against my back. He suddenly reached up and grasped my right nipple between a thumb and forefinger. He squeezed it several times then switched to the left one. I moaned softly and pressed against his sculpted chest, resting my head on his shoulder. I ground my ass against the steadily-rising lump beneath his breechclout. He pulled and twisted my nipples until they were fully hard, the small brown nubs poking out defiantly from my chest.

The chief then released my nipples and began trailing his fingers through the hairs on my chest and stomach. He curled them around the tips of his fingers and gently tugged on them. All the young men in the chief's party, himself included, had no hair on their chests and stomachs, and only a smattering on their arms and legs. Apparently my hirsute torso was intriguing to him. He ran his fingers down to my crotch and began playing with the profusion of hair that grew there. Grabbing my semihard dick in his right hand, he quickly stroked it to full rigidity.

One of the warriors noticed the action on the young chief's horse, and word quickly spread through the group. One by one they remounted their horses and quietly sidled over to either side of the chief's horse. Curiosity and a recognizable yearning was written plainly on each face. The chief, thoroughly absorbed with my cock, appeared not to notice our audience, or, if he did notice, didn't care. The Apache Ben was riding with was the last to join the group of onlookers, but he reined in the closest. Ben caught and held my gaze as the young chief continued to stroke my stiffer. The bruise on his cheek looked worse close up, and I also noticed a small cut above his left eye. There were also cuts and bruises on his arms and legs.

The chief suddenly bent me forward until my face was pressed into his horse's mane. I turned my head to the right, afraid of suffocating in the mass of hair. My ass was now completely at the chief's mercy. The idea excited me. My equipment was pressed firmly into the blanket beneath me, my prick laid out flat, and fully hard. The war chief slapped my right ass cheek, then the left. The sounds echoed through the rocks around us. I heard several snickers from the group of warriors. The chief proceeded to give me a sound spanking. It seemed to last forever, but was in truth only a couple of minutes in duration. I bit my lower lip to keep from crying out and closed my eyes so I couldn't see the smiles on the other Apaches' faces, nor the look on Ben's. When he was finished, the young chief rubbed my ass cheeks vigorously, taking some of the sting out of them.

Spreading the cheeks of my ass apart with his thumbs, the chief exposed the small, brown hole nestled between them. I squirmed as he pressed a thumb against the sensitive opening, then began slowly strumming it. I heard him spit, and felt the warm fluid hit my corn hole dead center. He spit once more and rubbed the fluid over and around the tiny opening. The chief continued pressing against my shit hole with his thumb until, suddenly, the ring of muscle relaxed, allowing the digit to slip inside. He didn't stop there, but pushed it deep up my chute. I clenched the muscles inside my asshole and squeezed his thumb hard. The chief grunted, then began pushing his thumb in and out steadily. I rocked back against him, matching his thrusts.

After a few more strokes he withdrew his thumb and placed the fat head of his cock against my opening. He grabbed my hips, his strong fingers digging in deeply. I pushed back against his swollen knob and it popped through the tight opening.

The war chief penetrated me slowly but insistently until I felt his crotch hair tickling my ass cheeks. At least I now knew that he had hair down there, I thought to myself. I grunted and closed my eyes as his large cock head banged into my secret muscle. He held his hawg inside me, allowing my hole to adjust to its girth, then pulled out slowly, moaning softly as he did so. I heard and felt the head of his dick pop out of my shitter. The young chief paused a moment, then slid back into me just as slowly, as if testing the waters, before he began pumping steadily in and out of me. His thrusts were long and deep, each one propelling me forward onto his horse's neck. The blanket beneath me rubbed against my equipment and soon my clear fluid had dampened a considerable spot.

Gripping my shoulders, the young chief pulled me back and upright against him, impaling me on his thick shaft. He placed a hand on my chest to steady me, then grabbed my dick and began sliding his hand up and down it, using some of my fluid to ease his strokes. As he pumped my tool, I suddenly remembered our audience. I opened my eyes to see what they were up to. The warriors hadn't remained idle. Strong, brown hands had reached beneath leather breechclouts and pulled out brown cocks of various lengths and widths. These same hands, some left, others right, all most likely covered with spit, were sliding up and down thickening shafts. The warrior riding behind Ben was busy stroking himself and Ben. Ben moved his hips in time with the warrior's hand.

The chief's hand moved faster on my member, and his thrusts up my asshole became even more powerful. Several times I almost slid sideways off his horse, but each time he caught and steadied me with a powerful arm. On his next plunge deep inside me, the war chief moaned long and loud. His fingers dug deeply into my waist as I felt his spunk flood my hole. When the chief was done shooting, he pushed me forward onto his horse's neck once more and collapsed upon my back. His dick was still hard and inside me, and his hand was still wrapped around my hawg. However, his hand was now pinned beneath me. I pushed up slightly against the chief, giving his hand room to slide on my stiffer. He understood immediately and quickly resumed his stroking. After only a few strokes, I felt my release approaching. I craned my neck just in time to see the first white drop shoot from the slit in the head and land in the horse's mane. As the chief pumped my cock with his left hand, he placed his right underneath the fat head, palm up. I watched as it filled with my sticky fluid. When he had milked the last drop from me, the chief withdrew his hand. He held it to his nose like he'd done last night in the cabin, sniffed the small pile, then titled his hand and let the white mound slide onto his tongue. He swallowed it without so much as a grimace, then licked his hand clean.

The warriors gathered around us were shooting their seed in rapid succession, catching it in the palms of their hands and eating it as the chief had done with mine. Their heated cries filled the quiet afternoon air. The warrior mounted behind Ben was bent around him at the waist, his face in Ben's crotch, his mouth sliding up and down on Ben's hawg. Ben suddenly twitched on his mount, and hollered as his eruption began. The warrior ceased his bobbing and simply held the large knob in his mouth as Ben emptied into it. When Ben was spent, he slumped back against the warrior, his chest heaving. No one spoke as brown hands were licked clean, and brown, softening dicks were tucked beneath leather breechclouts once more.

The chief pushed up off me, pulled his softening meat out of my hole, and yanked me back into an upright position. He uttered a single cry, then he kicked his horse in the ribs and off we galloped. His cry was echoed by the rest of the warriors as they fell in line single file behind us. We followed no discernible trail, but simply raced along the sand dunes, the wind whipping sand in my face. The chief guided his horse expertly with his knees around rocks and bushes, and up and down gullies and sandy washouts. We rode as if pursued, and I glanced back to see if, indeed, we were. It soon dawned on me, though, that the warriors were riding for the simple joy of it, reveling in the sun and fresh air, and probably their freedom as well.

We rode for hours, stopping once late in the afternoon to drink and water the horses again at a small spring (this one with clear, crisp water) where it seemed impossible for water to be. We drank our fill and headed out once more, this time at a slightly slower pace, but still a far cry from a leisurely ride. I saw several hawks, one scrawny coyote that two of the warriors briefly chased, and numerous jackrabbits, several of which the warriors pierced with deadly accuracy with their arrows. We descended a small sand dune and, upon reaching the bottom of it, emerged into a wide gully. I spotted wagon tracks in the sand. As we followed the well-worn trail for several miles, I noticed the warriors' increased alertness. We passed several battered and abandoned stagecoaches and wagons with bleaching bones strewn amongst them. Once we came upon a stagecoach where the passengers had been tied to the wheels and burned. Their black, empty eye sockets stared at us as we rode past. I wondered briefly if this band of warriors had played a role in any of these incidences.

The sun was just beginning its descent when we turned off the trail and started to climb into the rock-strewn hills. We rode uphill for miles, again following no trail that I could see. It was obvious, though, that the Apaches knew where they were headed because they never once halted to take any bearings. We rode through places I'd never thought a horse could go, and I began to wonder if my Apache captors and their mounts weren't half mountain goat. We reached a small plateau that ended at a long, steep rise. The group slowed to a walk as we started up it. When we reached the top, ahead, in the distance, gigantic sandstone cliffs faced us. We halted, and I saw a flash of light coming from the top of one of the cliffs. I wasn't sure if I was seeing things or not, but then the flash came again. The Apache riding with Ben came up beside us and conferred briefly with the war chief. He rode back to his place in line, and we started down the other side of the incline. When we reached the bottom, we broke into a run once more. We didn't slow down as we neared the cliffs, and I feared the Apaches were going to dash themselves into the rocks. But then I saw a break in one of the cliff faces. As we drew closer I could see that it was wide enough and tall enough to admit a horse and rider, with a few feet on each side to spare. The young chief rode straight for it, and we burst through the gap at a dead run. The passage was winding and narrow, the space never becoming wider than the entrance. We raced through it at breakneck speed. One misstep by a horse would have surely caused serious injury to its rider. We burst suddenly from the passage into fading sunlight, and I gaped in open astonishment at what lay before me. At first I thought I was suffering from a heat-induced hallucination.

The passage had opened onto a long, wide, grassy plateau, filled to almost overflowing with teepees. There must have been several hundred of them. Curls of white smoke rose lazily into the air from the tops of the teepees, along with whitish-gray smoke from the numerous fires burning on the ground around them. Painted images adorned the buffalo-hide walls of the teepees. The smell of roasting buffalo meat was heavy on the air. Off to my left I could see large fields of maize and a variety of melons. Other fields held vegetables that I couldn't distinguish from this distance. Apache women and small children were bent over, working among the rows. To the right of these fields a sizable stream forked; one branch meandered through the large village, the other disappeared from my line of sight. Beyond the fields of maize large herds of horses grazed.

As we rode toward the nearest teepees, we were immediately surrounded by a sizable circle of screaming Apache children and ferocious-looking dogs. The children hurled rocks and sticks at Ben and me, and yelled unintelligible words that I was certain weren't Apache words of welcome. The dogs nipped at the horses' feet and ran around and underneath them, barking furiously all the while. The chief yelled a few curt words, and the children ceased throwing things and edged back from our group, but they and the dogs still trailed us as we rode through the village. Apaches, both male and female, young and old, alerted by the cries of the children and the barking dogs, emerged from their teepees and eyed us in silence as we passed.

We splashed through the stream and rode up a short incline onto another small plateau, where more teepees were clustered, although considerably fewer than on the lower plateau. We rode to a large teepee that was set apart from the others and halted in front of it. The young chief dismounted, untied my feet and hands, and pulled me from his horse. The rest of the warriors also dismounted. Ben's hands and feet were untied and he was hauled off his horse as well.

The flap on the teepee was suddenly pushed out and flipped back, and a broad-chested, white-haired Apache stepped out and faced our small party. His head was adorned with a magnificent feather headdress that trailed down his back to his waist. He wore buckskin trousers and shirt, each adorned with colorful beadwork and buckskin fringe. I guessed we were in the presence of the head chief of the Chiricahua Apaches that lived in this valley. The war chief stepped forward, clasped forearms with the white-haired chief, then began speaking. He gestured with his hands as he did so, pointing to Ben and me several times. It was obvious he was relating to his chief how it was that he had returned with two naked white men as prisoners.

The white-haired chief listened to the young chief's narra-
tion impassively, his gaze traveling from the young chief to Ben
and me, and back again, several times. When the young chief
had finished speaking, the white-haired chief spoke a few words
in reply and motioned with his right hand toward the high, rock
cliffs visible behind his teepee. I looked in that direction and
could just make out the roof of a structure, outlined against yet
another small hill. The young chief nodded, walked back to me,
grabbed the end of the rope that bound my wrists, and half-led,
half-dragged me past the white-haired chief and up the hill. As
we crested the hill, I could see a rectangular structure about one
hundred feet away, at the base of a small hill that rose to meet
the sandstone cliffs. I glanced back over my shoulder and saw
Ben close on my heels, escorted by one of the Apaches from the
group that had captured us.

As we neared the structure, an Apache emerged from it and
stood to the right of the entrance. Additional warriors appeared
at each front corner, each of them wielding army-issue rifles.
I wondered what they were guarding inside the structure. We
paused in front of the entrance, and the chief untied my wrists
and then Ben's. He pulled back the buffalo-skin flap that served
as the door and pushed us inside. The chief, however, remained
outside the lodge and closed the flap behind us.

I stood just inside the entrance, awash in complete and
immediate darkness. I waited for my eyes to adjust to the dark
interior and, when they had, saw that Ben and I were not the
only occupants. Three men huddled against the wall to our
right. A shaft of fast-fading sunlight arced from a hole in the
lodge roof to the ground directly in front of them. There were
several such holes, designed to let out the smoke from fires.
Four fires were presently burning low within the lodge, in a
line down the center of it. I went to the wall opposite of what I
assumed were other prisoners and sank to the ground, my back
against the rough hide. Ben slumped down beside me. All three

of the men faced us, but only one eyed us steadily. The heads of the other two were slumped on their chests, either in sleep or in death. All three were dirty and naked.

I was hungry, thirsty, and tired. Most of the saddle grease had rubbed off, and my skin had turned a brighter red since leaving the cabin. My lips were blistered and starting to peel. My thoughts wandered back over the past couple of days. Since riding out of Deadwood in search of Ben, I'd had what you would call a string of shit luck. Since our capture last night by the Apaches, I'd been alert for any chance to escape while such a small number of warriors guarded us. There had been no such chance. Now that we were in what appeared to be their main village, with the number of Apaches having grown probably one hundred fold, I could see no way for Ben and me to make a break for it. Granted, we were untied, but even if we did manage to sneak out of the lodge, win our way through the village, and eventually out of this valley, I had no idea which trails to take to get to the nearest fort or settlement. We'd made so many twists and turns on the ride to the Apache stronghold that, even with the sun as a guide, I feared we'd easily get lost, and die from thirst in the desert.

A slight smile came to my mouth as I realized what I'd been thinking. Ben and me. As if there were no way I was leaving him behind. I was thinking of him as if he were my friend, or brother, or even a partner of some kind. I was becoming more and more concerned about the welfare of the desperado I had sworn to bring in, the same man who had inadvertently caused my capture by Chet and his band and, subsequently, the Chiricahua. Again, I pondered whether my concern was that of a lawman protecting his prisoner, or simply the concern of a man who was lonely for companionship in this vast western wasteland. As I considered it further, I realized suddenly that, outlaw or not, I had fallen in love with this red-haired, green-eyed man sitting beside me. The knowledge hit me hard, for I was unprepared to deal with it under these circumstances. Ben was still wanted on a murder charge back in Abilene. However, the realization that I loved Ben brought with it a new determination to win our freedom from our Apache captors and somehow help Ben prove his innocence.

I turned my head slightly to the right and found myself staring into Ben's eyes. There were dark circles under them, and the whites were interspersed with small, red lines, like tiny cracks. The blood from the cut above his left eye had dried to a dark-brown color. His face was coated with a mixture of trail dust and sweat. His skin was bright red from the sun, which had left his lips dry and cracked as well. His cheeks and throat were covered with several days' worth of dark-red stubble. His left cheek was now swollen, almost hiding his eye. I was pretty sure that, except for the bruises, I looked as bad as Ben.

"How'd ya git them cuts an' bruises, Ben?"

He stared at me a moment before replying. As I waited for him to speak, it dawned on me that, for the first time, I had called him by his given name.

"When I saw 'em put ya on a diff'rent horse, I figured they'd do the same to me, an' I thought that would be my chance. By the way they was carryin' ya I could tell ya was asleep. The Apaches were ready fer me, though, an' didn' take kindly to me tryin' to escape."

He turned his head away from me and was silent for a long time, then turned to face me once more.

"How we goin' to git out of this here mess, Jake?"

His voice was raspy and low. I was taken slightly aback, not so much by the question as by the fact that this was the first time he'd addressed me using my first name. Perhaps because I had done the same to him.

I stared at him for several moments before speaking. When I did answer him, my voice sounded as rough as his had.

"I don't rightly know, Ben. We'll just have to keep our eyes an' ears open fer the first opportunity that comes our way. I think we'll stand a much better chance of escapin' together than if'n just one of us tries."

Ben stared hard into my eyes, as if trying to gauge my sincerity.

"Is that the ranger in ya speakin', Jake, or do ya really care what happens to me?"

Afraid that I'd already revealed too much, I didn't respond. Encouraged by my silence, Ben smiled at me through cracked lips and reached for my hand. I opened it willingly, and his large, callused one slipped into mine. We sat quietly, holding hands, ignoring the huddled forms across from us. I was sure that Ben was as confused as I was about our newfound civility. My thoughts were suddenly interrupted by a voice from across the lodge. It took me a moment to realize that one of the men had spoken to us.

"I said, my name's Samuel. My friends call me Sam. How long have you two been pris'ners?"

I looked across the lodge and saw that the middle man was sitting up. Assuming he was the one who had spoken, I focused my attention on him. Ben's continued silence made it plain that I was to be the elected speaker for us.

"My name's Jake, an' this here's Ben." I indicated Ben with a jerk of my thumb. "They captured us last night. How many miles from here I couldn't tell ya. The rest of our party was killed."

True to the reticence of the West, I was unwilling to divulge to this stranger what had been transpiring when Ben and I were caught, or the circumstances that had brought us together.

The man rose and came over to where we sat, limping slightly on his right leg. He stopped a few feet in front of us. He was an older man, graying at the temples, dirty, but still quite handsome. However, I took an instant dislike to him. His eyes traveled the length of our bodies several times, lingering at our crotches each time.

"I can see why they didn' kill you two right off," he said roughly. "They must be gittin' tired of usin' the three of us ev'ry night."

I had no idea what he was talking about and, looking at Ben, I could tell by the puzzled look on his face that he didn't understand either. I was about to reply when the hide flap at the entrance was thrown back, and the young chief stepped inside. He walked over to us and without glancing at Ben or me, spoke directly to Samuel. To my surprise, Samuel answered him in the Apache dialect. The chief, apparently satisfied with Samuel's response, turned and left the lodge.

"I see ya speak their tongue, Samuel," I said, warily.

His eyes narrowed to slits. By calling him "Samuel" I'd established the fact that I didn' consider him a friend. Samuel eyed me steadily before replying.

"I've been here longer than I care to remember, stranger. I had to learn their language to survive."

His declaration dashed any hopes I'd had of making a quick escape.

"What did the chief say to ya, Samuel?"

"He warned me an' my friends to keep our hands off'n you an' yer good-lookin' friend. He's savin' you two fer his own needs. Also, I now know why they didn' kill the two of ya right off. He an' his warriors think you're both plumb loco, seein's how you're the first white men he's ever seen, or heard tell of fer that matter, ridin' through the desert buck-naked. Apaches fear an', at the same time, have a grudgin' respect fer crazy people. They think they've been touched by the spirits."

So, Chet's fears of pursuit had been well founded. The Apaches had indeed been following us through the Badlands.

"What did ya mean before when ya said 'usin' the three of us ev'ry night'?" I asked.

Samuel stared at me quizzically, a small smile playing at the corners of his mouth.

"It's a little-known fact, but the Apache are one of the randi-est tribes 'round, 'specially the Chiricahua. Couplin' with their squaws ev'ry chance they git, sometimes a half-dozen times a day, or with other squaws when they hanker to an' another war-rior is willin' to share. An' they can be quite the sharin' bunch, if'n ya git my meanin'. When their squaws are seven or eight months with child, or when their blood's flowin', warriors often turn to each other fer pleasurin'. Or they make do with any pris'ners they happen to have on hand, male or female. They also take male pris'ners along on huntin' parties fer their plea-surin', figurin' their women folk will slow 'em down. Fer awhile now it's been just the three of us, but I'm bettin' that's soon gonna change."

When Samuel finished speaking, I looked at Ben. He returned my gaze, a mixture of fear and anger in his eyes. I couldn't deny that I'd been aroused by the war chief and his equally good-look-ing warriors during the encounter at the stream this afternoon. I still could almost feel his large, hot cock inside me, his warm, rough hand grasping my dick. But I certainly had no desire to spend the rest of my days satisfying the lust of the warriors in this tribe. That is, until I was no longer of use.

"Have ya ever tried to escape?" I asked, hoping Samuel wouldn't notice the rising note of despair in my voice.

"Oh sure," Samuel replied. "We tried it once. Shortly after we first got caught. There were four of us in the beginnin'. My partner tried to escape when we were taken along on a buffalo hunt to keep the warriors entertained. They caught him real fast an' made him into a woman, if'n ya know what I mean. That was before they each had a turn with him, then slow-roasted him over a fire. Seein' him cooked took most notions of escapin' right out of our heads."

Before I could reply, four Apaches entered the lodge, each carrying a wooden gourd. Without another word, Samuel turned and limped back across the lodge to join his friends.

Two of the warriors went to them and set their gourds on the ground by their feet. The remaining two approached Ben and me. They set the gourds on the ground between us, and then all four warriors left the lodge. As soon as they'd gone, I inspected the gourds. One was filled with water; the other contained some type of stew. I picked up the latter and inspected its contents closely. It was indeed a stew, made with chunks of buffalo meat, maize, and some type of bean. I scooped some up with two fingers, placed them in my mouth, and sucked the mixture from them. It certainly wasn't the best-tasting food I'd ever eaten, but it would fill my stomach. I picked up the water gourd and took a long drink. The water was cold, sharp, and delicious to my parched mouth. I was ravenous and made short work of the stew, washing it down with the last of the water. Ben did the same with his portion.

The same four warriors returned soon after we'd finished eating and collected the empty gourds. They stoked the fires in the center of the lodge before leaving. As soon as they had gone, Samuel stood up. He was limping over to us when the flap opened up again. This time it was the young war chief. He was followed closely by nine brown, stalwart warriors. Samuel halted and watched the Apaches in silence. The torso of the warrior directly behind the young chief was painted similar to his, but with fewer feathers adorning his head. I reckoned he was a chief of lesser rank, probably a junior war chief. The rest of the Apaches were painted, but wore no feathers. Two of them carried a travois, laden with objects that were, as yet, unidentifiable. The two warriors behind the travois had a bow and a quiver of arrows slung over their shoulders. The last four warriors in line each carried a torch tied to the end of a long, wooden pole. The procession halted in front of Ben and me. The torch-wielding warriors stuck the torches in the ground in a line in front of us, then used a small piece of burning wood from the nearest fire to light them. They then formed a line facing us, behind the two chiefs and the rest of the warriors. The two warriors carrying the travois set it on the ground between us and joined the line formed by the four warriors. All the Apaches, except the young chief and the junior war chief, as I'd duly christened him, carried knives at their waists.

The young chief spoke and one of the bow-wielding warriors stepped to my right side. The second went to Ben's left. Not wanting to show the warriors my fear, I scrutinized the contents of the travois. On it were gourds of various shapes and sizes, similar to the ones that had contained our food and water. There were also bundles of the valley's rich, green grass and small pieces of cloth. Upon closer inspection I saw that the cloth was pieces of tanned buffalo hide. The young war chief motioned with his right hand for Samuel to return to the other side of the lodge.

The war chief spoke quickly and commandingly, and two warriors immediately stepped forward from the line. One knelt at my feet, and one knelt at Ben's. Grabbing our ankles, they unceremoniously yanked us forward. Ben and I were propelled backward, landing flat on our backs. The wind was forced from my lungs when I hit the hard ground. As I struggled to return air to my lungs, the Apaches released our ankles, and the bow-wielding warriors moved closer to us. Unslinging their bows, they each nocked an arrow and aimed them at our individual midsections. I braced myself for the arrow I was sure was about to pierce my flesh.

CHAPTER FIVE

The arrow that I anticipated would end my life never came. The warriors who had pulled Ben and me onto our backs stepped to the travois. Bending down, they each grabbed a piece of buffalo hide from the travois and dipped it into one of the larger gourds. I heard splashing water and deduced that Ben and I were about to get a much-needed bath. The young war chief stood at my feet as the two men squatted in the dirt between us. The junior war chief stood at Ben's feet. A second pair of warriors moved forward from the line, grabbed a piece of buffalo hide, dunked it in the water gourd, and joined their kneeling comrades. One went to my right side, the other to Ben's left. Apaches now squatted on both sides of us. Starting with my face, the warriors washed the sweat and grime from it. The buffalo-hide cloths and cold water felt good against my sunburned forehead, cheeks, and throat. Ben was being scrubbed as well.

The four men, in unison, dipped their cloths in the gourds, wrung them out, shifted slightly beside us, and began washing our chests. The two warriors attending to me ran the cloths slowly over my chest at first, then started scrubbing more vigorously. All the while they avoided contact with my nipples. As the chief had been, they were fascinated by the amount of hair on my chest and stomach. They ran the fingers of their free hands through the thick mass several times, once or twice even tugging the hair gently as if to see if, indeed, it was attached. Their curiosity satisfied, they moved down to my stomach. One inserted a finger into my navel, causing my hips to buck of their own accord. When they'd finished with my stomach, the two men dipped their cloths once more and placed them on the nipple closest to them. The cold water caused both nipples to harden immediately into stiff, brown nubs. Removing the cloths, the warriors made small circular motions around each nipple, coming close to the points several times but never actually touching them. After several passes, the cloths were set aside, and strong, brown fingers began twisting each teat. Soon the fingers were replaced by two eager mouths. The men proceeded to bite and suck the tender brown pieces of flesh. I moaned and writhed in the dirt of the lodge floor. My dick was rock hard, and stuck straight up from my crotch like a flagpole. I turned my head to my left and saw that Ben's nipples were receiving the same treatment from the two Apaches tending to him. The two chiefs suddenly spoke several words, sharply, and both sets of warriors immediately released Ben's and my nipples and took up the cloths once more.

My pair shuffled on their knees until they reached my hips, then began scrubbing my crotch. The soft cloths plowed through my mass of crotch hair. The smell of my crotch came strongly to my nostrils. The Apaches briefly played with the wiry hair, then washed the sensitive areas where my legs attached to my groin. The one on my left wrapped his cloth around my swollen dick and, making a fist, began sliding it up and down my shaft. I began moving my hips in time to his stroking hand. The warrior on my right watched for a moment, then bent down and lapped up the clear fluid bubbling from the tiny slit in the swollen head of my meat. When he was done, he engulfed the fat knob, pushed the first warrior aside, and quickly swallowed my cock to its thick base. He sawed back up and was licking the head once more when the young war chief stepped forward and back-handed him across the head. The man went sprawling. I was thankful that my stiffer hadn't been in his mouth at the time. The warrior picked himself up, grabbed his cloth, and both warriors went to work on my ball sac, carefully washing the twin globes of flesh and the wrinkled sac of skin.

When they were done with my nuts, the two men washed the fronts of my legs, then my feet, then rolled me over on my stomach. The cloths were dipped and wrung again, and then my back was vigorously scrubbed. They skipped my ass and washed the backs of my legs and then my feet, before returning to my ass. Both cheeks were washed, then held apart as the hairy crack between them was thoroughly scrubbed. Each time the soft cloth made contact with my brown spot, I moaned softly, and my ass involuntarily rose off the ground. The cloths were dipped once more and, suddenly, cold water cascaded directly onto my shit hole. The sensation was incredible, causing the skin on my arms and legs to turn to gooseflesh. The water ran down the crack of my ass and over my nut sac, causing my balls to retreat into my body. One of the warriors slipped two of his fingers roughly into my crevice. I gasped at the sudden intrusion. He plunged them in and out several times, then withdrew them and rinsed my crack again.

Evidently my bung hole wasn't cleaned to his satisfaction, for the warrior plunged his fingers inside me twice more, rinsed off my back door, and then I was flipped on my back again. My dick was still achingly hard, and fresh fluid was oozing from the slit in the head. Both men gazed at my stiffer, somewhat longingly it seemed, then they each grabbed a handful of grass and began drying me off. The grass was soft and soothing on my skin, and slightly ticklish. It smelled clean and fresh. When they had dried my body thoroughly, the two Apaches stood up and stepped away from me. When the warriors tending to Ben were done, they and the two who had washed me added wood to the fires, then returned to their places in line. The two warriors with the nocked arrows remained in place beside us, their eyes never leaving us.

The two chiefs stepped forward and knelt down on opposite sides of the travois, the young chief facing me and the junior chief facing Ben. The young war chief grabbed one of the smaller gourds from the travois and dipped his middle finger into its contents. The junior war chief swung around, grabbed a similar gourd, then faced Ben again. When the chief withdrew his hand from the bowl and extended it toward me, I saw that the finger he'd dipped was covered with what appeared to be blood. When it was beneath my nose, however, I smelled wild raspberries, not blood, and breathed a small sigh of relief.

The young chief pressed his fingertip to the end of my nose and traced the bridge with it, stopping just above the line of my eyebrows. He then drew a line across my forehead just above both brows. He sat back and studied his work for a moment, then dipped his finger again. Placing the tip of his finger once more on the end of my nose, the chief drew a second line along the thin piece of flesh that separated my nostrils. He continued across my lips, over my chin and down my throat, finally stopping equidistant between my nipples. Dipping his finger once more, he drew a horizontal line across my tits, directly through each nipple, then made similar lines across my chest and stomach down to my waist. From the point at which he'd stopped between my nipples, the young chief ran another line down my chest and stomach, through the deep cut of my navel, and into my crotch hair. He withdrew his hand, and I thought he had finished, but he dipped his whole hand into the gourd and proceeded to coat my cock and balls with the red berry juice. When he was done, he sat back on his haunches, again inspecting his work. I turned my head and saw that the junior war chief had similarly painted Ben.

The young war chief motioned with his right hand to the warriors standing in line. Two of them went to the travois, removed several of the small gourds, and placed them on the ground by each chief. Then they picked up the travois and carried it out of the lodge. The two warriors returned shortly and resumed their place in line. The whole procedure was so well executed that I wondered how many times it had been performed in the past. The two bow-wielding Apaches remained motionless, their arrows still aimed at Ben and me, their dark-brown eyes staring at us fixedly.

The young chief crawled over my left leg and knelt at my crotch in the v formed by my widespread legs. He ran his fingers slowly through my now bright-red crotch hair. He then bent down until his lips were almost touching the mass of hair, and blew gently on it. The chief blew into the patch twice more, then his tongue darted out and he began licking the thick forest of hair. I moaned softly and bucked my hips, burying his face deep in the dark thatch. He inhaled deeply several times as he nuzzled in it like a wild hog digging for roots. When he finally pulled his face away, his nose and the entire area around his mouth had turned a bright red from the berry juice. The young chief stared at me intently as he pulled several hairs from his tongue, which was also red. Bending down once more, he flicked his tongue around the thick base of my cock. From there he trailed it up the shaft, stopping when he reached the blood-engorged head. He licked the fat knob thoroughly, then ran his tongue through the leaking slit in the head, lapping up the fluid seeping from it. Grabbing my thick shaft in his hand, the young chief sucked on it softly and gently bit the loose skin.

I turned to look at Ben. The junior chief was bent over Ben's crotch at an angle, bobbing up and down on his tool. Ben's basket was cupped in the Apache's right hand.

My own chief released my cock head, pulled the skin back from it and engulfed the knob. He slowly swallowed my dick, his lips forming a perfect o of suction around it. Soon the head of my stiffer was lodged deep down his warm, wet throat. The young chief sawed slowly back up to the head, his lips tight on my shaft. He licked the plum-sized knob several times before sinking back down the shaft. His fingers found my right nipple and began teasing it while he continued sliding up and down my pole, trailing his tongue along it and twirling it around the thick base. Grabbing my hefty nut sac in his other hand, he roughly kneaded each nut.

I pumped my hips slowly to match the young chief's bobbing head, thrusting my stiffer deep into his throat on each of his downward plunges. Caught up in the moment, I placed my left hand on the back of the chief's head and forced him down on my cock. Without losing his rhythm on my dick, he immediately released my sac and raised his hand in the air. I understood my mistake when I saw movement out of the corner of my eye. The warrior on my right had drawn back his arrow, prepared to send it into my flesh. Apparently I'd crossed some unseen line of Apache sexual etiquette. To my immense relief, however, I realized the young chief's raised hand had stayed the incensed Apache. I quickly removed my hand, but the chief grabbed it and placed it on the back of his head once more. He seemed to welcome it, and didn't pause in his sucking as my fear quickly dissipated and my fingers boldly found a grip in his wild, night-black hair.

With eyes filled with lust, I scanned the line of Apaches standing behind the chief, then scrutinized the bow-wielding warriors standing next to Ben and me. Each warrior's face remained impassive as the two chiefs bobbed up and down on our dicks. The bulges beneath their leather breechclouts, however, belied their tranquil demeanor and attested to their own growing sexual excitement. The young chief increased his efforts on my stiffer; his sucking noises joining the moans and small audible sighs coming from Ben and myself. The chief's hot, wet mouth, Ben's strong male sex smell as he writhed next to me, and my rapt audience of silent warriors soon brought me to the point of shooting.

On the next thrust of my hips, I let out several harsh, guttural groans as my release was triggered and the first blast of spunk shot from the head of my cock. I bucked like a bronc as I flooded the chief's mouth with my cream. He continued to knead my balls as he quickly swallowed the flow. When I was spent, he released my still-hard dick. He ran his thumb across my piss slit and I bucked my hips a final time as a series of shudders passed through my upper torso. The young chief sat back on his heels, eyed me briefly, then turned his attention to the junior chief and Ben. I did the same.

Ben's furry chest was rising and falling with his rapid breathing, and he was yowling like a female bobcat in heat. The junior chief sawed up on Ben's pole once more, let the fat crown pop from his mouth, and started stroking it with his left hand. He moved to the right a little, apparently to give me and the young chief a better view. This confirmed in my mind my earlier deduction that this was not the first time the two chiefs had performed this ritual. The junior chief's hand moved faster on Ben's stiffer, and Ben's hips were pumping like a weathervane in a prairie storm. He hollered suddenly and a large white drop of cream shot from the head of his dick and landed on his thigh. More of his spunk shot forth, thick and white, landing in his crotch hair and on each of his thighs. The junior chief continued stroking Ben's meat until Ben was done shooting, then he leaned down and licked Ben's crotch and thighs clean while the rest of us looked on.

When the junior chief had finished cleaning Ben, the young chief turned back to me. He grabbed my dick again and played with it as it grew soft, then released it and stood up. He stared down at me as he reached behind him. I couldn't see what he was doing, but when his breechclout fell to the ground at his feet, I had my answer. And I finally got a good look at what had plugged my shit hole earlier today by the stream. His pole was long and fat. Two light-blue veins snaked along the shaft. The plum-sized head was still hidden beneath its skin cover. His large sac was darker in color than the flesh of his cock. Each ball was the size of a hen's egg, the left one hanging slightly lower than the right. A small triangle of black crotch hair grew just above the base of his hawg. As I stared at the thick shaft, it quickly swelled to its full proportions, the bulbous head emerging from its skin cocoon. The knob was the same color as his ball sac.

The young chief pulled on his dick a few times, then knelt down once more between my outstretched legs. He dipped his fingers into a heretofore unused gourd. When he drew them back they were covered in a light-brown substance. He motioned to the warriors standing in line; one stepped forward, grabbed me around each ankle, and flipped me unceremoniously onto my stomach. Ben was similarly turned. The chief spread my ass cheeks and filled the crack with the brown stuff. It was cool against my back door. A small tingle swept through my upper body, causing my nipples to harden again. The same young warrior flipped me on my back once more, then took his place in line again. The young chief dipped his fingers again and coated his massive cock with the brown substance. Ben was on his back again as well, and the junior chief was applying the substance to his cock.

Grabbing me by the back of each thigh, the young chief lifted my legs and pushed them up and over me until my toes touched the sides of my head. I arched my back slightly to ease the strain. He shuffled forward on his knees and I felt the large head of his dick push against my back door. I pushed back against it and gasped when it suddenly popped through the tight opening. The young chief held the head just inside my asshole and turned to look at Ben and the junior chief. I followed his lead. Ben's legs were also in the air above him, his feet beside his ears, his teeth gritted as the junior chief entered him. The junior chief's member was as thick as that of the young war chief.

Satisfied that the junior chief was in and tending to business, my own chief slowly and relentlessly slid inside me. His thick member spread the walls of my asshole until the blunt head was nestled deep inside my channel. The walls of my chute quickly reshaped around his dick. I squeezed the fat pole tightly as the young chief slowly withdrew. He grunted his appreciation. When the head popped out, he grabbed my feet and placed each one over his shoulders, then slowly thrust back inside me. I could feel the heat of his rod against the sensitive lining of my asshole. The chief began slow, deep thrusts, taking his time and making me feel every inch of him. Waves of lust swept over me each time the head of his cock poked my secret muscle. My own stiffer was hard again, but the chief ignored it for the time being as he concentrated on plowing my ass.

The chief grabbed me behind each knee, his fingers digging into my skin as he increased the strength of his plunges. My whole body was dripping sweat, and my chute was on fire. The junior chief was slamming into Ben as hard and as steadily as I was getting it. I gazed at our audience. They were watching our couplings with slack mouths and glazed eyes. Under several breechclouts I could see erect cocks clearly outlined. On the chief's next powerful plunge, he cried out, and I felt his seed flooding my back door. He continued to plow into me force-fully as he pumped me full of his cream. After a final thrust, he collapsed on top of me, his thick pole still deep inside me. His weight felt good upon me. I wrapped my legs around his waist, locking my heels in the small of his back. I heard a sharp cry, and turned to see the junior chief collapse on top of Ben.

The young chief lay atop me for several moments, his chest rising and falling, then pushed up off me. As he withdrew his softening cock, the head made a sucking noise as my puckered opening reluctantly released it. Some of his spunk oozed from my hole and ran down the crack of my ass. I laid my aching legs flat on the ground once more.

Kneeling once again between my legs, the chief grabbed a small gourd filled with water and drank noisily from it. When he had slaked his thirst, he shuffled around to my right side and held the gourd to my lips. I lifted my head and took a drink. The water was cool and refreshing. When I'd finished, the chief handed the gourd to the junior chief, who drank from it before holding it for Ben. The young chief grabbed a second gourd, dipped his fingers into its contents, and scooped out the familiar stew that Ben and I had eaten earlier. He sucked the stew off his fingers, chewed contentedly, dipped his fingers a second time, and passed the gourd to the junior chief.

My dick was still fully hard, as was Ben's. When the young chief had finished his second mouthful of stew, he grabbed my stiffer with his left hand. He eyed it for a moment, then dipped the fingers of his right hand into the gourd containing the brown substance he'd used to grease my ass. I happened to look over the young chief's shoulder, and saw that the Apaches forming the line were almost completely naked. Each warrior's breechclout lay on the ground at their feet, which left them clad only in leather moccasins. Six brown cocks of varying lengths and thicknesses were being stroked by six brown hands. The two chiefs and the bow-wielding warriors paid no attention to the Apaches behind them. As the young chief slathered the brown stuff on my hawg, I settled back and waited for his grip on it to tighten and his stroking to begin. However, he dipped his fingers in the same gourd and raised up on his knees, reaching behind him as he did so. I couldn't see what he was doing, but, when I looked over at Ben and the junior chief, the mystery was solved. The junior chief was spreading the brown substance between the cheeks of his ass.

When my chief was done, he wiped the excess on his thigh, stood up, and placed a foot against each of my hips. He then squatted above my crotch, looking as if he were about to relieve himself. It suddenly dawned on me what he was up to. The young chief grabbed my cock around its thick base and maneuvered his asshole over it and down onto the fat knob. The head parted his ass cheeks and poked against the tiny opening. Resting his weight on the head of my dick, the young chief pushed down against it. His shit hole suddenly loosened, and the head of my cock slipped inside his tight, hot channel. He didn't stop there, but slid down onto my pole until his basket was resting on my patch of crotch hair and my balls were pushed flat. I moaned softly as the young chief repeatedly squeezed my dick with his talented ass muscles. Without thinking, I grabbed him at the waist. This time the bow-wielding Apache made no move to stop me. The war chief rose up on my shaft slowly until my cock head had almost popped from his hole. Grabbing his thick member in his left hand, he began pumping it with long, lazy strokes as he sank down on my hawg once more.

He started riding me as if I was a horse, his long, black hair tossing wildly about his face and shoulders as he bucked up and down. Each time he rose up until just the fat crown was still inside him, then he plunged back down, his ass cheeks squashing my nuts. I began pumping my hips to match his bucking. The junior chief was astride Ben as well, and stroking his fat, brown dick. My chief planted his hands flat on my stomach and began bouncing wildly up and down on my stiffer. I could feel the pressure building in my balls, and knew that I was getting ready to blow. The next time the young chief plunged down, he stayed there, fiercely clenching my hawg with his hole, determined to milk the spunk from it. I yelled as my explosion started, and I began filling the chief's chute with my cream. His own savage cry echoed mine as white ropes of his spunk squirted from his cock and landed on my stomach.

The chief continued to ride me until I was done shooting then rose up suddenly, letting my dick slide out of his opening, and knelt between my legs. He scooped up his spunk from my stomach with his fingers and held them up to my mouth; the smell of his seed was strong. I opened my mouth wide, he shoved his fingers inside, and I sucked them clean. When the chief withdrew his hand, his face broke into a smile. It was the

first one I'd seen from him, or the entire group for that matter. As he sat back on his haunches we both turned to watch
Ben and the junior chief. The muscular warrior was feverishly
bouncing up and down on Ben's cock. Ben's eyes were clenched
shut and his mouth was partially open, the tip of his tongue protruding from the right corner. Ben suddenly cried out, grabbed
the junior chief at the waist, and held him still as his eruption
overtook him. The junior chief's own explosion soon followed.
His seed shot from the slit in the large brown knob, crisscross-
ing Ben's stomach. When the junior chief was spent, he slid up
and off Ben's cock. As my chief had done with me, the junior
chief scooped up his thick, white cream from Ben's stomach
and fed it to him. Ben ate it eagerly and licked the chief's fingers
clean. When Ben was done, the junior chief crawled over and
squatted beside the young chief. They passed the water gourd
between them again and gave Ben and me another drink.

Their thirst slaked, the chiefs stood up and turned to face the
line of Apaches. The young chief spoke a few words, and four
of the six warriors stepped forward simultaneously, two moving to Ben's side and two to mine. One warrior knelt between
my outstretched legs, the other at my head. The two warriors
near Ben similarly positioned themselves. The Apache kneeling between my legs scooped up some of the brown stuff and
coated his cock with it. He shuffled forward on his knees to my
crotch, grabbed me by the back of each thigh, lifted my legs in
the air, and pushed them up and over my torso. The Apache
kneeling at my head grabbed me by the ankles and pulled my
feet toward him until my toes were once more alongside my
ears. Then he leaned over me so that his crotch was positioned
above my forehead. The cock head of the first warrior pushed
against my hole. I grunted as he entered me effortlessly. He
didn't waste any time. His strokes were full, rabbit-like, and
deep, each one striking the still-throbbing and swollen muscle
buried within my asshole.

One of Ben's warriors had penetrated him as well, and was plowing into him furiously. The sound of flesh slapping against flesh filled the lodge. The second Apache straddled Ben's face from behind, filling Ben's mouth with his fat, brown pole. His ball sac rested on the bridge of Ben's nose. It was the last thing I saw before a pair of smooth, brown, hairless ass cheeks lowered onto my face. I reached up and spread the cheeks apart with my thumbs, exposing the tiny brown spot. I ran my tongue along the dark, hairless crack, tasting the warrior's gamy-smelling ass, then swathed the tiny opening. He moaned steadily and started sliding his wrinkled opening back and forth across my tongue. The other Apache continued plowing into me and, on his next plunge, his seed flooded my channel.

The warrior sitting on my face suddenly pulled his ass away and quickly swung around to straddle my face, placing the head of his dick against my lips. I opened my mouth in time to catch the first spurt of his spunk. I swallowed repeatedly as the warrior emptied his cream into my mouth. When he was spent, he withdrew his stiffer, wiped the dripping head on my cheek, and sat back on his haunches. The other warrior pulled his cock out of my asshole none too gently. The bow-wielding warrior to my right immediately laid down his bow, stepped between my outstretched legs, and knelt down. A second warrior from the line moved to my head. When I glanced at Ben, I saw that his warriors were finished with him as well. The warrior guarding Ben set down his bow and knelt between Ben's legs. The last warrior from the line positioned himself at Ben's head. My former guard entered me, his stiffer much bigger than his fellow warrior's, and began steadily drilling my back door. Two of the warriors that had been replaced took up the bows, while the remaining two returned to where the original line had been formed.

I quickly lost all track of time as my world narrowed down to brown cocks in my mouth or asshole, spunk flooding both holes or splattering onto my body, and corn holes in my face. When the Apaches were finally done with Ben and me, it was evident from the burned-out torches that a good while had passed. Each of us had been serviced by both chiefs at least twice, and each of the warriors had two turns with us as well. I was also sure that Samuel and his companions had joined in on the fun. I recalled Samuel grinning at me as he knelt between my outstretched legs. I watched the warriors gather up the gourds and the dead torches, and leave the lodge. The last thing I remember was Ben crawling over to me and curling up beside me, his head on my chest.

When I woke, sunlight was filtering through the ragged smoke holes in the roof. Ben was still curled up beside me, his left arm slung across my stomach, his head on my chest. His breathing was deep and even. I could feel the warmth emanating from his hairy, brawny arm. He smelled of sweat, spunk, and the brown substance the Apaches had used repeatedly on us the night before. My morning stiffer was wide awake and peering at the world inquisitively through its one tiny eye. I could still taste spunk on my tongue. My chest and stomach, as well as the crack of my ass, were spotted with dried seed. I tried to move Ben's arm off my stomach without waking him, but he moaned and stirred slightly. Then his green eyes opened and stared into mine. I smiled at him warmly, put my arm around him and held him tight as I looked sleepily around the lodge.

Samuel and the two other captives were sprawled on the ground across from us, formless blobs under thin, woolen blankets. Their loud snores drifted over to us. After a moment I sat up, pushing Ben's head gently off me as I did so. I reached between my ass cheeks and tentatively felt my opening with a fingertip. When I withdrew the finger it was covered with the telltale greasy brown stuff. I began exploring my chute slowly and methodically with the same finger. It was a little tender from last night's activity, but other than that it was intact.

Ben had just sat up next to me when the flap at the entrance was thrown back and five stalwart Apaches entered. They carried with them the now familiar gourds. I watched as two of the warriors approached us. The other three walked over to Samuel and his friends. They kicked the three men awake, somewhat belligerently, and placed the gourds on the ground in front of them. When the warriors reached Ben and me, both men set their gourds on the ground at our feet. Two gourds held water and two were heaped with more of the buffalo stew.

Ben and I made short work of the stew, then drank the cool, refreshing water. The warriors stood silently in front of us while they waited for us to eat. When we were finished, they and the other three warriors gathered the gourds and left the lodge as silently as they'd entered.

Shortly after they left, two more Apaches came into the lodge. One carried two pairs of moccasins and two breechclouts; the other carried two of the ubiquitous gourds. They set their bundles on the ground in front of us, grabbed us around the ankles, pulled us onto our backs, then flipped us onto our stomachs. Out of the corner of my eye I could see that the warrior carrying the gourds had knelt between my outstretched legs. Spreading the cheeks of my ass, he washed my crack thoroughly, then slathered the contents of the second gourd on and around my asshole. It was some type of unguent, for it was cool and soothing on my well-used hole. When he was finished with me, the warrior did the same to Ben's shit hole. We were then flipped onto our backs, and the warrior also applied some to the cut above Ben's eye, as well as his swollen cheek. Lastly, the berry juice was washed from our faces, chests and stomachs, as well as our crotches.

When the warrior was done with Ben, the second Apache kicked a pair of moccasins and a breechclout toward me; the other set was sent flying in Ben's direction. They left while Ben and I were getting dressed. The moccasins fit reasonably well, but it took awhile for me to lace them all the way to just below my knees. Ben helped me tie the breechclout behind my back at my waist, and I did the same for him. The leather pouch beneath the front flap was snug on my equipment, and the back flap stretched firmly over my butt. I walked around inside the lodge to get accustomed to the moccasins. As I did so, the leather pouch exerted a pressure on my crotch area that was quite pleasurable.

While I strode around the lodge, I also searched for a way to escape. I avoided the three white captives. I found no weaknesses in the hide-covered walls. The smoke holes in the ceiling were too high to be considered. And even if I'd been able to reach one of them standing on Ben's shoulders, the holes themselves were too small for my body to pass through. The lodge was snug and secure. As I turned and started back in Ben's direction, Samuel threw off his blanket, stood up, and limped to intercept me. I stopped short when he was only a few feet from me and stared into his eyes.

"On behalf of myself an' the boys," he said, a sly smile playing at the corners of his mouth, "I'd like to thank you an' yer friend fer those sweet asses that ya gave us last night."

Before I realized what I was doing my hands were around Samuel's throat. I wrestled him to the ground and straddled his chest as my grip around his throat tightened. He struggled feebly, but my anger lent me strength. His eyes were starting to close when I was hauled violently off him by a firm grip. I rolled several times, managing to end up on my back. A muscular knee landed squarely on my chest. As the wind was driven from my lungs, a wicked-looking blade was pressed to my throat. I looked up into the angry eyes of the young war chief.

CHAPTER SIX

The chief continued to press the knife blade against my throat, and I braced myself for it to pierce my skin. He suddenly stopped, got up off my chest, grabbed my right foot, and dragged me over to Ben. The dirt floor of the lodge scraped my sunburned skin. The young chief dumped me next to Ben and quickly returned to Samuel. A young warrior was covering Ben with a rifle, which explained why Ben hadn't tried to prevent me from killing Samuel.

Samuel was still laying on the ground. His hands were at his throat, and he was gasping as he desperately tried to draw breath into his lungs. The chief pulled him roughly to his feet, heedless of the man's struggles, and spoke rapidly to him, gesturing at Ben and me several times, then left the lodge. Samuel stared after him, his hatred written plainly on his face. When the chief was gone, Samuel limped over to us. He face was still red from my recent attempt to strangle him. The warrior guarding us eyed him warily.

"The chief wants me to tell ya that he an' the junior chief are goin' on a little huntin' party. You two are accompanyin' 'em. It seems you've struck their fancy," he continued, sneering at us. "He says you're furry like the grizzly, hung like the buffalo, an' yer holes are tighter than his squaw's. The group's leavin' shortly. I'm goin' along as interpreter."

He swung around and had started back toward the other two men when he stopped suddenly and walked back to us. He stared down at me intently.

"Don't think this is over, my friend," he growled. "I'm thinkin' that one of us might not return from this huntin' trip, an' I don't

aims it to be me." Without another word he turned and headed
back to his companions.

"That was a risky thing ya did, Jake," Ben said softly. "You
could have been killed."

"I know. I let my anger at our situation override my better
judgement."

Ben grabbed my hand and squeezed it tight.

"We have to play it safe, Jake, an' bide our time until the
opportunity presents itself to escape."

I knew he was right, but I made no reply. My fury still had a
strong hold on me. We sat in silence, the young warrior watching us intently. The young chief soon returned, accompanied by
two Apaches. He motioned for Ben and me and then Samuel
to rise and follow him. The three of us fell in line behind the
young chief, Samuel ahead of me, Ben behind, and the three
warriors close on his heels. When I stepped outside into the
morning sunshine I was momentarily blinded.

As my eyes adjusted, I saw a semicircle of a dozen warriors, on painted horses, in front of the lodge. The junior chief
was among them. He rode up to us and held out his hand to
Ben, obviously not expecting him to refuse it. Ben grabbed the
strong, brown hand, and the chief pulled him up behind him
on his horse. The young chief spoke a few words and a warrior rode forward leading two horses. One was the Black. He
recognized me and nickered softly. None of my other horses
were in the group. The warrior handed the Black's rope bridle
to the young chief. He leaped onto the Black's broad back and
held out his hand to me. Grasping it, I swung up behind him.
Samuel mounted the second horse. It was evident that Ben and
I weren't trusted to ride by ourselves. The chief wheeled the
Black around, kicked him in the sides with his heels, and away
we galloped, the rest of the warriors falling in line behind us.
The three warriors that had escorted us from the lodge were
left behind.

Our small band rode across the short plain that lead to the lodge, down the hill past the old chief's teepee, down the next hill, and through the main village. Several Apache warriors raised their hands in greeting as we rode by them, but the women we passed ignored us. The familiar circle of screaming children and barking dogs trailed us as we left the village. When we emerged from the cliff passage, we headed along the cliff face, ignoring the trail that had brought us to the Apache stronghold the day before. As the miles fell away, the sameness of the terrain caused my thoughts from yesterday to hit home once more: if Ben and I did manage to escape, we would be hard pressed to find our way out of this maze of rocks. We finally emerged onto level ground, and headed north. Even though I was their captive, I had to admit to myself that the Apaches were quite resplendent astride their painted mounts. The sun highlighted the rich brown of their skin and the deep black of their hair. They sat tall in the saddle, their backs straight and proud. The rope bridles mostly hung idle in their hands, as they preferred to guide their horses using only their knees. Their eyes scanned the landscape as we rode, missing nothing.

We rode without stopping until the sun was high overhead, then halted briefly at a small, muddy stream to drink and water the horses. We ate a couple handfuls of pemmican, then were on our way once more. Just as the sun was starting its descent, we came upon a well-worn trail. Eventually it led us to a small clearing beneath an overhang of crumbling rock. Here we made camp. A trickle of water ran from a crack in the base of the rock wall, forming a small pool. The rock wall protected us from any enemies approaching from the rear. A large stand of cactus protected our front and left sides. The only way into our camp was by the trail we'd entered on. As soon as we halted, a single warrior scrambled up the rock wall. When he reached the top, he scanned our back trail, then melted into the landscape.

When we were settled in, two warriors loped off down our

back trail. They returned shortly carrying several large jackrabbits by their ears. They skinned them and we ate the meat
raw. After we ate, Ben's and my hands and feet were tied. I slept
curled up next to the young chief, a wool blanket covering me
to keep off the night chill. The chief wrapped his strong brown
arms around me and held me tight. Ben slept across from us,
held tightly in the arms of the junior chief. The young chief
awakened me shortly before dawn and untied my hands and
feet. Ben's ropes were undone as well. We ate more of the dry,
tasteless pemmican for breakfast. As I studied Ben, I could see
that the swelling in his cheek had gone down considerably.
When we finished eating, we drank from the small pool, then
Ben and I mounted behind our chiefs, and the party rode out
once more. After a few miles we veered off the trail and struck
out across rough terrain.

The Apaches rode without hesitation, following no discernible trail as they wound through the cactuses, rocks, and
sagebrush that dotted the landscape. Around midmorning we
happened upon a small oasis. Several large rocks offered inviting shade. The sound of running water came from a stand of
scrub trees a few feet away. I could see sunlight shimmering on
water. The young chief spoke for several moments, the longest
I'd ever heard him talk. When he was done, he, the junior chief,
and Samuel dismounted. The war chief motioned for Ben and
me to get down as well. They then led their horses through the
thicket, Samuel in the lead, Ben and I between the chiefs. The
rest of the warriors remained behind. We emerged into a small
clearing, where a good-sized pool was formed by a small stream
cascading between two boulders. Rich, green grass grew right
to the water's edge. When the three of them had watered their
horses and had their own fill, and Ben and I had taken a drink,
the war chief gave a quick yelp like that of a coyote. The rest of
the warriors entered the clearing single file, dismounted, and
led their horses to the water. They let their horses drink before

quenching their own thirst. When the warriors were done, they mounted once more and rode from the clearing, leaving the two chiefs, Samuel, Ben, and myself. The young chief immediately addressed Samuel. When he had finished speaking, Samuel turned to face Ben and me, a smile lighting up his face.

"The chief wants both of ya to wash yerselves in the pool," he said. "He says not only are ya both hung like the buffalo, but after that night in the lodge ya smell like one too."

He laughed when he finished translating the young chief's words.

The thought of the cool water was enticing. And after being used by all the warriors the other night I had no qualms about being naked in front of this trio. They'd seen it all before. I looked at Ben, and he nodded his head in assent. We walked to the edge of the pool, removed our moccasins and breechclouts, laid them in the soft grass, and stepped into the water. It was bitingly cold and caused gooseflesh to quickly spread upward through my body. As Ben stood beside me, I once again found myself admiring his burly, hairy body and his soft though sizable cock. In silence we waded toward the center of the pool. The floor of the pool was made up of sand, and the water never rose above our thighs. We sat down on the sandy bottom, shoulder to shoulder. We faced away from our three spectators, but I could feel their eyes boring into my back.

I grabbed a handful of sand and began to wash my arms and upper torso. Ben did the same. The sand was invigorating to my skin, and my nipples were soon hard and tingling. As I scrubbed, I started thinking once again about the weeks that had passed since I first started out in pursuit of Ben. Suddenly, Ben spoke, bringing me sharply out of my reverie.

"What do ya think our chances are of gittin' away while we're on this huntin' excursion, Jake?"

He kept his voice low, but I still wasn't certain that our words wouldn't carry to Samuel.

"Splash 'round a bit, Ben, so that white devil won't hear what we're sayin' an' relay it to the chief."

I was loath to answer his question because I had nothing encouraging to say. His green eyes stared into mine, imploring me to toss him a tiny thread of hope. I thought carefully about what I should say before replying.

"That depends on a great many things," I said, splashing a great deal as I'd told him to do. "I'll tell ya one thing fer sure; I wouldn't count on any help from Samuel. He seems pretty resigned to his lot. Besides, I don't trust him one bit. We just need to keep our eyes an' ears open, an' take advantage of the first chance we git to make a break fer it. I'm bettin', though, that bein' free of the Apache village will provide us with a better opportunity to escape."

"Why is that?" Ben asked, loud enough so I could hear above our splashing, but not so it would carry to our audience.

"Well, I doubt very much that I could find my way from the village to the nearest town, fort, or other sign of civilization. The trail to their stronghold has too many twists, turns, an' backtracks. Even usin' the sun as a guide we could still take a wrong turn an' wind up hopelessly lost, an' die from thirst."

I scooped up another handful of sand and scrubbed my legs and crotch beneath the pool's surface. The water was crystal clear, and I could see that Ben was washing his lower body as well. Despite the cold water, my cock made a valiant attempt to respond to the ministrations of my hand. It had reached a state of semihardness by the time I began working on my feet.

"Ya heard what Samuel said happened to his partner that tried to git away, Jake. I wouldn't want the same thing to happen to you."

I stared into his eyes a moment before answering.

"I wouldn't want that to happen to you either, Ben. Or anythin' else fer that matter."

My concern was evident in my voice.

"But I don't aim to be no object of Apache lust fer the rest of my days. Or, that is, until they plumb wear us out."

He stared into the pool, as if mulling over what I'd said. I felt a sudden yearning for him, sharp and deep.

"If'n we don't git away, Jake, then I won't be able to find Bart in Silverton an' prove to ya that I'm innocent. I can't live out the rest of my days with these Apaches with ya thinkin' I killed that ranger."

"I don't think ya killed that ranger, Ben, an' I aims to help ya prove it."

The words were out of my mouth before the thought was even done forming in my head.

Ben's mouth dropped open and he stared at me, wide-eyed. He reached over and touched my cheek with the tips of his fingers, then traced my lips with the middle one. I felt his hand on my leg, and then it was wrapped around my pole. I grabbed his manhood and began squeezing it. The warmth of his hand fought against the cold water of the pool, and eventually won as my cock swelled to its full size. Ben's own member thickened and grew as I continued to squeeze it. Without losing his grip on my hawg, Ben swung around and knelt in front of me. I rose up on my own knees to meet him. Our bodies pressed together in the frigid water, our dicks throbbing and pulsing against each other. I sought his lips with mine, and pushed my tongue deep inside his mouth. He grabbed it gently between his teeth and eagerly sucked on it. I wrapped my arms around him and held him tight. Laughter and several loud whoops suddenly came from the pool's edge. I turned around and saw the chiefs and Samuel avidly watching us. The young chief spoke rapidly to Samuel.

"The chief says to tell ya not to stop on our account, boys," Samuel snickered.

As I stared at the three men standing near the pool, all my rage and frustration from the past few days rose to the surface for the second time that day. I wanted to put my hands around one of their throats, it didn't matter which one, and choke the life out of them. I turned and started wading toward shore. My intent must have been plainly evident, for both chiefs drew their wicked-looking knifes. That didn't deter me, though. I'd only taken a half-dozen steps, however, when Ben grabbed my arm and swung me around to face him. His concern was written plainly on his face. In my rage I almost struck him, but his powerful grip on my arm restored my senses.

"Don't do it, Jake. It's three against one, an' you're bound to be killed. If'n they want a show, let's give 'em one. It ain't nothin' the three of 'em haven't seen before. Or had, fer that matter. Besides, this could be the last chance fer just the two of us to be together in this way."

He pulled me to him and wrapped his strong arms around me. He kissed me deeply and passionately, and I eagerly returned his kiss. The head of his cock poked into my stomach. Grabbing my hand, he led me to the shallower water at the edge of the pool. Neither of us glanced at our audience. The edge of the pool was muddy, but I sat down heavily, heedless of the muck. The mud oozed over my legs to just below my knees. I still held Ben's hand, and I pulled him down onto his knees beside me. He quickly straddled my lap and I grabbed him at the waist to steady him. Once more he covered my face with kisses, and I readily returned them.

Ben leaned back, gazed into my eyes with his lust-filled ones, then pushed me flat on my back in the mud. The brown muck oozed out from underneath me. He lay atop me, the hair on his chest scratching my nipples, his thick shaft throbbing against my own. I grabbed his ass cheeks and roughly kneaded them, then pulled them apart and poked at his tiny hole with a fingertip. He ran his tongue over my stubbled cheeks and throat, then tongued a swath through my chest hair to my tits. He began working my nipples, biting and sucking the sensitive nubs. I continued to probe Ben's back door with my finger. He pushed against it insistently, and suddenly my finger was inside him. Moaning softly, he rubbed his stiffer against mine.

Ben bit each nipple a final time, then licked a path down through the hairs on my stomach. He paused briefly to flick the tip of his tongue in and out of my navel several times before burying his face in my crotch hair. I'd been forced to pull my finger from his hole as he slid down me, and I now held it to Ben's lips. He grabbed it with his teeth, took it into his mouth, and sucked on it eagerly. My dick was hard and straining against his cheek. Finally releasing my finger, Ben grabbed my hawg and squeezed it several times.

Taking the fat head into his mouth, Ben sucked on it softly for a good while, then swallowed the entire shaft. He gagged slightly, but took the whole thing deep down his throat until his lips were nestled in my thick, dark-brown crotch hair. He sucked hard on my stiffer, his lips tight around the thick base, then slid back up to the crown, his tongue trailing along the shaft as he did so. With just the large knob in his mouth once more, Ben bit down on it gently and scraped his upper teeth across it before letting the plum-sized head pop from his mouth. He swirled his tongue over the tip, licked down the fat pole to my balls, and took the large sac of flesh into his mouth. Rolling the twin globes around, he sucked on them avidly. Finally releasing my ball sac, he tongued the sensitive area below it, above where my ass crack started. I gasped aloud and grabbed a handful of his hair. Eventually he worked his tongue into the crack. Pulling my cheeks apart, he drove his tongue into my bung hole, then began eating it as if it were his last meal. I pulled his hair, urging on his efforts.

Ben pulled his face from the crack of my ass and spit several times onto my hole. As the saliva ran down my crack, he shifted quickly onto his knees and placed the large head of his cock against my puckered opening. He pushed hard, and I pushed back against him, just as hard. I gritted my teeth as the large knob popped through and the rest of Ben's dick quickly followed, sliding into my warm wetness. It pushed the walls of my chute apart until the head of his dick lodged against the hidden muscle deep within me. As he held it there, waves of pleasure raced through my body. I moaned softly as he slowly withdrew until just the knob was still inside me, then plunged in to the hilt once more, striking the secret muscle once again. Ben stretched out, his weight resting fully upon me, and began thrusting slowly and steadily into me. The hair on his chest repeatedly scraped across my nipples. I could hear and feel Ben's balls slapping against my ass cheeks. With each deep thrust Ben drove my ass into the mud, producing a loud squishing noise.

"Give it to me, Ben," I whispered fiercely in his ear.

I wrapped my arms around his back and my legs around his waist, locking my ankles in the small of his back. Using my arms and feet, I pulled him to me on each of his thrusts, forcing his pole deep inside me. Grabbing my bottom lip with his teeth, Ben gently pulled it, then began biting the lobes of my ears. Chills ran through my body. He pushed my arms up over my head, inhaled deeply from each armpit, then tongued the patches of dark hair that grew there. Then, pushing himself up and off me, he grabbed my leaking hawg and began furiously jerking it. The group of onlookers on the bank were completely forgotten as I urged Ben with my mouth and my body to pound my ass harder. I grabbed my cock out of his hand and began stroking it myself, wanting to shoot my load when he shot his. Our rhythm was perfect. Ben slammed his dick into me one last time and cried out my name as his eruption was triggered. He held his dick inside me as his spunk flooded my insides. My own cream shot from the slit in the swollen head of my cock and splashed onto Ben's abdomen.

When Ben was spent he pulled out and collapsed on top of me. His lips sought mine, and he kissed me, deeply. I held him tight, reveling in his nakedness. Suddenly, I heard a series of moans and sharp little cries. Ben had heard them also, for he raised his head and stared over my right shoulder at something on the bank behind us. I pushed him off me, flipped onto my stomach, and saw what held Ben's attention. Samuel was naked and on his hands and knees in the grass a few feet from the pool's edge. The young chief was plowing him from behind, and the junior chief was stuffing his substantial brown cock into Samuel's mouth. Any previous cries must have been drowned out by ours. Before long, the thrusts of both chiefs intensified, and all at once they cried out as one as they released their individual flow into Samuel's eager mouth and ass. When the two chiefs were spent they withdrew from Samuel, stood up, and readjusted their breechclouts. The young chief pulled Samuel roughly to his feet and spoke sharply to him. Samuel faced us and began donning his clothing.

"Okay, boys," Samuel said, when he was fully dressed. "Git yerselves rinsed off; the show's over. The chief is anxious to move on. By the way, that was quite a show, fellas. I definitely think it's goin' to be fun havin' the two of ya around. Or at least one of ya, that is."

Neither Ben nor I responded to his taunt. Ben stared into my eyes then got to his feet. He held out his hand and helped me up. I kissed him one last time, unselfconsciously. We rinsed off in the cold water, retrieved our moccasins and breechclouts, and quickly dressed. Ben tied my breechclout for me and I did the same for him. I brushed his cheek lightly with my fingertips and gave him an encouraging smile. I walked to the young chief's horse and he held out his hand and helped me mount. Ben swung up behind the junior chief as Samuel mounted his own horse.

We rode back through the scrub trees, joined the rest of the warriors, and set out once more. Shortly thereafter we came across a well-used trail, deeply rutted by wagon wheels and horses' hooves. As we followed it for several miles, I began to suspect our party wasn't hunting quarry of the four-legged variety at all. We slowed to a walk, then our small party halted completely. One of the warriors dismounted, knelt down, and placed an ear to the ground. When I realized he was listening for the sounds of anyone approaching on the trail, my heart sank in my chest. My suspicion was correct: our band of "hunters" was going to ambush the next unwary traveler or travelers that passed this way. Images of the previous burned-out stagecoaches and skeletons flashed through my mind. Ben and I would be witnesses to the slaughter. Ben turned to me, an anxious, worried expression on his face. I knew immediately he'd also figured out what the Apaches were planning. However, there was nothing either of us could do about it. We rode slowly and silently for a few more miles, then stopped once again as the warrior knelt and listened. Suddenly, he voiced a sharp cry and raised his right hand in the air. He must have finally heard what he'd been listening for. A stagecoach, rider, or group of riders was headed our way. A sick dread filled me because neither Ben nor I had any means to warn the approaching party of its impending doom.

The young chief spoke loudly and excitedly, and the warriors rode off the trail, leaving the chiefs, a warrior, Samuel, Ben, and me behind. The Apaches melted into the landscape, disappearing behind rocks, sagebrush, and cactuses. The young chief surveyed the area, checking to make sure the warriors were out of sight and that everything appeared normal. Satisfied, our small party turned their horses around and headed along our back trail. We traveled about fifty yards on it, then turned onto a smaller trail that ran parallel to the stage line. We rode for a short distance, then the chiefs and the warrior suddenly halted and dismounted. Samuel remained on his horse. The chiefs pulled Ben and I roughly from their horses and shoved us toward a large cactus. Pushing us down in the meager shade it offered, they bound our hands and feet, and gagged us with vile-smelling strips of cloth. They quickly remounted and, followed by Samuel, rode back the way we'd come, obviously to join up with the rest of the Apaches. Apparently Samuel was going to take part in the attack. The warrior that remained took up a position to our right, his rifle resting across his thigh, black eyes regarding us intently.

Ben and I stared into each other's eyes. I could see in his the rage that he felt about the situation that was going to unfold shortly. I heard a faint noise off in the distance. As the sound grew steadily louder, it became several distinct sounds: the creaking of wooden wagon wheels, the snorts of horses, the jingle of harnesses, and frequent loud cries accompanied by the crack of a whip. A stagecoach was approaching, and fast. The speed at which it was traveling attested to the fact that the driver was aware of the Apache menace along this stretch of his run. Heavy rifle fire interspersed with Apache cries suddenly drowned out the noise from the stagecoach. The young warrior guarding us jumped to his feet, obviously eager to be a part of the conflict. The rifle reports continued for some time, and were added to by pistols and shotguns. I felt a small measure of relief. At least the travelers weren't giving up without a fight. After a while though, the gunfire came less frequently, then stopped altogether. Silence descended over the area. It seemed to stretch on forever until it was suddenly broken by a woman's scream, which was abruptly cut off as it reached its crescendo. Silence settled once more, this time lasting twice as long as before.

All at once I heard the sound of running horses. It grew louder, and suddenly the Apaches came galloping down the small trail. They pulled up a few feet from Ben and me, crowding the narrow trail with their milling horses. I noticed with satisfaction that there were three missing warriors. The junior chief was one of them. I was disappointed, however, to see that Samuel was still alive. The young chief rode up to us. The Black was snorting and rolling his eyes as he fought the chief's strong grip on the rope bridle. Several fresh scalps hung at the young chief's waist, as well as from several of the other warriors'. One dangled from Samuel's waist as well. My hatred for the white man swelled. The young chief leaped from the Black, untied Ben and me, and removed our gags. He pushed me roughly toward his horse. Something had sure spooked him, and he was in a big hurry to get moving. Not waiting for me to mount on my own, he hoisted me onto the Black and climbed up behind me. A warrior rode up next to us and hauled Ben up on his horse so quickly that Ben almost slid off the other side. The warrior who had guarded us mounted his horse as well. I turned and saw thick, black smoke billowing into the air: the stagecoach was burning.

The Apaches galloped wildly down the short side trail and emerged onto the stagecoach line right as the sharp notes of a bugle pierced the air. We came to a halt at the y formed by the two trails. The burning stagecoach was about thirty yards down the trail. Bodies were scattered among the wreckage. A group of men on horseback was fast approaching the section of the trail where the warriors had laid their ambush. As they drew closer, I spotted the yellow guidon flapping in the breeze and made out dark-blue uniforms. It was a column of cavalry. As they neared the stagecoach, several riders broke off from the main group and reined in at the burning wreckage. The rest continued on in our direction. Making a quick count, I determined that the remaining Apaches in our group were outnumbered three to one. Another bugle blast pierced the air as the column broke into a full gallop. They'd spotted us. The young chief scrutinized the oncoming troops. He appeared to be gauging his chances in a confrontation with the cavalry. He must not have been feeling lucky today, for he gave a sudden shrill cry, and we raced away from the approaching soldiers.

We rode at breakneck speed, the young chief urging the

Black ever faster with his hands and feet. We veered off the trail and set a reckless pace across the uneven terrain. I looked over my shoulder and saw the blue-clad horsemen turn off the trail at the same place we had. They quickly closed the distance between us. We didn't slow down as we galloped headlong down a steep washout and up the other side. We leapt over rocks and sagebrush without breaking stride, the Apaches whipping their horses into a frenzy with their hands. My heart was in my throat, for I knew that a horse could go down from one misstep, its leg broken, its rider receiving a broken neck. Rifle fire erupted from behind us. The Apache riding beside us fell backward off his horse. Two more Apaches tumbled from their mounts as the warrior carrying Ben moved up alongside us. I saw Samuel ahead and to my right. Why couldn't a bullet take him, I thought to myself, bitterly.

We climbed a small, steep hill, and plummeted down the other side. A horse stumbled and rolled, tossing its rider. The warrior sprang to his feet and quickly caught a riderless horse running with our fleeing band. As we reached the bottom of the hill a small plain stretched out before us. I looked back and saw that we were starting to put distance between ourselves and the soldiers. As we started across the plain, the young chief turned to the warrior still riding beside us. Some unseen signal must have passed between them because, without warning, the young chief turned and shoved me from the Black. As I fell I saw, out of the corner of my eye, Ben being pushed from his horse as well. I landed hard on the packed, sandy ground, the air forced from my lungs. I rolled several feet, over rocks and sagebrush, until I was brought up hard by a large rock. I lay against it, gasping for breath, my entire body covered with cuts, scrapes, and scratches. I felt my arms and legs for any broken bones. I found none. I'd been very lucky. I got slowly and shakily to my feet and stood there, looking around for Ben. I could see the fleeing Apaches in the distance, now mere dots on the sandy plain. I walked a few feet before I finally spotted Ben. He lay in a heap at the base of a large cactus. He sat up as I approached him, then slowly struggled to his feet. He limped to me, holding out his arms. I stepped into them silently. He hugged me fiercely, then his lips were on mine. We kissed for several moments, then I stepped away from him and held him at arm's length. I looked him over from head to toe. He was covered with cuts and scrapes as well, but other than that he appeared to be intact.

He held my gaze, concern written plainly on his face.

"Are ya okay?" he stammered.

"Just a couple of scrapes. I've been through worse. Don't worry, I'll live."

The sound of approaching hooves echoed off the rocks around us. As I looked at Ben, I suddenly realized the danger our physical appearance could put us in. Our skins were burnt a deep reddish-brown from the unrelenting sun, and we were clad in leather breechclouts and moccasins. There was a good chance the soldiers would mistake us for Apaches.

"Get on yer knees, Ben, quick, an' raise yer hands in the air."

I dropped to my knees before the words had left my mouth, but Ben still stood there, a puzzled expression on his face, a reply forming on his lips.

I cut it short.

"Just shut yer mouth, git on yer knees, an' raise yer hands in the air. These soldiers might mistake us fer Apaches, shoot first, an' ask questions later."

Understanding dawned in his eyes, and he dropped to his knees beside me. We knelt, waiting for the soldiers. Two of them were several yards in advance of the rest of the detail. As they drew nearer, my heart sank when they suddenly brought their horses to an abrupt stop, raised their rifles, and pointed them at us.

CHAPTER SEVEN

"Don't shoot!" I cried. "We're white men." Ben quickly echoed my words.

I saw the startled looks on their faces. Ben and I repeated the phrase over and over, trying to make our voices loud enough to be heard over the thundering hoofbeats. The remainder of the column halted behind the two soldiers, who hadn't lowered their rifles but were no longer pointing them at Ben and me. One of them raised his hand in the air and turned around to face the men behind him. He quickly ordered four of them to stay with him and the second front rider, and dispatched the rest in pursuit of the Apaches. The soldiers who had been ordered to remain reined in next to the man who'd given the orders. The rest of the men charged past us in a thick cloud of dust. I could see startled and curious looks on the soldiers' faces as their eyes roved over Ben and me. The six left behind rode up to us and dismounted. The soldier who'd ordered the column to split up stepped in front of us. His light-gray eyes scanned our faces as he towered over us. The other five men held their ground.

He stood six foot two, maybe three, give or take an inch. His dark-blue cavalry hat rested on a mass of dark-brown, curly hair. Tiny gold crossed sabers adorned the front of the hat. Thick, brown stubble covered his sunburned cheeks and throat. A full mustache hid his upper lip; the lower one was full and chapped from too many hours under the grueling desert sun. A dirty yellow ascot was tied at his throat. His dark-blue shirt outlined his powerfully built shoulders and arms, as well as his broad chest and flat stomach. The gold buttons lining the front of his shirt were chipped and faded. The muscles in his thighs and legs bulged beneath the thin light-blue material of his trousers. My gaze lingered at the lump at his crotch, underneath a row of dusty gold buttons. I could see his fat cock head to the right of the buttons, straining against the worn material. Thick black boots covered his feet, ending just below his knees. A Spencer carbine was in his right hand, its barrel pointed at the ground. A saber hung from his right hip; a pistol was at his left.

An equally handsome soldier walked up beside gray-eyes. I knew from the foragers cap he wore he was of a lower rank.

"It looks like we've rescued some Apache pris'ners, Major."

The soldier's voice was rich and deep. The man he addressed as major didn't respond as he continued to scrutinize Ben and me.

"Git up off'n yer knees you two, you're free men now, compliments of the Seventh Calvary. I'm Major Stephen Preston. Tell me yer names, an' how ya came to be pris'ners of the Apache."

Ben and I stood up. I didn't miss the quick scan the major made of my body, nor the lingering look at my crotch. I introduced myself first, then Ben, and started our tale, beginning with our capture by the outlaw band, and our ride to their hideout. I went on to describe the Apache raid, how we'd been taken prisoner, and our brief stay in the Apache village. I ended with the war party ambushing the stagecoach. I purposefully left out the sexual escapades that had taken place with Chet and his men, as well as the Apaches. I also omitted the reason for my pursuit of Ben, but did tell the major we had been headed to Silverton. When I finished speaking, the major stared at me thoughtfully for a moment, as if weighing the validity of my story in his mind.

As he stood there eyeing me, the troops dispatched to pursue the fleeing Apaches returned. I was disappointed to see Samuel with them. The lead soldier pulled his horse up short a few feet from the major and fairly leaped from the saddle. He ordered Samuel to dismount as well, and strode purposefully to the major, Samuel close behind him. The young soldier's right hand went so sharply to his forehead in a salute that I thought for sure he'd given himself a concussion.

"Major Preston. We pursued the Apaches fer several miles, but eventually lost sight of 'em, an' then we lost their tracks altogether. We did, however, shoot three more of the red devils before they eluded us, an' we rescued another pris'ner."

"Sergeant," the major said, a note of weariness creeping into his voice, "please don't refer to the Apache as 'red devils.' They're human, like you an' me. They're desperately fightin' to preserve a way of life that existed long before the white man came along. A way of life that we're as desperate to destroy through our ignorance of 'em. That will be all, Sergeant."

I was surprised by the major's short speech, and apparently the sergeant had heard similar words before. A look of distaste spread across his face, and he started to reply but the major cut him short.

"I said that was all, Sergeant."

The sergeant saluted once more, turned on his heel, and fairly stomped back to his horse.

The major asked Samuel his name, then asked how he had come to be a prisoner of the Chiricahua. Samuel related the events of his capture, then corroborated the account I'd given, from the time Ben and I were brought to the Apache village up to the raid today. To my dismay, however, he proceeded to describe in great detail our sexual encounters with the Apaches, himself, and the two other white prisoners. Luckily none of the other soldiers were close enough to Samuel to hear him. When Samuel had finished speaking, the major turned to Ben and me.

"Is what Samuel says true, Mr. Slater?"

His penetrating gaze made it impossible to withhold the truth.

"It is, Major Preston. I saw no reason to relay our dealings with the Apaches. Also, there's somethin' else ya don't know. Samuel was part of the raidin' party you encountered today. When he returned from the stagecoach, he had a fresh scalp at his waist. It might be gone now, but Ben can testify that it was there."

Samuel turned and started to run, but two soldiers quickly grabbed him. One checked his waist and, sure enough, a fresh scalp was tucked beneath his shirt. Evidently he had hidden it, but had forgotten to dispose of it before the soldiers caught up with him. Without saying a word, the major walked calmly over to Samuel and shot him point-blank in the forehead with his pistol. Samuel crumpled silently to the ground at the major's feet.

The major returned to Ben and me.

"We'll take ya with us back to Fort Benson fer now. I know a fort's not a very hospitable place fer civilians, but the next stage is due at the fort in a few days, and you can leave with it. Silverton is only seven or eight hours travel time by stagecoach. Because of the recent Indian trouble, a larger than usual number of my troops are spread through the region fer the next few days, but I should be able to spare a few men to provide a partial escort to Silverton. I have no extra clothin' to give ya right now, so I'm afraid you'll have to suffer the sun until we reach the fort."

When he finished speaking, the major eyed us up and down again, his gaze lingering once more at the sizable lumps beneath our breechclouts. He turned abruptly and faced his troops.

"Sergeant Billings, bring two mounts fer these men, give 'em food an' water, an' make it quick. I want to be headed to Fort Benson before those Apaches git the notion to circle back an' harass us."

A youngish man led two dusty mounts over to Ben and me. He pulled a dented canteen from the saddlebag on the nearest horse and tossed it to me. I popped the cap and held it to my lips. The water was slightly warm, but still refreshing. I passed the canteen to Ben. The sergeant then handed each of us several pieces of hardtack. The stuff was old and tough as shoe leather, but I ate every bit of it as if it were a fine Sunday dinner. I stepped to the nearest horse and swung up into the saddle, careful not to crush my cock and balls against the pommel. Ben mounted the remaining horse. Major Preston ordered the column to reform. When it did, we found ourselves in the middle of it. The major surveyed his troops, then gave the order to move out. We headed back toward the stagecoach line, and soon merged onto it.

We halted when we reached the stagecoach. The soldiers left behind had pulled the bodies away from the wreckage and were busy digging graves. I averted my gaze from the victims. No one spoke while the soldiers completed their grisly task. When the men were done, they mounted up and we took to the trail once more. As I rode beside Ben, I gazed at him repeatedly. He didn't notice as he stared straight ahead, lost in his thoughts. He suddenly turned to me and caught me gawking at him. He stared at me steadily for what seemed like a lifetime, his face expressing no emotion. All at once, a smile lit it up. I was sure it was a smile of relief because of our newfound freedom.

We rode for the rest of that morning with no sign of the Apache raiding party. I hoped that Ben and I had seen the last of our captors. We halted briefly at a sluggish stream to water the horses, then rode on. The sun was high overhead as we started to climb a large sand dune. When we reached the crest, I could see a vast plain spread out below us. In the center of the plain stood a log fort. The ground around the outside of it had been cleared of rocks, scrub trees, and cactus; in effect, anything that could offer cover to an approaching enemy. Even from this distance I could see tiny figures moving to and fro inside the post. We continued down the other side of the dune and struck out across the plain. As we approached the fort, a sentry on the parapet cried out. His cry was echoed from within the compound. I hadn't seen many forts in my day, but Fort Benson resembled the numerous descriptions I'd heard and read about. The walls were made of rough-hewn logs, the bark still intact, measuring at least twenty feet in height. They were laced together with thick rope at the top, middle, and bottom. The gaps between them had been chinked with mud. The tops of the logs were fashioned to resemble large stakes. I could see numerous blue-shirted soldiers watching us from the parapet that ran the length of the front wall. The sun glinted off the barrels of their rifles.

As the detail neared the gate, the wooden doors swung inward. We rode through them and into the compound, the soldiers standing at the gate saluting the major as we rode past. The ol' Stars and Stripes waved proudly from a wooden pole in the center of the compound. Off to my left several columns of troops were performing drills. Beyond them I could see a low clapboard barn and a wooden corral overflowing with horses. To my right were several low, rectangular rough-hewn log buildings that I assumed were the soldiers' barracks. A ragtag garden was laid out adjacent to the furthest one. A good-sized well stood next to it. Another rectangular building, larger than the barracks, stood kitty-corner to the garden. Based on its size, the smoke that curled up from a pipe in the roof, and the smells of roasting meat, I was pretty sure it was the mess hall. To the right of the mess hall was a low, square building, also made of logs. This was probably the major's personal quarters.

We rode past the barracks and the mess hall and halted in front of the square building. The major dismounted and walked back to Ben and me.

"You two come inside my office. I'd like to hear yer story again, from start to finish."

As Ben and I swung down from our horses and followed the major inside, the soldiers turned around and headed toward the corral, leading our three mounts with them. The interior of the square building was cool, dim, and sparsely furnished. A large wooden desk monopolized most of the area, facing the door we'd entered. The accompanying chair was pushed against the back wall. On that same wall hung a portrait of President Lincoln. Two rough-hewn, wooden chairs hung on pegs on the wall to our right.

"You boys hold tight while I see if'n I have any spare clothin' fer ya, besides that which the government issues."

The major went to a second door to the left of the desk. It was slightly ajar. I caught a glimpse of a large bed as he stepped into the room and closed the door behind him.

Ben and I stood silently in front of the desk while we waited for him to return. I studied the few items on the desktop. These consisted of an inkwell and quill pen, several sheets of foolscap, and a daguerreotype of a rather severe-looking woman. The major returned shortly with two sets of shirts and pants. He set these on the desk and went back into the room, immediately returning with two pairs of boots, socks, bandanas, and a bottle of whiskey. He set the bottle on the desk and dropped the boots at our feet. Grabbing the chairs from the wall, he set them in front of us.

"I couldn't find any spare civilian clothin', so these old cavalry shirts an' pants will have to do. When the stage arrives in a few days it will be bringin' supplies, includin' clothin'. With the Apaches raisin' such a ruckus, however, there's no guarantee the stage will even make it through to the fort. Ya both saw what happened today."

Ben and I each grabbed a shirt and pair of pants, stripped off our breechclouts and moccasins, and began to dress. With everything I'd been through in the past few days, I was not concerned about the major seeing me buck-naked. In fact, the idea excited me. Out of the corner of my eye I could see him staring at Ben and me as we stood momentarily naked in front of him.

When we finished dressing, the major seated himself behind his large desk. Ben and I sat in the chairs the major had provided. The major produced three glasses from a desk drawer, pulled the cork from the bottle of whiskey, and filled each glass. He pushed two toward us, grabbed his own, and leaned back in his chair. He eyed us silently for several moments.

"Now, Mr. Masters, tell me yer version of yer and Mr. Slater's story, from the beginnin'. And Mr. Slater, don't interrupt him."

Ben looked at me and I nodded my head slightly. To my immense relief, Ben related our story as I had, ending it with the major rescuing us from the Apaches. He omitted the fact, as I had done, that he was a wanted man and that I was a Texas Ranger pursuing him. The only difference between our versions was the fact that he recounted our sexual activity with the Apaches, but to a much lesser extent than what Samuel had portrayed. Ben looked the major squarely in the eye as he finished speaking. The major returned his stare, somewhat suspiciously. I knew that our story was filled with big gaps of missing information.

"Are ya sure that's the whole story, Mr. Masters? You're not leavin' out any details, as Mr. Slater did this afternoon?"

Ben stared calmly back at the major.

"That's the whole story, Major."

"If'n ya say so, then I have no choice but to believe ya. It's just that I've got a nose fer lawmen, an' right now my nose is tellin' me that one of you fellas is the law. Am I right?"

The major's last remark took Ben by surprise, and he simply stared at the major without responding. I spoke up quickly, to allay Major Preston's suspicions.

"I can assure ya, Major, that neither one of us is associated with the law in any way, shape, or form."

"I'll take yer word fer it then, Mr. Slater. You'll find empty bunks over in the barracks, thanks to a raid by our Apache friends earlier this week. Supper's served at six o'clock sharp in the mess. Stragglers don't eat. As long as you're stayin' at the fort fer a few days, you're goin' to earn yer keep. There are plenty of chores 'round here to keep both of ya busy. An' the men are always hungry fer fresh meat, so there's always huntin' to be done. I'll walk ya over to the barracks an' git ya settled in."

We finished our whiskey and followed the major, entering the first barracks we came to. Inside it was dim and cool, like the major's quarters had been. The barracks was deserted at this time of day. A row of bunk beds lined the outside walls to the right and left of us, perpendicular to the wall, forming an aisle down the center. Between each bunk stood a large trunk I assumed was for the soldiers' gear and perhaps personal belongings. At the end of the aisle, against the back wall, stood a huge pot-bellied stove. Several rough-hewn wooden chairs and some oak barrels formed a semicircle in front of it. We walked down the aisle and stopped at the last bunk bed.

"This bunk here isn't being used. Feel free to lay down an' rest fer a spell. I know you've been through a lot these past few days. The bugler will announce when supper's ready."

He turned and walked down the aisle. I watched him until he disappeared out the door, then took a seat on one of the oak barrels in front of the stove. Ben took the one on my right. I felt his eyes upon me, and I turned to meet his gaze.

"Thanks, Jake, fer not tellin' the major you was chasin' me because I'm wanted fer killin' the ranger. He would have strung me up fer sure."

"I didn' like lyin' to the man, Ben, but I told ya at the pool this mornin' that I no longer believe ya killed the ranger. But my thinkin' so won't matter much unless we git to Silverton, find Bart Jensen, an' wring a confession out of him. This is a lonely an' dangerous territory we're in. I figger two men workin' together have better odds than two men workin' against each other. Besides, I . . . ."

I cut myself short when I realized that I'd been about to tell

Ben that I cared very much what happened to him because I had fallen in love with him. I saw understanding dawn in his eyes. He didn' speak; he just simply grabbed my hand and squeezed it tight.

"Let's git some shut-eye before supper. I'll take the lower bunk an' you can have the top one."

"Okay, Jake."

I took off my shirt and hung it on one of the posts of the bunk bed. Ben took his off also, stepped onto the lower bunk, and hoisted himself onto the top one. I stretched out on the lower bunk and was soon fast asleep.

Ben and I were in the Apache lodge again, and Apache warriors were mounting us one after the other. I looked up to see a line of warriors the length of the lodge and out the door. Next in line was Samuel, a grin on his face from ear to ear.

I cursed him, and woke myself up. A good-looking young soldier was kneeling at the edge of my bunk. His upper torso lay across it. He was swirling his tongue over the head of my cock. He had undone the buttons on my pants and pulled them down past my thighs without waking me. I rose up on my elbows and glanced quickly around the barracks, checking to see if any other soldiers were present. We were alone. The soldier's eyes met mine as he explored my piss slit with the tip of his tongue. The young man licked from the crown down along the shaft to the thick base. He ran his tongue around the base several times, then continued down to my nut sac. He grabbed it and tugged back the excess skin, outlining the full size of the twin globes. The soldier slurped at them like a thirsty coyote drinking from a desert stream, then took the entire sac into his mouth. He rolled my nuts around and sucked on them softly, then let my sac drop from his mouth. He then ran his tongue up and down my shaft. After several turns, the young man returned to the blood-engorged head and lapped up the fluid bubbling at the slit.

Taking the large knob into his mouth, he slowly sank down
the length of my stiffer. The fat head hit the back of the young
soldier's throat then slid deep down his gullet. His mouth was
stretched wide around the thick base. The young soldier gagged
slightly as he struggled to breathe while keeping my whole
dick buried down his throat. He alternated between sucking so
hard I was sure his intent was to pull my tool out by its roots
to sucking softly as if he was a nursing newborn. Finally, he
slid his mouth back up my pole and began licking the crown
once more. He teased the swollen slit briefly with the tip of
his tongue, then swallowed my cock again. When his lips were
pressed against my crotch hair, he slid back up to the knob, then
began steadily sawing up and down on my stiffer. I grabbed
a handful of his hair and used it to control the up and down
movement of his head. Grabbing my nut sac in his right hand,
the soldier squeezed firmly.

"Suck my cock, soldier," I whispered, hoarsely.

He needed no further encouragement. His efforts on my
hawg quickly doubled in intensity. In addition to the noisy cock
sucking of the soldier and my soft moans, I suddenly heard a
slight rustling. I saw movement out of the corner of my right
eye and turned my head just as Ben was easing himself off the
top bunk. He dropped lightly onto the floor to left of the soldier. The man didn't see or hear Ben, though, because he was
too busy enjoying my dick. There was a large bulge beneath
the gold buttons of Ben's faded cavalry-issue trousers. His
nipples were hard, poking through the blanket of hair covering his chest. Stepping beside the bobbing soldier, Ben quickly
undid the buttons on his pants and pushed them down over
his muscular thighs to his knees. I admired his by-now-familiar hawg as he thrust his hips forward and poked the young
soldier in the left ear with the head of his cock. The man fairly
spat my dick out of his mouth and whirled to face Ben. He was
promptly whacked in the face by Ben's huge stiffer. Luckily for

me, the young soldier was on an upward swing, or he would probably have choked on my pole when Ben startled him. The soldier sized up the situation immediately and swallowed Ben's pole and began bobbing up and down on it as eagerly as he'd done on mine. Ben moaned softly, placed his right hand on the soldier's head, and began slowly pumping his hips to match the man's pistoning head. One his next upward saw, he let Ben's hawg slip from his mouth.

"Get up on the bunk with him," he said softly to Ben.

I slid over and Ben lay down beside me. He placed his left arm across my pillow, and I laid my head in its crook. I began playing with Ben's tits, strumming them with my fingers and pinching the dark-brown nipples. Ben moaned his appreciation. Meanwhile, the soldier had crawled onto the bunk and positioned himself on his hands and knees above Ben's crotch. He swallowed Ben's manhood to the root and resumed his bobbing. After a dozen or so bobs, it was my turn, and once again my fat staff was deep down his throat. The soldier began alternating between our dicks, never quite staying on either one long enough to bring either one of us to the point of shooting. I continued to work Ben's nipples, squeezing the tender points of flesh. Ben squirmed beside me and started pulling my tits in return, bringing my nipples to instant hardness.

I watched the young man saw up and down on Ben's cock. When it was my turn again, the soldier grabbed my trousers, pulled them down past my knees, and began exploring the crack of my ass with his finger. Running it lightly up and down my sweaty, hairy crack, he came close to, but never quite touched, my puckered opening. I humped my ass against his hand, urging him to explore my hole fully. He obliged by rubbing my shit hole, slowly at first, then faster and faster. Soon I was thrashing on the bed beside Ben. The soldier withdrew his finger, spit twice on it, then pushed it against my hole once more. I grunted loudly when it suddenly popped through the opening. The soldier slid his finger inside me to the second knuckle, but was unable to reach my hidden secret muscle. I began moving my hips to match his finger as he slid it in and out of my channel. He took my stiffer into his mouth, sawed on it several times, then spit it out, pulled his finger abruptly out of my asshole, and swung back to Ben.

The young soldier gave Ben the same treatment I'd just received. Ben grunted softly when the man's finger slid into his chute, and he also began pumping his hips to match the in and out movements of the large digit. Ben stopped playing with my nipples and, placing his hand on the back of my head, pushed my face into his tit. I sucked the whole muscle into my mouth and chewed on it noisily. Placing his other hand on the back of the soldier's head, Ben forced his dick deep into the young man's throat on each of his downward plunges. Ben's moans and cries increased in length and intensity as he writhed on the bunk beside me. His breaths were coming in deep, ragged gasps, and I was sure he was close to shooting his stuff. The young soldier apparently sensed this as well. He grabbed Ben's ball sac in his right hand, engulfed Ben's cock to the root one last time and stayed there, his nose buried in Ben's thatch of reddish-brown crotch hair. I bit down hard on Ben's nipple, triggering his explosion.

"I'm gonna blow, boys," he cried softly, his ass rising off the bed.

I could see and hear the soldier's throat muscles working as he swallowed Ben's seed. Ben spasmed one last time, then settled back on the bed. The man held Ben's shaft in his mouth until it started to soften. When he finally released it, a final drop of spunk oozed out of the piss slit. The soldier scooped it up with his tongue, then swung back to my fat pole and swallowed it once more. Grabbing my balls in his right hand, he started kneading them.

Ben turned on his side, facing me, and ran his fingers through

the hair on my chest. He then leaned into me and began working my nipples with his lips and tongue. The combination of
the soldier's warm, wet mouth on my stiffer, and Ben's mouth
on my teats quickly pushed me over the edge. I moaned like a
whore in heat when my balls pulled out of the young soldier's
grasp and rolled up snug to the base of my dick.

"Get ready to swallow, soldier boy," I gasped.

The first drop of my seed erupted into his mouth. Ben held
me tight as the intensity of my explosion gripped me, and I
filled the young soldier's mouth with my cream. He swallowed
every bit of it, then released my dick and licked it clean.

When he was finished, the soldier crawled off the bed without a word. I thought he was going to leave but, instead, he
stood next to the bunk, staring down at us. He slowly unbuttoned his shirt and pulled the tucked in portion out of his
trousers. His chest was thickly muscled and hairless. Quarter-
sized, light-brown nipples capped his tits. His stomach was
ridged with muscle, and also hairless. A substantial trail of black
hairs started just below his navel and disappeared beneath the
waistband of his pants. He undid the row of buttons that lined
them. I could see the white of his drawers and the pronounced
swell underneath the row of buttons on them. He undid these
as well, and pulled his trousers and drawers down his beefy,
hairy thighs to his knees. His dick sprang free, slapping up hard
against his stomach. It was semi-hard, the large head still clearly
outlined inside its cocoon of skin. His balls were of considerable size, hanging low in their sac between his legs. Sparse black
hairs sprouted from the skin of the sac. A considerable thatch
of black hair covered the v of his crotch. What hair the young
man lacked on his chest and stomach was more than made up
for by the hair on his legs and at his crotch.

The young soldier shuffled to the edge of the bunk. The
smell of his crotch was strong. Grabbing his stiffer in his left
hand, he pulled the skin back from the head. The tiny slit was

already dripping clear fluid. Sliding his thumb through the slit, the young man caught the fluid, put his thumb in his mouth, and sucked on it as he stared into my eyes. Ben stirred beside me, and my own dick was quickly coming back to life. The soldier's pole was fully hard now. His equipment was of a generous size and length. The soldier spit into his left hand then coated his shaft with it. He encircled the thick base with the thumb and forefinger of his left hand, and slid them up the shaft and over the knob, squeezing it as he did so. After several strokes, more drops of clear fluid oozed from his piss slit. Catching the fluid with his thumb once more, he sucked it clean.

The soldier then grabbed his hawg and began stroking it in earnest. With his right hand he played with his tits, running his fingers over the swells of flesh and teasing the nipples until they were rigid. Once hard, he twisted them savagely, wringing small moans of pleasure from deep within him. He began thrusting his hips to match his stroking hand. His hefty basket swayed between his legs.

I was mesmerized as I watched the young soldier give himself relief. My cock was standing at attention, leaking its own fluid. I was so intent on the soldier that I didn't see Ben reach for my stiffer. I jumped when his fingers encircled it and he started slowly pumping it. His hand was rough and, with no spit, I winced after just a few strokes. Ben immediately understood, spit into his hand, spread it onto my dick, and resumed his stroking. I leaned back on my elbows and spread my legs. After numerous strokes, Ben switched to his right hand. Leaning into me, he worked my left nipple with his teeth and lips. I placed a hand on the back of his head and pushed his face into my tit.

"Suck it, Ben," I gasped.

My words evidently spurred him on, for he redoubled his efforts on the tiny nub of flesh.

On Ben's left, the soldier was moaning incessantly. His

head lolled on his right shoulder, and his mouth hung open, his tongue protruding from the right corner. He was thrusting his hips violently as he furiously stroked his pole. His fingers were frantically pulling and twisting both nipples in turn. Ben's skilled hand and mouth and the sight of the lusty soldier quickly triggered my second explosion of the evening.

"I'm gonna shoot," I said, through clenched teeth.

Ben released my nipple, moved down to my crotch, and took my swollen cock head into his mouth. I cried out repeatedly as I filled his mouth with my seed. He gulped steadily. When I was spent, he licked the crown and shaft clean. Ben turned to face the young man right as the first glob of spunk blasted from the soldier's dick. It caromed off Ben's right cheek and landed on my chest. Ben leaned forward and swallowed the young soldier's swollen knob. The man placed his hands on Ben's shoulders to balance himself as he emptied into Ben's waiting mouth. As he pulled the head of his stiffer from Ben's mouth, a bugle blared outside.

CHAPTER EIGHT

"That's the call to supper," the young soldier stammered. He quickly pulled his pants and drawers up, buttoning them over his still swollen cock with great difficulty. He buttoned his shirt, then leaned over Ben to reach me, his lips seeking mine. His tongue pushed past my lips and briefly explored my mouth, then the young man withdrew it and leaned back to kiss Ben as well. When the soldier was fully dressed, he ran from the barracks.

I looked at Ben, a smile lighting up my face.

"Isn't it bad manners to have dessert before the main course?"

His hearty laughter was his only reply. He bent down and licked the blob of the young soldier's seed from my chest, then kissed me full on the mouth and hugged me fiercely. We scrambled off the bunk and dressed in silence. I adjusted my semi-hard dick beneath the tight, blue pants to hide the still-sizable lump. I glanced down at my crotch to gauge my success and noticed a small damp spot at my crotch where the large, oozing head of my cock was nestled. I looked up just as the major came down the aisle toward us.

"Supper's ready in the mess hall if'n you're hungry, boys. It's army food, but there's plenty of it, an' it'll fill ya up."

"We're both starvin', Major. We're right behind ya," I replied.

He turned to go, but suddenly stopped. He faced us again, then glanced at the rumpled blanket on the bottom bunk. His gaze traveled to my crotch, lingering at the slowly spreading circle of stain, before returning to my face to bore into my eyes.

He sniffed the air several times, his eyes never leaving mine.

"I take it that you are now well-rested, gentlemen?"

"Very much so, Major," I replied.

Ben nodded his assent.

He studied us a moment longer then turned smartly on his heel and strode from the barracks without saying another word. We were right behind him.

The major walked across the compound with us as far as the mess hall, bid us a curt farewell, and went on to his quarters. Apparently he didn't eat with his men. As Ben and I entered the mess hall, the sight of so many men, and the sounds and smells that accompanied them, immediately overwhelmed my senses. The chuck line was to our right. A large man in an apron stood at the front of the line, handing out tin plates, forks, and cups. Another man, even larger than the first and also wearing an apron, this one soiled, was spooning something onto the metal plates that the passing soldiers held up to him. A third man, wearing no apron, was at the end of the line, filling the tin cups. Ben and I grabbed a plate, a fork, and a cup, and took our place in line. When it was my turn to hold my plate up to the middle man, he slopped a generous portion of what looked like stew onto it. When I reached the end of the line, the man there took my cup and filled it with steaming coffee. I spotted a table in the far corner with empty seats on its bench. As we sat down, Ben and I introduced ourselves to the men seated around us. The food was indeed stew, and to my surprise it was good and filling. We both went back for a second helping.

The soldiers at the table quickly made us feel right at home. They listened, open interest expressed plainly on their sun-reddened faces, as I related how Ben and I were captured by the Chiricahua. When I finished, they took turns telling of their own misadventures with various Indian tribes in the region. The soldiers were a mixed lot, made up of young and old, greenhorns and veterans. My eyes wandered from handsome faces, bearded and mustached, to hairy, beefy forearms exposed by rolled-back sleeves. I hadn't been around this large a group of men since leaving Abilene in pursuit of Ben. When we finished eating, two of the soldiers offered to show Ben and me the fort. We walked around the compound, checking out the barn, the corrals, and the meager garden in the deepening twilight. Darkness was creeping over the fort as we made our way back to our barracks.

Once inside, the two men excused themselves and went to their individual bunks. A half-dozen soldiers were sitting by the pot-bellied stove. One of them invited Ben and me to join in a friendly game of poker. We agreed, and took seats atop two of the large, wooden barrels. A fire was burning in the stove, its heat fighting the chill of the desert night. Several of the soldiers rolled smokes while the soldier sitting closest to the stove shuffled and dealt the cards. I'd just picked up the cards dealt to me when I saw the major coming down the aisle. He walked purposefully up to the small group gathered around the stove, his gaze taking in each of us individually, finally coming to rest on me.

"Mr. Slater," he said, his voice brisk and brimming with authority, "would ya mind joinin' me in my quarters fer a short time? I have a few more questions to ask ya 'bout the band of Apache that held you an' Mr. Masters captive."

Even though it was posed as a question, I knew I couldn't refuse the major's request.

"Sure, Major. Do ya want Ben to join us as well?"

"No, Mr. Slater, yer presence is sufficient."

I rose from the barrel, handed my cards to the soldier who'd dealt them, shot Ben what I hoped was a comforting look, and followed the major to his quarters. The chairs Ben and I had sat in earlier today were still in front of his desk. I sat down as the major seated himself behind his desk. He produced the same bottle of whiskey, along with two glasses, and filled them with the light-brown liquid. He downed his and refilled the glass.

"Now, Mr. Slater, tell me yer story again, from the time the Apaches captured ya. I'm interested in learnin' the number of warriors in their village."

I drank my whiskey in one gulp, waited while the major refilled my glass, then started my tale. I began with the moment the half-dozen Apaches had burst into the bandits' hideout, killing every last one of them, and sparing Ben and me to take us to their mountain stronghold. When the major asked if I could pinpoint the location of the Apache village, I reluctantly told him no. His face registered his disappointment. However, he was somewhat mollified when I proceeded to tell him the number of teepees that made up the village, the number of horses I'd seen, and the amount of food that was being grown. I paused a moment to sip my whiskey, then launched into the details of our sexual escapades with the Apaches while we were their captives. The major listened attentively, now and then interjecting a question. When I was done, he finished his second whiskey, poured another for himself, and topped off my glass. He stared at me for a moment, then cleared his throat, somewhat nervously.

"I've often heard that the Apache will take pleasure from a man the same's they do from a woman. I know the same thing often occurs between white men. When ya live in a remote, frontier place such as this, Mr. Slater, where the women are few an' far between, an' the unmarried ones are even scarcer, ya quickly learn to take yer pleasurin' when an' from whom ya can."

"Please, Major, call me Jake," I stammered, my heart pounding loudly in my chest as it dawned on me where this conversation might be headed. I took another sip of my whiskey, praying that my shaking hand wouldn't cause me to spill some, thus betraying my excitement.

"Okay, Jake. An' I'll refer to Mr. Masters as Ben. An' you can call me Stephen when it's just the two of us. It wouldn't do to have a nice-looking feller like you callin' me Stephen in front of my men now, would it?"

He paused for a moment, waiting for his words to sink in.

"Are you an' Ben familiar with each other as a man and a woman are, Jake, or, in these parts, as many men are?"

I didn't answer Stephen; I just sat there, staring at him.

"Don't be alarmed. I've bedded many a man in my time, several of them right here at this fort. Take fer instance that young corporal I saw leavin' your barracks tonight right before supper. That young corporal has sat right where you are now, on several occasions. I know the smell that's produced from men having sex, Jake. Also, I saw the telltale stain on the crotch of yer pants."

When he finished speaking, he chuckled softly.

I gulped the remainder of my whiskey and set the glass on the desk. The major got up slowly from his chair, his light-gray eyes staring into mine. He stepped around the desk and walked past me. I turned in the chair when he passed beyond my line of vision to see where he was headed. I couldn't help but notice how nicely his cavalry-issue pants outlined the contours of his muscular ass. He stopped at the door to his office, but didn't open it. Instead, he grabbed a piece of wood, about four foot long by two foot wide, that was leaning against the front wall. I hadn't noticed it before. Upon closer inspection of the door, I saw two wooden brackets, shaped like l's, mounted to the wall on either side of the door. The major slid the piece of wood into the brackets, barring any unwanted entrance. When he turned around and faced me again, there was no mistaking the rising swell at his crotch.

"Just holler if'n ya want out, Jake, an' I'll happily oblige. Not many do the first time, an' none do the second. I'm a gamblin' man, Jake, an' I'm bettin' you'll be stayin'."

"You'd win that bet, Stephen," I replied.

He laughed heartily as he walked back across the room toward me. Turning back around in the chair, I faced his desk once more. I was willing to let Stephen take the lead in this game, because I was still unsure whether or not I should tip my hand to him concerning Ben and myself. Stephen's footsteps stopped directly behind me and I felt him brush against my back. I jumped when he placed his hands on my shoulders. I could feel the heat and strength in them through my thin cotton shirt.

"There are a lot of ways a man can satisfy another man, Jake. An' my gut feelin' is tellin' me that you an' Ben are familiar with several of these ways."

Before I could think of a reply, he took his right hand from my shoulder and placed it on the back of my neck. The heat of his hand was more pronounced against my bare skin. He began stroking my neck with his fingers. The roughness of them against my sunburned skin made me wince slightly, and caused the hairs on my entire body to stand on end. Stephen's right hand was soon joined by his left, and he began kneading the muscles in my neck. My cock stirred in my pants. He worked on my neck for a good while, then switched to my shoulders. His strong fingers fiercely gripped the knotted muscles there, forcing them to loosen up. I suddenly felt warm breath in my ear, which carried with it the smell of whiskey. Stephen licked the sensitive lobe of my ear, then took the entire end into his mouth and gently nibbled on it. He then sucked the lobe briefly before releasing it and flicking his tongue inside my ear. I moaned softly and squirmed on the chair as Stephen's tongue slid around inside. He didn't miss a single sensitive spot. My nipples had turned to hardened, fiery points of flesh on my chest. I reached down and adjusted my stiffer to give it room to swell to its full proportion.

Stephen licked the inside of my ear once more, then began nuzzling the back of my neck. Soon he was covering it with soft kisses. I pressed back against his chest, forcing the back of the chair to push into his crotch. He planted a final kiss, then stepped around my right side to face me. I stared into his eyes.

They were full of mischief combined with a recognizable manly yearning. Without a word, he straddled my lap. His face was inches from mine, and he kissed me, deeply. His mustache tickled my upper lip as it meshed with the hair that grew above my own. His mouth tasted of whiskey and tobacco. Forcing his thick, wet tongue past my lips, Stephen explored the inside of my mouth, running his tongue over my upper and lower teeth, then twining it around my own tongue like two lovers at a barn dance. Stephen grabbed my tongue between his teeth and sucked it into his mouth. As I strained forward, Stephen ground his crotch into mine. I felt the wetness where the fat head of his dick was pinned against his trousers.

Finally releasing my tongue, Stephen tore his gaze from mine and began undoing the buttons on my shirt. When the last one was free, he pushed the shirt over my shoulders and partway down my arms, for a moment effectively pinning me to the chair. I shifted forward slightly to allow him to pull the shirt off my arms completely. Stephen stared at my chest as if hypnotized, then placed his hands on the swells of muscle that formed my tits and pinched my nipples none-too-gently. I squirmed in the chair, my soft cries and moans spurring him to greater efforts.

Stephen twisted each nipple once more, then released them. Leaning into me, he took each teat into his mouth in turn, sucking and biting on the hardened nubs until small cries and moans issued from me nonstop. He bit the right nipple one last time, causing me to jerk forward in the chair, then slid off my lap and knelt on the floor at my feet. He leaned into me once more and, as he did so, I inhaled deeply of his raw maleness. Starting at my throat, he licked down through the hairs on my chest, this time ignoring my swollen and aching nipples. Several times he gathered tufts of my dark-brown chest hair between his teeth and gently tugged on them. Working his way down to my deeply cut navel, Stephen teasingly licked around it several times, then drove the tip of his tongue deep into the opening. I again jerked forward on the chair when the tip hit the back of my navel and a current of sensation swept through my upper torso. Driving the tip of his tongue home twice more, Stephen licked down to the waistband of my pants, and from there to my swelling crotch. He squeezed the large mound several times; the pressure felt good on my cock and ball sac. Undoing the row of buttons that lined my crotch, he slid his hand inside. He traced my dick and nut sac with a finger, then withdrew his hand and grabbed my pants by their waistband.

"Lift yer ass," Stephen whispered.

I rose slightly off the chair and he yanked my pants down my thighs to my knees. My hawg sprang free, slapping hard against my stomach and depositing a small drop of clear fluid below my navel. I lifted my feet off the floor, allowing Stephen to slide my trousers over my knees and down my legs to my ankles. He sat on the floor, grabbed my right boot, and tugged it off. The left one followed suit, as did my socks and pants. I was now completely naked.

Stephen stood up in front of me again, his gaze traveling the length of my naked body.

"Ya sure are a fine-lookin' man, Jake."

He reached behind him and grabbed the bottle of whiskey off the desk. Tilting the bottle to his lips, Stephen took a long pull from it then wiped his sleeve across his mouth. Stepping closer to me, he raised the bottle to my lips. I gulped the liquid, feeling it burn its way down to my stomach. As I licked the residue from my lips, Stephen bent over my crotch and poured a goodly amount of the whiskey directly onto it, soaking my swollen tool and nut sac as well as the patch of thick hair. I could feel the whiskey running beneath my sac and onto the chair beneath my ass. Setting the bottle on the floor beside the chair, Stephen knelt in front of me and began lapping the whiskey from my crotch.

He slid his tongue up and down my shaft, then moved down

to bathe my heavy, swollen balls. Twirling his tongue around the twin globes, he lifted and rolled them inside their protective sac of flesh. When he was done with my balls, Stephen licked his way to my crotch hair, and buried his face in the thick patch. He sucked big clumps of hair into his mouth and pulled on them gently with his teeth.

Pulling his face out of my crotch hair, Stephen pressed my hawg against my stomach and held it there with his hand while he focused his attention once more on my nut sac. He swallowed the entire sac of flesh and began sucking fiercely on the hens-egg-sized balls. I moaned uncontrollably as he worked the swollen orbs for a good while, then let them drop from his mouth. He slid his tongue along the underside of my thick shaft to the blood-engorged crown. Lapping first at the large knob, he then gently scraped his upper front teeth over it. Stephen suddenly let up on my slit, engulfed the fat head, and proceeded to swallow the entire length of my cock, his mouth wet and warm, his lips forming a tight ring of suction around the thick shaft.

Holding my pole in his mouth, Stephen sucked on it softly, then slid back up to the knob. He nibbled on it briefly then swallowed my dick once more. Grabbing my basket in his right hand, he squeezed it several times, seemingly determined to milk the seed out of me. I grabbed handfuls of Stephen's hair and used it to propel him up and down on my stiffer, gagging him a few times in the process. Saliva ran copiously from the corners of his mouth, further dampening my crotch hair and nut sac.

"Suck my cock, Major," I cried as I began pumping my hips to match Stephen's pistoning head. The sucking noises he was making, combined with his soft groans, added to my heightening arousal. I was moaning uncontrollably and thrashing on the chair. The smell of my own crotch wafted to my nostrils. The familiar tingling flooded my crotch as my eruption began.

"I'm gonna shoot!" I hollered just as the first glob of seed shot from my dick and into Stephen's mouth. He swallowed it without hesitation and gulped repeatedly as the rest of my spunk emptied into him. When I was spent, Stephen held my hawg in his mouth while it slowly softened.

When I was completely soft, Stephen released my cock then rose from his knees and straddled my lap once more. He kissed me deeply and passionately, then probed my mouth with his tongue, which tasted of my spunk. He withdrew his tongue, stood up suddenly, grabbed my right arm, and pulled me roughly onto my feet. He spun me around and pushed me against the desk. Reaching behind me, Stephen gripped the cheeks of my ass, picked me up, and lifted me onto the desk as if I weighed no more than a child. I stared into his beautiful gray eyes for a moment, then spread my legs, allowing him to step between them until his own legs were pressed against the desk. Stephen unbuttoned his dark-blue shirt and let it fall to the floor. He undid the buttons on his undershirt and pulled it off over his head, revealing a forest of thick, black, fleecy hair covering his chest and stomach. The hair disappeared beneath the waistband of his trousers. His dark-brown nipples were already taut, poking out defiantly from the dense jungle of fur that surrounded them. He undid the buttons on his pants and drawers, and slid both down to his ankles.

I stared in lust at the naked man in front of me. Stephen's dick was completely hard, and enormous, both in length and circumference. It stuck straight out from beneath a patch of profuse black crotch hair that blended in with the hair on his stomach and legs. The head of his cock was easily the size of a plum. His nuts were enormous, hanging low in their flesh sac between his legs, the right one slightly below the left.

Stephen placed a hand on my knee for support, tugged his Calvary-issue boots off, then his socks, and stepped out of his trousers and drawers. He pushed me back until I lay flat on top of the desk, my legs dangling over the edge. He grabbed me behind each knee, raised my legs in the air, and pushed them over my upper torso until my heels were touching my ears. He held my legs there as he bent down and began licking my ball sac. After a final lick, he trailed his tongue down to the dark, moist, hairy crack of my ass. I grabbed my ass cheeks and spread them wide, giving Stephen plenty of room to work on the dark hole hidden between them.

Stephen tongued around the puckered opening for a good while, teasing but never touching the edges or the tender center. He paused suddenly, lifted his head slightly, stared into my eyes, then dipped his head once more and drove the tip of his tongue deep into my hole. I cried out, arching my back and pushing against his tongue as he probed my secret spot. After licking the tiny hole thoroughly, he ran his tongue across it several times, the stubble on his chin rasping along the crack of my ass. I heard him spit, and jumped when the cold liquid hit my back door. He spit twice more, stood upright, and placed the head of his hawg against the puckered opening. He pushed against my corn hole, and I pushed back just as hard, desperately wanting his pole deep inside me. My hole put up a brief fight before allowing the large knob to pop through. I gasped and clenched my teeth from the slight pain as his huge dick slowly slid up my chute. It pushed the walls of my asshole apart, penetrating deep, until Stephen's crotch hairs were tickling my ass cheeks.

Stephen held his cock inside me, allowing my shitter to conform to its large intruder. I repeatedly squeezed it as hard as I could with my eager hole. Stephen moaned his appreciation and sprawled on top of me, his lips once more seeking mine. I locked my arms across his broad, sweaty back and, easing my legs down, planted my heels against the cheeks of his ass. He slowly withdrew his stiffer, paused with just the knob still inside me, then slid steadily and determinedly back in. He started pumping into me with slow, deep thrusts. The pain was soon replaced by an intense pleasure. Pushing himself upright once more, Stephen placed his hands flat on my stomach, all the while continuing to plow my ass.

"Pound my ass, Major!" I yelled.

I slid my feet up from his ass and locked them in the small of his back. With my arms and my feet, I pulled Stephen to me on each of his lunges, urging him to increase the force of his penetration. In response, Stephen started hammering me with a renewed vigor. The desk was rocking with the force of his thrusts; soon it was banging loudly against the floor. I unwrapped my arms from around Stephen, grabbed my pole in my right hand, and began stroking it in time with his thrusts. With my left hand I began pulling on his nipples.

"I'm gonna blow, Jake," he gasped.

He slammed into me one last time, yelling incoherently as his eruption began. His spunk flooded my asshole. My own hawg erupted, spraying white seed across the hairs on my stomach. When he'd shot his load, Stephen collapsed on top of me. As I wrapped my arms around him he covered my lips and face with kisses. He stayed inside me until his cock began to soften, then slowly pulled out. I swore I heard my chute breathe a sigh of relief. Stephen wiped the head of his dick on the back of my leg, stepped back, and plopped into the chair, his chest heaving from his recent exertion. He grabbed the bottle of whiskey off the floor and took a long pull from it. I sat up and slid off the desk. My legs were wobbly as I stepped over to Stephen. He handed me the bottle and I took a hefty swig from it myself, then handed it back.

"Ya know, Jake, it's been a long time since I've had a man like you," he drawled. "Too long. Now I know why Ben looks at ya the way he does. I'm sure he's received his fair share of pleasurin' from ya."

"What do ya mean by the way Ben looks at me?"

My heart was pounding in my chest, and the eagerness in my voice was hard to miss.

Stephen stared at me without replying. The silence dragged on as Stephen continued to eye me steadily. He looked down at the floor briefly, then into my eyes once more.

"I was reluctant to bring this to yer attention, Jake, because I've only known you an' Ben fer a few days. I've taken quite a fancy to ya but it's nothin' compared to how Ben feels. I can tell just by the way he looks at ya an' acts toward ya that he's in love with ya. An' I think it's safe to say that you feel the same 'bout him. Don't let him slip away from ya, Jake," he finished, quietly.

I was fairly certain that Stephen was correct in his assessment of Ben. On several recent occasions Ben had shown me that much. I also believed that Ben and I were both reluctant to express those feelings until this Bart Jensen matter had been dealt with.

"It's best ya be gittin' back to the barracks, Jake. My regular boys will be thinkin' I'm playin' favorites with ya."

Stephen got up from the chair and stepped to me, his arms outstretched. I moved into them and we embraced, his warm, hairy body pressed tightly to mine. We kissed long and hard, then he pushed me gently away.

"Go to Ben, Jake, an' tell him how ya feel. Don't wait until it's too late."

I dressed slowly. I could feel Stephen's eyes upon me, but I didn't look at him. When I was clothed once more, I walked to the door, lifted the board from its brackets, and paused to look back at Stephen. A bright smile lit up his face, and he nodded his head in the direction of the barracks.

"One more thing. Before you an' Ben leave, I'd like a crack at both of ya."

"I'm sure that can be arranged."

CHAPTER NINE

I opened the door and stepped out into the dark, silent night, closing the door gently behind me. I walked across the sandy compound to the barracks. When I entered, complete silence greeted me. As I walked between the rows of bunks I heard the snores of the sleeping soldiers. The smell of their combined sweat was heavy in the air. My mind was still filled with Stephen's words. I reached my bunk and stood by it, staring at the sleeping man in the bed above mine. Ben was on his side, his face turned to me. His chest rose and fell with his even breathing. Slight snores escaped his slightly-opened mouth.

I undressed and crawled beneath my blanket. I lay awake a long time, once more going over in my mind the series of events that had occurred since I'd first set out in pursuit of Ben. I suddenly realized just how much I loved this supposed outlaw. As I drifted off, I knew in my heart and mind that Ben was innocent. And I also knew that I wouldn't let him slip away from me.

I awoke with the sun's rays spilling through the window beside my bunk. I threw off my blanket and sat on the edge of the bed. I stood up and turned to see if Ben was still sleeping. I found myself staring into a pair of green eyes, full of mischief. He smiled at me and hopped down off the bunk. Taking me into his arms, he began passionately kissing me. I returned his kisses, then pushed him gently away. Several of the soldiers were already stirring, and I didn't want to be caught embracing Ben. From past experience I knew that not all men were as understanding as Stephen and many others I'd met when it came to the desires between two men. I told Ben what had happened last night between Stephen and myself, and I also passed along Stephen's invitation for Ben to join us the next time. Ben eagerly accepted. We dressed quietly but hurriedly and joined a small group of soldiers headed for breakfast in the mess hall. I was surprised when Stephen joined us at our table. The three of us made small talk about issues concerning Fort Benson.

After breakfast Stephen assigned Ben and me several chores to keep us busy during the course of the day. The first one was weeding the garden. That didn't take long, for few weeds grew in the hard, sandy soil, and fewer vegetables. A couple of rows of squash, both Indian and summer, sucked what little moisture they could from the rocky soil. Several straggly rows of maize grew next to the squash, and that was the extent of the garden. Everything else had withered and died. Ben and I took turns drawing water from the well and wetting the rows of vegetables. When we finished in the garden, we headed over to the horse barn. Our second chore of the day was to clean the horse stalls. As we neared the barn door, the smell of horse shit lay heavy in the air. Black flies swarmed continuously around our heads as we worked. When we finished in the barn, we ate a quick lunch in the mess hall then took part in a hunting expedition with several of the soldiers. The hunt took the rest of the afternoon. We returned to the fort just as the sun was starting to set. We'd managed to bag several large hares, a couple of rattlesnakes, and a few small grouse.

After supper Ben and I returned to the barracks with the group of soldiers we had eaten with. They occupied their time with various mundane activities: rolling smokes, cleaning their Spencers and Colts, and polishing their boots and sabers. A burly soldier named Jeremiah suggested a game of poker, and Ben and I joined a half-dozen men in front of the stove. Among the group was the young soldier who had serviced Ben and me yesterday afternoon in the barracks. I'd since learned his name was Matthew.

Jeremiah dragged his wooden trunk over to use as a table.

As darkness swiftly closed in around us, Matthew lit several oil lamps, placing one on top of the stove and the other on the trunk. Their flickering flames cast grotesque shadows onto the log wall behind us. We played for matchsticks only, since none of these poor soldiers could rustle up enough money for a kitty. A whiskey bottle suddenly appeared and was eagerly passed around. I'd learned in my brief stay here that although whiskey wasn't specifically against Army regulations (some leniency was shown to soldiers living on these lonely outposts), it was most assuredly against the major's strict orders. If these soldiers only knew what went on in Stephen's office, I thought to myself. Then again, probably some of them did. Two soldiers were designated to watch the door and give the alarm if the major happened to check in on his men before retiring for the evening.

When the first bottle of whiskey had been consumed, another miraculously appeared. As the whiskey continued to flow, the conversation naturally turned to man's favorite pastime and greatest obsession: sex. Stories were shared of frantic couplings with willing girls back home, and each soldier had a tale to relate concerning the talents of the sensual señoritas down along Mexico way. Ben and I contributed no stories of our own, but no one seemed to notice. Or if they did notice, they chose not to comment on the fact. As the night progressed, the rest of the soldiers that were not a part of our group retired to their bunks.

I was surprised to find myself becoming aroused by the voracious sexual appetites of these lonely, randy men. When the next hand had been played out, Jeremiah, whose turn it was to deal, cleared his throat.

"Seeins' how it's almost time to turn in, boys, why don' we make that the last hand. Then we can play a quick game of Sucker before we hit the sack."

Each of the men quickly nodded his agreement, smiles appearing on each face. I'd never heard of the game Jeremiah

HOT ON HIS TRAIL · 157 ·

had just mentioned. I knew a sucker was someone who was easily fooled, but I'd never heard of a game made up about it. I glanced over at Ben, and I could tell by the blank expression on his face that he'd also never heard of it.

"What is Sucker?" I asked the brawny soldier.

"Johnny," Jeremiah said, speaking to the young soldier sitting to my left, "explain the rules of the game to our new friends."

The young man looked at each of us in turn before speaking, a smile still on his face.

"It's a very simple game, gentlemen. Each of us is dealt one card, face down. The player with the lowest card has to eat the other players' spunk, startin' with the player with the highest card an' workin' his way down."

"That's the whole game?" I stammered. My heart was pounding in my chest.

"That's it," Johnny replied. "Are ya up to it? Word has it that ya might be."

I glanced at Matthew, who smiled back at me steadily, then I looked at Ben to see what his reaction was. The smile on his face said it all.

"I'm in, boys," I replied. Ben's "me too" echoed it.

I took a slug from the whiskey bottle that was passed to me as Jeremiah shuffled the deck and dealt the cards. When he'd dealt a card to himself, an expectant hush fell over the group.

"Okay boys," he drawled, "let's see what you've got."

One by one we turned our cards face up on the trunk. I was disappointed to see the jack of hearts staring back at me. I had hoped to get the low card because I'd wanted a crack at the beefy Jeremiah. Ben had been dealt the queen of hearts. Matthew was staring at the two of spades. Jeremiah and Johnny each had an ace, but I was sure Jeremiah would get first dibs on Matthew. The three remaining soldiers each had a king. The thought ran briefly through my mind that this game had been set up, but no one was complaining, least of all Matthew. He looked at each of us in turn, stood up, pushed the trunk out of the way, and knelt on the floor. It was obvious this wasn't the first time he'd "lost." The soldiers stood up, and Ben and I followed their lead. We formed a circle around Matthew, shuffling closer to him so that we were easily within his reach. Ben was to my immediate right.

Matthew swung around on his knees and faced Jeremiah. I had guessed correctly that Jeremiah would be the first. All eyes were on the two men. Jeremiah undid the buttons on his shirt, peeled it off, and tossed it aside. He wasn't wearing an undershirt. His chest was massive and covered in dark-brown hair. His well-muscled tits were enormous, capped by half-dol-lar-sized brown nipples. His stomach was covered in the same dark hair as his chest. Jeremiah smiled as he undid the buttons on the front of his trousers. He slid them down to his knees, exposing his white drawers and the sizable lump at his crotch. He unhooked the buttons on his drawers as well and tugged them down to join his trousers, revealing his hairy, beefy thighs. I found myself staring at the fattest cock I'd ever seen, and I'd seen a few in my day. The man wasn't even fully hard yet, but his shaft was thicker than my wrist. The head, slowly emerg-ing from its covering, was larger than a hen's egg, and his balls, in their enormous sac of skin, were the size of small apples. Several blue veins ran the length of the shaft. His crotch hair was dark, thick, and profuse, and there was no separation as it continued up onto his stomach.

Matthew grabbed Jeremiah's horse cock with his right hand and began stroking it. The piece of flesh hardened fully, sticking out at least a foot from the burly soldier's crotch. His nuts rolled in their fleshy sac as Matthew pumped his pole. I tore my eyes away from that massive dick long enough to glance at the group encircling Matthew. The soldiers, and even Ben, were all staring slack-jawed at Jeremiah's hawg. Pushing Matthew's hand away, Jeremiah spit into his own hand several times, smeared the fluid over his stiffer, and began stroking it. His hand moved along the long, thick shaft like an old lover, caressing each of the veins and squeezing the large crown before moving back to the base and starting over again. Matthew grabbed Jeremiah's ponderous, swaying nut sac and fondled it as the manly soldier's hand moved faster on his stiffer.

Jeremiah's broad chest was heaving and running with sweat. He grabbed Matthew by the shoulder, pulled him roughly toward his crotch, and positioned Matthew's face just below his enormous cock head. On Jeremiah's next stroke he placed his hand over his mouth. I didn't know why until I heard his muffled cries. I quickly deduced that not all of the soldiers in the barracks were privy to this game, and Jeremiah didn't want to make them so with the noise of his release. I wondered if this small group comprised Stephen's "boys."

Matthew opened his mouth wide in anticipation. A thick white blob of spunk flew from the large slit in the head of Jeremiah's hawg, splatting onto Matthew's cheek. Matthew raised up on his knees slightly, grabbed Jeremiah's cock, and aimed the head at his mouth. The next drop flew right into it. It was followed by several more, all of which Matthew swallowed. The spunk continued to spray from the rugged soldier's monstrous pole so quickly that Matthew had a hard time keeping up with the flow. A few more drops landed on his cheeks, and one plopped onto his nose.

Jeremiah heaved a final time and deposited one more blast of spunk in Matthew's mouth. The burly soldier then stepped back and sat down heavily on a barrel. His strong odor permeated the air around our group. Matthew crawled to Jeremiah, licked his dick clean, then returned to the center of the circle. Jeremiah stood up, pulled his drawers and pants up, donned his shirt, and rejoined the circle.

Johnny was next. He dropped his pants and drawers as Jeremiah had done, and removed his shirt and undershirt. His chest was completely hairless, but well-muscled, the nipples large and dark. His pole wasn't of any great length, but it was incredibly fat, almost club-like. The head was a darker color than the shaft. Spitting into his hand, Johnny spread the saliva on his cock and began slowly stroking it. Matthew shuffled forward on his knees, his face only inches from Johnny's crotch. Then, to my surprise, Johnny turned around, offering his hairy butt to the young soldier. And Matthew knew exactly what to do with it. Placing a hand on each cheek, he spread them apart with his thumbs. His tongue darted out and disappeared into the crack of Johnny's ass. Johnny moaned softly and ground his ass against Matthew's eager tongue.

I felt a tug on my arm and, tearing my eyes from Johnny and Matthew, I turned to the young soldier to my left. He tugged on my sleeve again, this time impatiently, and I realized that the circle was re-forming as a semicircle to give each of us a bird's-eye view of Matthew going to town on Johnny's shit hole.

Johnny's hand moved faster on his hawg, and Matthew's tongue was darting in and out of Johnny's crack. Holding the cheeks of Johnny's ass apart with one hand, Matthew reached between Johnny's massive legs and cupped his heavy, swaying sac. Johnny's moans increased in volume as Matthew kneaded his nuts. He swung around to face Matthew, never breaking the rhythm of his stroking. He put his hand over his mouth as Jeremiah had done, but the sounds caused by his eruption could still be heard within our semicircle. A white drop flew from his dick and, caroming off Matthew's cheek, landed on the floor by Matthew's knee. Matthew opened his mouth wide and stuck out his tongue as Johnny pointed his swollen dick at the opening. The next blast landed squarely on Matthew's tongue, as did the rest, until a substantial pile had formed. Matthew held his tongue out until Johnny had squeezed the last drop from his stiffer, then he swallowed the entire offering. He licked Johnny's dick clean and sat back on his heels as Johnny slowly dressed.

Matthew repeated his performance on Jessie, Luke, and Zachary, the three remaining soldiers. Each of their dicks was equally impressive, but none of them was as large as Jeremiah's. I was beginning to understand why these men were referred to as horse soldiers. All three had undone shirts, undershirts, pants, and drawers, revealing hairy, brawny chests, stomachs, and legs, but nothing matching Jeremiah's hirsuteness or bulk. Matthew had knelt expectantly in front of Jessie until the soldier had pumped his spunk into his mouth. Luke had altered the routine a little by allowing Matthew to do most of the stroking on his pole, and had even allowed Matthew to lick the fat head a few times as he pumped it. When it was Zachary's turn, Jessie and Luke immediately stepped to either side of him and began sucking and biting his dark-brown nipples. Zachary groaned and thrust his hawg into Matthew's face. Matthew promptly swallowed the thick shaft and began sawing up and down on it. Zachary pumped his hips to match Matthew's bobbing head. None of the other soldiers protested Matthew's cock sucking. It was apparent that here in the West each man had his own limits as to what he would allow in the form of pleasuring from another man. Each man in this group appeared to respect those limits.

Zachary was soon squirming from the servicing his tits and stiffer were receiving. Releasing his left nipple, Jessie began kissing Zachary fervently on the mouth. His kisses were ardently returned. Placing his hand on top of Matthew's head, Zachary began thrusting his dick faster in and out of Matthew's mouth. Zachary was soon thrashing wildly, and muffled sounds were escaping between his kisses with Jessie. Luke suddenly grabbed Zachary's shoulder, placed a hand over his mouth, and held him tightly as Zachary spasmed with his release.

When Zachary was spent, he stepped away from Matthew. Now it was Ben's turn. As Matthew swung around on his knees, Ben pulled down his pants, revealing that he wasn't wearing any drawers. I stared openly at his burly, hairy legs and his big, fat hawg, which was fully hard. Ben didn't even get a chance to touch his pole before Matthew had it clasped firmly in his hand and was pumping it vigorously. As he stroked it, Matthew swirled his tongue over the fat crown and worked Ben's piss slit. Ben moaned loudly and rested his hand on the top of Matthew's head. Matthew ducked beneath his stroking hand and took each of Ben's balls into his mouth in turn and sucked on them while never losing his rhythm on Ben's hawg. Jeremiah and the rest of the soldiers stared at Matthew and Ben with lust-filled eyes. I caught and held Jeremiah's gaze, and he stared back without speaking. I turned my attention back to Ben, unbuttoned his shirt, and started playing with his tits. Ben was moaning uncontrollably now, and the intensity of his cries of pleasure was increasing, so I placed my hand over his mouth. Ben's scent was heavy about me, heightening my arousal and prompting me to throw caution to the wind. I began licking his throat, and eventually worked my way down to his taut nipples. I took the right one into my mouth, sucking on it noisily and nipping it with my teeth. I did the same to the left one, then began alternating between the two. Ben was squirming and thrashing beside me, and from our past experiences together I knew he was getting close to releasing his juice. His body jerked forward suddenly. I looked down at Matthew right as the first blast of Ben's spunk erupted from the slit in his cock head, hitting Matthew just below his right eye. Not missing a stroke, Matthew engulfed the head of Ben's cock and then half the length. Matthew milked the seed out of Ben with his lips and greedily swallowed it.

When Ben had finished shooting, I removed my hand from his mouth. Matthew eased off his stiffer. Ben shuddered as a final drop of spunk oozed out and plopped onto his right leg. Matthew licked it up without hesitation, then looked expectantly up at me. I nodded my head slightly. He deftly unbuttoned my pants and tugged them down to my ankles. Ben was panting loudly next to me, and I could hear low, excited murmurs from the soldiers standing around us.

"Lick it," I whispered, hoarsely.

Matthew trailed his tongue up and down my shaft, then ran it over and around the fat crown. Ben undid the buttons on my shirt and pulled it open, revealing my hairy chest. He leaned into me, flicked his tongue over my right nipple, then began biting on it and pulling it with his teeth. I moaned softly and, placing my hand on the back of Ben's head, held him to my breast. Matthew licked the head of my hawg, then swallowed it until his nose was buried deep in my crotch hair. He stayed on my pole for several seconds, sucking for all he was worth, then sawed back up to the head. He twirled his tongue over it before taking it into his mouth once more to begin sawing steadily up and down. In the meantime, Ben had switched to my other nipple, giving it the same treatment.

Zachary stepped to Matthew's side and knelt on the floor by him. He began tugging at the buttons at Matthew's crotch. When he'd undone them all, he pulled Matthew's dick out through the flap in his drawers, and began slurping on it noisily. Johnny came to my left side, knelt down, and wormed in behind me. He pried the cheeks of my ass apart and began sliding his tongue along the crack and over and around my asshole. Jeremiah had pulled out his horse cock and was busily stroking it. He moved closer to our little group until he was standing directly behind and almost over Matthew. Evidently everyone's limits were being pushed this evening.

Johnny's tongue working my ass crack was driving me crazy. The air around us was heavy with the scent of our combined sweat and spunk. Matthew was writhing below me as Zachary bobbed up and down on his stiffer. My nipples were on fire from the combination of Ben's lips and tongue, and I felt my explosion approaching. Ben began kissing me on the lips, smothering my groans and, before long, I was shooting my seed into Matthew's mouth. As I did so, I pushed back against the tongue working my hole. As Matthew swallowed my seed, he began moaning as his own release overtook him. Soon Zachary's throat muscles were flexing as he swallowed Matthew's cream.

Ben grabbed my cock and began jerking it as I emptied into Matthew's mouth. Jeremiah's hand moved faster on his dick, and suddenly he grunted "Matthew." Matthew pulled his still-dripping pole out of Zachary's mouth, let my still-spurting dick plop from his mouth, and turned just in time to catch the first blast of Jeremiah's cream. While Matthew drank Jeremiah dry, Ben knelt down in front of me and finished me off, then licked my stiffer clean.

Jeremiah tucked his softening member back into his pants as he stepped away from Matthew. Zachary got up from the floor, licking Matthew's spunk from his lips as he did so. I pulled my pants up and buttoned them, then buttoned my shirt. Ben buttoned his shirt and hugged me fiercely. Matthew remained on the floor where he was, his now-soft dick hanging out of his pants. Jeremiah was the first to break the silence with a soft chuckle.

"Ya know, boys," he said, "I think I like our friends' version of Sucker better than the way we've been playin'."

The rest of the soldiers murmured their assent, Matthew the loudest. We said our goodnights and went to our individual bunks. I kissed Ben on the lips, this time without worrying that we might be seen, then crawled onto my bunk and fell immediately asleep.

CHAPTER TEN

The next morning we joined Jeremiah and Matthew in the mess hall for breakfast. No one mentioned the card game from the night before, but several secret smiles were exchanged between the four of us. When we were done eating we stood on the low front porch, enjoying the early morning sunshine and talking idly. Matthew excused himself after a few minutes, saying he had chores to do, leaving Ben and me alone with Jeremiah. The rugged man turned to us.

"The major has asked me to lead a small huntin' party up into the hills behind the fort this mornin'. I was wonderin' if'n you an' Ben would like to join me."

"I'm up fer it, Jeremiah," I replied. "We don't have any chores to do today. An' I'm sure no one will miss us while we're gone."

"How does that sound, Ben?"

"It sounds like fun."

"I'll grab extra rifles an' canteens from the barracks," Jeremiah said, "an' meet ya at the horse barn."

As he turned to go, a sudden thought occurred to me.

"What about the Apaches? Is it safe fer just a small group to go off huntin'?"

"The major beefed up the outlyin' details several weeks ago because of Indian trouble. Our troops are scourin' a wide area 'round the post day and night. Don't worry, we'll be just fine. We're not goin' that far."

With my concern partially allayed, Ben and I headed to the horse barn to await Jeremiah. My thoughts were swirling in my head. Why Jeremiah's sudden interest in Ben and me? Did the handsome soldier have more in mind for us than hunting?

When we entered the barn, Matthew was there, cleaning out the stalls. We told him of our plans, and he wished us luck. When Jeremiah arrived, he chose mounts for the three of us as well as saddles and bridles, and we quickly equipped our horses. Jeremiah handed a canteen to Ben and one to me, and we hung them from our pommels. I grabbed the reins of the dark-brown gelding Jeremiah had chosen for me and swung up onto its back. Ben swung up on a large, black gelding. Jeremiah handed me a Spencer rifle, which I slid into the scabbard at my right knee. He gave Ben one also.

"Is it just the three of us, Jeremiah?" I asked.

"Yes. All of the other lazy bastards I asked suddenly had chores to do an' couldn't come with us. No one wants to go any-where in this heat unless they absolutely have to. Like I said, don't worry, we'll be fine."

Jeremiah mounted his horse and we left the barn. We rode at a slow walk, single file, across the compound toward the large, wooden gates. Two soldiers stationed there swung them open for us, and we rode out onto the plain. The heat and wind hit us like a sharp slap in the face. I pulled my bandana up over my mouth and nose to keep out the dust, and Ben and Jeremiah did the same. We headed due north, circling around the fort toward the low foothills. As we approached their base, it was refreshing to see vegetation and rocks dotting the landscape once again, although calling the dried grass, stunted sagebrush, and small cactuses vegetation was a stretch. We began our ascent of the low, flat hills. As we topped the crest of the first hill, we paused to drink sparingly from our canteens. I wiped the sweat and grit from my face with my bandana, then retied it over my mouth and nose. More low, flat hills spread out endlessly before us, all dotted with the by-now-familiar cactus and sagebrush inter-spersed with large, rocky outcrops of various shades of browns and grays. No one spoke, the oppressive heat making it hard to form words in our throats. We gazed at the panorama before us for several minutes before starting our descent. When we reached the bottom, we entered a small ravine that had once been an old riverbed.

We rode for the next few hours, stopping occasionally to drink from our canteens or water our horses. So far we'd been fairly lucky. Jeremiah and I had each shot two large jackrabbits, and Ben had shot a rattlesnake he spotted sunning itself on a large, flat rock. We were still following the riverbed when, suddenly, an antelope erupted from a stand of sagebrush almost beneath our noses, surprising all three of us and getting away before anyone had a chance to get off a shot. When the sun reached its noontime position, we stopped and ate a quick meal of jerky, then headed out once more. We'd been riding for about an hour when the sound of rushing water came faintly to my ears. We headed in the direction of the sound, its volume increasing considerably as we did so. It was either a substantial stream or a waterfall of considerable size. I looked at Ben and Jeremiah and, as smiles broke out on their faces, I knew that we shared the same thought. We coaxed our horses into a slow gallop and headed toward the innervating sound. Down a gentle slope and between two rocky buttes we rode, emerging into a tiny oasis. A small pool shimmered in the afternoon sun. Bunch grass, sagebrush, and cactuses crowded the edges of the pool. The water that fed it burst forth from a large fissure in the rock wall a few feet above our heads, cascading down the cliff face to form the inviting pool.

Our horses nickered at the smell of water and when we gave them their head, they ran eagerly to the pool for a much-needed drink. We dismounted as one, letting our reins drop to the ground. I stepped to the edge of the pool, knelt down, cupped a handful of the cold water, and brought it to my lips. It was delicious. I scooped more handfuls as Ben and Jeremiah slaked their thirst as well.

"Well, boys," Jeremiah growled, "I don't know 'bout you fellas, but I could sure use a coolin' off."

Unbuttoning his shirt, he peeled it off and tossed it in the grass. He faced us as he bent down to tug off his worn boots and socks. Tossing both next to his shirt, he undid his pants as well as his drawers. Shucking both garments off as one, he added them to the pile of clothes. His cock was as I remembered it from the card game last night: long and fat, even though flaccid. His impressive balls hung low in their sac of flesh. Jeremiah scratched his ball sac absent-mindedly then turned around and stepped into the pool, giving us a full view of his hairy ass. I glanced over at Ben, winked, and began shedding my own clothing. He smiled back and did the same.

Jeremiah waded out about ten feet, then silently disappeared beneath the water's surface. When he resurfaced, a huge grin was on his face.

"The bottom is all sand," he hollered. "Ya can sit down just like it was a washtub."

He waded back toward the shore a few feet, his huge dick flopping against his right leg, and promptly sat down facing away from us. Ben and I waded out a few feet past Jeremiah, gooseflesh breaking out on our skin as we did. We sat down on the sandy bottom, facing Jeremiah. The cold water came up to our waists. After the initial shock wore off, the water was soothing to my hot and aching body. I nestled my ass firmly in the sand and closed my eyes.

All of a sudden I heard splashing coming from in front of us. I opened my eyes to see Jeremiah wading toward Ben and me. His hawg was starting to fill out—only half-hard, it would still put my daddy's prized cucumbers to shame.

He stopped directly in front of me, his huge dick only inches from my face. Drops of water fell from his furry chest; small trails of it were running down his stomach and through the thatch of dark-brown hair growing in profusion above his cock. The water continued down along the crack where his right leg joined his crotch, eventually disappearing in the hairy nether

regions below his ball sac. He caught and held my gaze with
his own, then grabbed his stiffer with his right hand and began
stroking it slowly, quickly bringing it to full hardness.

"Open yer mouth, Jake," he commanded, not expecting me
to refuse him. His voice was thick with lust.

I opened wide, and he guided the fat head into my mouth.
It was like trying to stuff a small apple into my mouth, whole. I
sucked the large knob and swirled my tongue around the crown.
The skin of it was warm and smooth, and I could taste the fluid
that was already gathering in his piss hole. Jeremiah grunted as
I probed the slit with my tongue. Something brushed against
my right shoulder. Out of the corner of my eye I could see Ben.
He dropped to his knees and wormed in between myself and
Jeremiah and began lapping at Jeremiah's giant balls. Ben then
tugged gently on Jeremiah's basket with his teeth before pulling
the right nut into his mouth and sucking on it hungrily. After a
moment he switched to the left one. When he tried to take the
entire sac into his mouth, he was unable to do so.

Jeremiah let out a low moan and began pulling and pinching his rock-hard nipples with his right hand. He placed his
left on the back of my head. I was certain I couldn't take all
of his massive pole down my throat, but his hand on my head
was insistent. I opened my mouth as wide as possible, and he
pushed his stiffer steadily in. The enormous knob hit the back of
my throat, lodged there momentarily, then slid free and headed
down my gullet. When I started to gag I gripped his thighs,
halting his forward progress until my throat could adjust to
the girth of his member. When I had swallowed a little over
half of his hawg, I knew I couldn't take any more of it; it was
just too big. Jeremiah sensed this as well, and his hand relaxed
on the back of my head. Enough of his cock remained outside
my mouth for me to wrap my hand around. I sucked softly on
his stiffer, while inhaling deeply the smells emanating from his
crotch. Ben was still busy licking Jeremiah's balls.

I slid slowly back up Jeremiah's dick until just the large crown was still in my mouth, then slid back down. He began pumping his massive hips. I placed my hands on his hairy, muscular thighs to steady myself when the force of his thrusts increased. Soon the muscles in his legs started quivering, and I realized he was getting close to shooting.

"Not yet, lads," he said, his voice barely above a whisper. "This feels too damn good to end this quickly."

Jeremiah pulled his pole out of my mouth, slapped the fat head against my right cheek, pushed Ben gently away from his ball sac, and waded to shore. He stepped out of the water and made his way to a large grassy area near where our horses were grazing. He lay down on his back in the lush grass, facing us, and spread his legs wide. His large nuts hung down upon the grass. His hawg resembled a small club protruding from his crotch. Ben and I waded to shore and knelt in the grass beside Jeremiah.

"One on each side of me, boys," he growled. "There's plenty here fer both of ya."

I crawled to Jeremiah's left, tight against his massive, hairy thigh, and Ben took the right. I started licking the mammoth cock, sliding my tongue up the thick shaft while Ben resumed working Jeremiah's nuts. As Ben and I licked and sucked contentedly, the late afternoon sun quickly dried our bodies. After a while, Ben and I switched. I ran my tongue over Jeremiah's ball sac, tracing the outline of each huge nut, and tasting his sweat and pungent maleness. I then took each ball into my mouth in turn, rolling the fat orbs around and sucking on them hungrily. As Jeremiah's groans and grunts became louder and more urgent, I moved from Jeremiah's sac to the thick shaft and licked one side of his stiffer while Ben tongued the other. We made our way up and down the thick piece of meat, then met at the large knob. We took turns running our tongues over and around the crown, and probing the swollen piss slit. I pulled away and Ben immediately swallowed half of Jeremiah's cock.

He bobbed up and down on it a few times, then released it to give me a turn. I opened wide and took in as much of the fat pole as I could.

"Get yer dicks down here where I can reach 'em, boys," Jeremiah panted.

Ben and I swung around so our crotches were aligned with Jeremiah's hairy armpits. He grabbed a stiffer in each meaty fist and began vigorously pumping them. Soon Ben and I were bucking our hips to match the giant's strokes.

As Ben took his next turn on Jeremiah's tool, I wet two of my fingers and began probing beneath the big man's bull-sized balls, intent on his back door. My fingers encountered a mass of sweaty hair as I worked them closer to the sensitive opening. Jeremiah slid forward a little in the grass and spread his legs wider, giving my fingers greater access to his hairy hole. When the tips of my fingers found the puckered spot, I pushed hard against it. It gave way almost immediately, and I slid two fingers into his hot moistness up to the second knuckle. Surprisingly, Jeremiah's asshole was not that deep for such a large man, and my fingers quickly made contact with the hidden muscle inside him. I rubbed it repeatedly and felt it swell beneath my fingers. Jeremiah bucked like a wild horse as I began sliding my fingers in and out of his hot hole.

Ben let Jeremiah's fat cock head pop from his mouth, and I quickly took it up in my own. Ben added two of his fingers to my pistoning ones. With four fingers plunging in and out of him, Jeremiah was grunting like the bear he resembled. He was thrashing so violently that it was hard to keep his stiffer in the mouth of whoever's turn it was. He continued to pump both our hawgs, and soon I felt my release building. I thrust my hips faster while continuing to drive my fingers deep into Jeremiah's asshole. I released Jeremiah's swollen knob and buried my face in his thick crotch hair. The odor of his crotch quickly triggered my eruption, and I shot my seed onto his hairy chest, completely covering his left nipple. When I was spent, Ben's body began to spasm with his own explosion. Soon he was spewing thick globs of white cream onto Jeremiah's right nipple.

"I'm gonna blow!" Jeremiah suddenly cried.

The large man's chest was heaving, and he was thrusting his hips savagely, forcing our fingers against his secret muscle again and again. Ben and I withdrew our fingers and positioned ourselves over Jeremiah's fat cock head. When the first blast of spunk flew out it landed squarely on Ben's cheek. I quickly took the large knob into my mouth and swallowed several drops of his seed before letting Ben have a turn. We switched back and forth until Jeremiah had shot his load. I had the last turn and, after releasing the swollen dick head, I leaned over and kissed Ben full on the mouth. I could taste Jeremiah's spunk on his lips.

"That sure was nice, fellas," Jeremiah said, his furry chest rising and falling rapidly. "I wish you two were stayin' at Fort Benson fer a little while longer, at least until my term is up. That'll be in another three months, an' then I'm headin' to California to try my hand at minin'. You guys would certainly make those months go by fast, an' I certainly would enjoy takin' you huntin' with me again."

"Believe me, Jeremiah," I replied. "If'n we was goin' to stay at the fort, we'd gladly go huntin' with ya any day."

He smiled, tousled my hair, but didn't reply to my declaration. We licked Jeremiah's cock and ball sac clean, then lapped up our seed from his chest. When we were finished, the three of us dozed in the soft grass, Jeremiah's large, beefy arms around our shoulders; our heads resting on his massive chest.

When I awoke, the sun was just starting its descent. When I licked my dry lips I could still taste Jeremiah's fluid. I roused Ben and Jeremiah, and we took a quick dip in the pool to rinse off. We dried off with handfuls of the lush green grass, dressed, and started back to the fort. It was close to dusk when we descended the hills and started across the plain toward the log structure.

Stephen was waiting for us just inside the gate.

"I'm glad to see ya boys made it back in one piece. We was startin' to worry 'bout ya."

"Sorry, Major," Jeremiah replied. "We stayed out a little longer than we had planned. We had good luck though."

He held up the jackrabbits and the rattlesnake for the major to see.

"Nice work, Jeremiah. Any fresh meat is much appreciated 'round here."

The major turned to me.

"Mr. Slater, the stagecoach came in while you boys were out huntin', carryin' a passenger who's also headin' to Silverton. He'll be beddin' down in one of the barracks fer the night. The supplies have been unloaded, an' I now have spare civilian clothing fer ya. The stage leaves in the mornin' at first light. I informed the driver he'll have two additional passengers when he leaves. You an' Mr. Masters should be in Silverton by tomorrow night, barrin' any unforeseen circumstances. Since tonight will be yer last night at the fort, I'd like fer both of ya to join me in my quarters fer a farewell supper as soon as it's convenient."

"We'd be much obliged, major. Ben an' I will take our horses to the barn an' join ya shortly."

Ben, Jeremiah, and I rode to the horse barn in silence. Once inside, we dismounted, removed bridles and saddles from the horses, and turned them over to a young soldier. We went outside and stood in front of the barn for a moment, watching the activity within the compound.

"Well, boys," Jeremiah said, "thanks again fer the huntin' trip. It was pure fun. I'd best be gittin' over to the mess hall fer supper. I can't afford to miss a meal."

Ben and I laughed heartily at Jeremiah's jest.

"I have the midnight watch on the wall tonight, so I won't be seein' ya this evenin'. But I'll be 'round in the mornin' to say good-bye."

As he finished speaking, he turned to face Ben and me. He shook our hands and hugged us fiercely, then turned and walked away without looking back.

We watched him approach the mess hall and disappear inside, then we headed for Stephen's quarters. We stepped onto the porch and I knocked on the door. Silence greeted my first knock. After my second, I heard a muffled "come in." I opened the door and we stepped inside. The major was nowhere in sight. Everything was as I remembered it from the other night: the desk, the chairs, the picture of Lincoln. One thing was different, however; the door to Stephen's bedroom was open. From where I stood, though, I was unable to see into the room.

"Stephen," I called out, "are ya here? Ben an' I are here fer supper."

"I'm in the bedroom, gentlemen. Drop the bar in place behind ya an' come on in."

I dropped the length of wood into the brackets and Ben and I walked to the bedroom door. When we reached it, I could see the room was deep in shadows. The only light came from two low-burning oil lamps in opposite corners. Ben and I stepped through the doorway and stood just inside it, allowing our eyes to adjust to the dimness. As the shadows slowly took shape, I saw Stephen. He was completely naked, spread-eagled on a large four-poster bed, propped up against numerous pillows. I glanced around the room, looking for signs of the supper we'd been invited to. I saw no table set for three. A bottle of whiskey stood on a small table to the right of Stephen's bed. Other than the table, the bed, and a large trunk, there was no other furniture in the room.

"Come in boys, an' join me on my bed. It's the one luxury I've allowed myself in this hellhole."

I closed the door and Ben and I approached Stephen's bed. His enormous cock pointed straight up at the ceiling like a flagpole. His huge fleshy pouch lolled between his legs, resting on the blanket covering the bed. I scanned his hairy, well-muscled body.

"Did we miss supper, Stephen, or is one of yer 'boys' bringin' it along shortly?"

He stared into my eyes, his own full of mischief and an easily identifiable lust. A smile spread across his face. He grabbed his dick in his right hand and began slowly stroking it. His early fluid glistened on the fat head in the light cast by one of the lamps.

"Ya haven't missed supper at all, Jake. It's right here in my hand an', as ya can see, there's plenty fer both of ya. Now, git out of those clothes an' git yer butts on this bed."

"Is that an order, Major?" I asked.

"Very much so, Jake."

Ben's laughter echoed mine as we quickly undressed. The sight of Stephen's naked body had brought my cock to instant hardness. Ben's dick was in the same state of arousal. I sat on the bed on Stephen's right, while Ben scrambled over him and sat on his left. Stephen leaned over me and grabbed the bottle of whiskey from the table. He removed the cork, and we passed the bottle between us. After several swigs, he placed the bottle back on the table.

Stephen grabbed me by the back of my neck and pulled me to him. He kissed me deeply several times, then his tongue pushed past my lips and began probing my mouth. He grabbed my tongue gently with his teeth, pulled it into his mouth, and sucked hard on it. Soft moans were escaping from me as I ran a hand over his hairy chest, playing with his tits. His nipples hardened immediately. I tweaked them repeatedly until Stephen was squirming on the bed beside me. Finally releasing my tongue, he planted kisses on my cheeks, forehead, and throat. I slid down and replaced my fingers with my mouth, biting and sucking on Stephen's nipples. He groaned loudly in appreciation. I grabbed his hawg and squeezed it hard.

Stephen grabbed Ben's stiffer and gave it a few tentative strokes. When he released it, Ben scrabbled backward and up onto the pillows that rested against the headboard. This new position placed his crotch at Stephen's eye level, his cock only inches from the major's face. Ben placed his right leg across the pillow behind Stephen's head, and planted his left foot on the major's stomach. Stephen inclined his head toward Ben's pole and began licking the blood-engorged crown. He tongued the slit in the head, lapping up all the clear fluid that had gathered there, then engulfed the fat knob. As Stephen noisily sucked on it, he placed his hand under Ben's hefty basket and jiggled the twin orbs. After sucking briefly on the head, Stephen rose up slightly on one of the pillows and swallowed Ben's dick. He paused at the root, then sawed slowly back up, his lips tight to the shaft. When he reached the head, he swirled his tongue over and around it, then took Ben's hawg into his mouth and proceeded to bob up and down on it as he kneaded Ben's balls.

I slid down on the bed until my face was at Stephen's crotch. I lifted his right leg and slid beneath it, laying flat on my stomach between his legs. Stephen's enormous pole towered before me. The odor of his crotch was a combination of piss, soap, sweat, and his pungent maleness. I hefted his heavy nut sac, then licked the large globes and rolled them around inside their sac with my tongue. Taking the left nut into my mouth, I sucked on it fiercely. Stephen placed his hand on the back of my head, pushing my face into his sac. I spat his left nut out, gave the right one the same treatment, then licked around the thick base of his dick.

From there I ran my tongue up and down the shaft, tracing the blue veins with the tip. Starting again at the base, I licked up to Stephen's fat cock head. I ran my tongue around the crown, then worked the tip in and out of the tiny piss hole, lapping up the fluid and savoring its flavor. Stephen squirmed on the bed, his moans muffled by Ben's stiffer. I placed my lips around the head of his dick, sucked on it briefly, then slowly swallowed

Stephen's hawg until his dark crotch hair poked into my nostrils. I sucked hard around the thick base, then slid back up to the knob, trailing my tongue along the underside of the shaft as I did so. I lapped up the new fluid in the slit, then began steadily sawing up and down on his fat pole. On each saw I released the knob completely, giving it a gentle scrape with my upper teeth as I did so.

After a dozen or so saws, I glanced up to see how Ben was faring. Supporting himself with a hand on either side of Stephen's head, Ben was thrusting his hawg in and out of Stephen's mouth, using it as if it were a big corn hole. Despite the difficult position, Stephen was taking the entire length with no protests. With a firm grip on Ben's ass cheeks, he pulled Ben deep into his mouth on each plunge. I could see the head of Ben's dick pushing against the skin of Stephen's throat.

I resumed my bobbing on Stephen's stiffer and worked it for a good while. After one final bob, I released it. I wanted his dick deep inside me. Spitting into my hand several times, I spread the saliva onto and around my corn hole. I wet two fingers and pushed them determinedly against the tiny opening. When the ring of muscle gave away, I jammed my fingers straight up my chute. I plunged them in and out several times, then withdrew them. I quickly straddled Stephen's crotch, wrapped a hand around his stiffer, held it up straight, and lowered myself until I felt the knob slide between the cheeks of my ass and push against my hole.

I paused for a moment to watch Ben as he plowed in and out of the major's mouth. His balls smacked loudly against Stephen's chin. Stephen thrust his hips upward, trying to force his cock head through my puckered opening. I tore my gaze from Ben's plunging hawg and forced my weight down onto Stephen's pole. My opening relaxed and I plunged the full length of Stephen's shaft. I moaned loudly, my cry followed quickly by Stephen's muffled one.

I sat impaled on Stephen's hawg without moving as I allowed my asshole to adjust to his massive member. The pain from his rapid entry soon turned to a pleasant, warm tingling. I began to rock back and forth on his stiffer, scraping the head of his cock over my secret muscle and causing waves of pleasure to course through my body. Finally, I slid up off his hawg, glancing once more at Ben as I did so. I could smell the familiar odor of Ben's crotch.

When only the head of Stephen's cock was still inside me, I slid back down his pole until his crotch hair was tickling my ass cheeks. I then began riding him, slowly at first, then faster as he proceeded to plow into me. I hunched forward a little to reach Stephen's tits. Grabbing each nipple, I pulled and twisted them repeatedly. Stephen writhed beneath me as his thrusts became even more powerful. I let go of his nipples and started jerking my stiffer as I bounced up and down wildly on his cock. My stroking hand and the intense pummeling of my secret muscle were quickly pushing me to the edge.

Ben was moaning uncontrollably as he continued to plow Stephen's mouth. He plunged deep down Stephen's throat once more, then pulled out of his mouth completely.

"Open wide, Major, here it comes," Ben cried.

He stroked his pole one last time and yelled when his eruption started. The first drop landed between Stephen's nose and upper lip. Stephen stuck out his tongue and Ben emptied the rest of his seed onto it. When Ben was spent, Stephen swallowed all of it. On my next plunge on Stephen's stiffer, my own explosion was triggered.

"I'm right behind ya, Ben," I yelled.

My spunk sprayed across Stephen's hairy stomach. As the last drop was deposited, Stephen lunged up into me a final time and yelled "Jake!" as his hot seed began flooding my hole. When Stephen was done shooting, I held his hawg inside me as it softened, then slid up off it. The knob pulled out of me with a wet squishing sound, and some of Stephen's spunk dribbled out and ran down the back of my pouch.

Ben lay back on the pillows, his chest rising and falling with his labored breathing. Stephen lay panting and heaving beneath me. I bent down and licked my cream off his stomach, then slid up his torso and kissed him on the mouth. Stephen returned my kisses as his hands explored my body. Ben resumed his position on Stephen's left, and I moved to his right. Stephen grabbed the bottle of whiskey once more and we passed it between us until it was empty. Stephen set the bottle on the table, then wrapped an arm around each of our shoulders. I was starting to doze off when he stirred beside me.

"I have to take a piss, Jake."

"I do too," Ben echoed.

I felt the urge as well.

Stephen crawled over me and climbed off the bed. I followed him, with Ben right behind me. We went to the bucket in the corner that I hadn't noticed before. We stood shoulder to shoulder, forming a small semicircle in front of it. Stephen grabbed my cock and held it. I held his in return, and Ben's as well. Stephen was the first to let go. A bright stream of piss arced from his dick, and I aimed it into the bucket. Ben was next, and I quickly followed. The stench of our combined piss in the bucket was strong. I shook a few last drops from their dicks, and Stephen got a last drop from mine. We then walked back to the bed and lay down once more, this time with Ben in the middle.

"Did ya enjoy yer supper, boys?"

Ben and I both replied with a somewhat sleepy, "Yes."

"Good, because now it's time fer dessert."

Stephen turned on his side to face Ben, and began biting and chewing his still-swollen nipples. Ben forgot his sleepiness and began moaning softly and squirming between us. Stephen bit each nipple once more, then tongued his way down Ben's chest and stomach to his crotch. Pausing briefly to lick Ben's equipment, he continued down his hairy legs to his feet. Stephen grabbed Ben by the ankles and expertly flipped him over onto his stomach. Pulling his legs apart, Stephen licked back up them to Ben's ass. He swabbed both cheeks, then spread them apart and drove his tongue between them. As he buried his face in the crack of Ben's ass, Ben's moans grew louder and he began thrashing on the bed. He also grabbed my slightly hard dick and quickly stroked it to its full proportions. Stephen tongued Ben for a while longer, then suddenly pulled his face away and raised up onto his knees. He slid the head of his cock between the cheeks of Ben's ass. Ben arched his back and raised his ass slightly. Small whimpers escaped from him as Stephen's fat hawg steadily penetrated his hole.

"Boy, yer tight," Stephen murmured.

Soon all that was visible was Stephen's thatch of crotch hair. I got up on my knees and shifted around in front of Ben so that my crotch was in his face. Ben was unable to take my dick into his mouth, though, because of the position Stephen had him in.

"Okay, Major," I said. "Are ya goin' to share him, or not?"

Immediately understanding what I needed, Stephen grabbed Ben at the waist. In one quick, smooth movement, and without breaking his connection with Ben, Stephen pulled him up onto his hands and knees. This placed the head of my stiffer only inches from Ben's mouth. He opened wide and I slid inside and deep down his throat. I began rapid in-and-out lunges, and Stephen timed his own thrusts to match mine. The only sounds in the room were my balls slapping against Ben's chin, Stephen's thighs slapping against Ben's ass, and our varied grunts and cries of delight.

Stephen was plowing Ben's ass with everything he had in him, his urgent cries coming more frequently. I was sure he wasn't far from his release. Ben's mouth was hot and wet on my cock, and my explosion came all too soon.

"I'm gonna fill yer mouth with my cream, Ben."

I plunged into Ben's mouth a final time, crying out as spasms wracked my body. I flooded Ben's mouth with my seed, and he swallowed every drop of it. When the last glob landed, Stephen panted and gasped as his own eruption started.

"I'm gonna fill yer bung hole, boy," he hollered.

When Stephen had shot his load, he collapsed onto Ben's back. I pulled my dick from Ben's mouth and held it in front of him. He eagerly licked it clean. When he was done, I lay back against the pillows. Stephen pulled out of Ben, rolled off his back, and lay beside him. Ben collapsed on the bed, panting like a dog. The three of us stayed in our separate positions for a long time without speaking. Stephen suddenly cleared his throat.

"Would ya gentlemen do me the honor of sleepin' in my bed on our last night together?"

"What about yer regular boys?" I quietly asked.

"They'll just have to understand, Jake. They'll still be here long after you an' Ben are just a memory."

"Then it would be an honor."

Ben echoed my sentiment. We stretched out on opposite sides of Stephen. He wrapped his strong arms around our shoulders once again, and we drifted off to sleep.

I woke to find Stephen sucking my cock. Through the window next to the bed, I could see the gray of predawn. Ben was sound asleep.

"Good mornin,' Major. I can't think of a more pleasant way to greet a new day."

Stephen bobbed on my dick once more, then let the fat knob pop from his mouth. He smiled up at me.

"Damn, Jake, it's 'bout time ya woke up. I've been workin' yer stiffer fer a while now."

He crawled over to Ben, grabbed Ben's hawg, stroked it until it grew hard, then swirled his tongue over the large crown and swallowed the fat pole. He bobbed up and down on it a half-dozen times before Ben woke up, grinning from ear to ear.

"Good mornin', Ben," I whispered.

Ben turned to me, the smile still on his face.

"Good mornin' to you too, Jake. An' a very good mornin' to you, Major. Fer a moment there I thought I'd died an' gone to heaven."

Stephen released Ben's cock and lay flat on his back between us.

"Before ya head back to the barracks, there's somethin' I'd like to try with you boys. When I was a young man, before I joined the cavalry, I met up an' traveled with two Jicarilla Apaches. They had abandoned their tribe to live among the white man an' learn his ways. Durin' our time together, they taught me quite a bit 'bout the diff'rent ways men can relieve each other. One thing they showed me I've never done since we parted company. The three of us tried it ev'ry now an' then, though I was always on the givin' end, not the receivin'. I've never had the gumption to be on the receivin' side until I met you two. Are ya game?"

"We're game fer anythin' with ya, Stephen," I replied.

"Okay then, boys, let's have at it."

Stephen quickly straddled my crotch, his back to me. I ran a finger through the patch of hair that grew just above where the crack of his ass began. Stephen spit several times into his hand, rose up on his knees, and spread the spit along his ass crack. He spit again, grabbed my stiffer, and coated it with his saliva. Stephen then shifted backward and slid the head of my cock between his cheeks until it pushed against his hole. I thrust my hips upward as Stephen pushed against the fat knob. The muscle in his asshole relaxed, and he slid slowly down onto my pole until all that was visible was my crotch hair. Stephen sat still for a moment, then rose up my shaft, moaning loudly, before sinking back down to my balls. He eased backward until he was laying flat on top of me, my dick filling his tight channel. He wrapped his arms around my neck and began to slide up and down on my stiffer. After a dozen or so times, he stopped and lay still.

"Okay, Ben," Stephen whispered. "Now come over here an' stick yer big dick in me alongside Jake's."

I could see the look of surprise on Ben's face. I was stunned myself.

"Are ya sure, Stephen," he stammered. "Won't that hurt ya?"

"Well, Ben, it sure as hell never hurt the two Jicarillas I hung with. An' if'n it does start to hurt I'll just have ya pull out of me."

Ben moved to Stephen's crotch, spit into his hand, and spread the spit along his pole. He inched forward on his knees and I felt the soft head of his dick touch the base of mine. Slowly, yet surely, Ben slid his hawg into Stephen's asshole right on top of mine. I could feel the heat of his cock and even the veins in the shaft as it slid along my stiffer. Stephen yelped when Ben's fat knob hit mine and both of them banged into his secret muscle at the same time. Ben now lay prone on Stephen, his heavy pouch resting on mine. He kissed him soundly, then kissed me when Stephen turned his head to the side to allow Ben to do so.

Ben lay still for several moments, then slowly slid his hawg out of Stephen until the crown rested on the thick base of my meat once more. Ben paused, then entered Stephen once more and began drilling steadily in and out of him. I wrapped my arms around Ben's back and started pumping into Stephen as well. Soon Ben quickened his thrusts and I did the same. We both plowed in and out of Stephen fiercely. Before long, Stephen was moaning uncontrollably, jerking between us and crying out repeatedly.

I slid my hands down Ben's back and kneaded the cheeks of his ass. I trailed a finger into his hairy ass crack and probed his puckered opening. I pushed firmly against it, and my finger slid in to the second knuckle. I began thrusting it in and out of Ben's hole in time with our thrusts into the major. The combination of Stephen's hot hole and Ben's dick sliding against mine on each of his thrusts quickly triggered my eruption.

"Shoot with me, boys!" I cried.

I let out a series of moans as I filled Stephen's ass with my seed. Ben followed shortly with his own explosion, and I felt his spunk flowing around the head of my cock. Suddenly, Stephen was spasming between us. He cried out repeatedly and shook several times, then was still. Ben lay quietly for several moments before pulling out of Stephen. A sizable puddle of Stephen's spunk coated the hairs on Ben's stomach. He flopped onto his back beside us. Stephen lay atop me for a moment, then slid off my pole and rolled onto the bed to my left.

"Well, Stephen," Ben gasped beside me, "was it worth the wait?"

"It certainly was, boys," Stephen replied. "I will definitely never fergit you two now. Especially when I can't shit fer the next week."

Ben and I laughed. He crawled over me and wormed in between us, and we lay quietly. I was the first to stir.

"We should be gittin' back to the barracks, Stephen. It wouldn't do fer us to be seen leavin' yer quarters at this hour of the mornin.'"

"You're right. Of course, Jake."

Stephen watched in silence as Ben and I dressed.

"The stagecoach will be leavin' in 'bout an hour, Jake. I'll join ya in the mess hall fer breakfast, an' then I'll see you an' Ben off."

We hugged and kissed him good-bye then stole silently from his quarters. No one was stirring yet in the compound as we walked back to the barracks and lay on our bunks. I was still wide awake when the first soldier stirred. I could hear Ben snoring above me. I stayed on my bunk until the bugler gave the call to breakfast, then woke Ben and we headed for the mess hall. Stephen joined us shortly thereafter. When we finished eating, we lingered, making small talk. Finally, Stephen rose from the table.

"A few of the soldiers are waitin' in the barracks to say goodbye to ya before ya leave," he said. "I'll go there with ya if'n ya don't mind."

"Not at all, Stephen," I replied.

We went to our barracks and, when we entered, Jeremiah, Johnny, and Matthew were sitting in front of the stove. We walked down the aisle and joined them. They each wished Ben and I well, shook our hands, then went down the aisle and out the barracks door. Jeremiah turned before he disappeared from sight and gave us a small wave.

"I think there's somethin' on Jake's bunk fer each of ya," Stephen said, casually.

I turned and saw several wrapped bundles on my bunk. I hadn't seen them when I came in. I stepped to the bunk for a closer look. Each bundle had either Ben's or my name scrawled on it. When Ben and I opened the bundles we each discovered a Spencer carbine and a Colt, along with a complete change of civilian clothing, minus hats. There were also two small cloth sacks. When we opened them we found several gold coins.

"Some partin' gifts fer ya boys," Stephen said. "By no means is there a fortune, but it's enough to buy horses an' supplies fer each of ya when ya git to Silverton. I'm certain I still don't know the whole story that brought ya to Fort Benson, but I know in my heart that you two belong together. Ya have my fervent prayers that yer trouble will soon be straightened out."

Ben and I hugged and kissed Stephen, then dressed in our new clothing. Stephen walked outside with us and over to the stagecoach, which was drawn up by the front gate. Two grizzled drivers, one with thick white whiskers, the other with black whiskers, were already seated on their platform above the horses. The four pairs of horses stamped their hooves, as if impatient to be on their way. A column of a dozen blue-clad soldiers sat patiently astride their horses in double file behind the coach. It was the escort Stephen had promised us.

"Are we ready to go, Major?" the black-whiskered driver gruffly asked.

"Not yet, driver. I'm waitin' fer the other passenger. I'm not sure where he is. I didn' see him at breakfast."

As Stephen finished speaking, a man emerged from the horse barn and headed in our direction. I saw Luke for a moment, standing just inside the barn door; then he disappeared. I had a pretty good idea of what had been keeping the other passenger.

CHAPTER ELEVEN

As the tall stranger drew near, I noted his black cloth pants, black cloth coat and hat, and his white cotton shirt. His coat and pants were spotted with trail dust, but his boots were shiny and black, obviously having been recently polished. I'd only seen his like a few times in my life, but I was certain the man was a preacher. He walked directly to the stagecoach, stopped in front of Stephen, and tipped his hat to him.

"Good mornin', Major."

"Good mornin' to ya, Mr. Hamilton."

Hamilton had addressed the major with a thick accent that I couldn't place right off. He stared at Ben and me intently, his gaze traveling from head to toe and lingering at our crotches. I returned his stare and gave him the same once-over. His hat rested on curly hair as black as coal. He was clean shaven, but the darker skin of his cheeks and throat clearly indicated where his facial hair grew. Most likely, in a few hours dark stubble would begin to reappear. His eyes were pale blue, set apart evenly by his nose, which was curved slightly to the right. His lips were full and moist, undoubtedly from an unguent he applied to them. No one in this arid region had lips that weren't dry and chapped. His cloth pants outlined the muscles in his legs, and the broadcloth coat he wore couldn't hide the width of his chest and shoulders. A Colt rested on his right hip, a practice common for preachers in this turbulent region.

"Good mornin' to you fine gentlemen as well. I understand we'll be travelin' together to Silverton. I'm sure the pleasure of yer company will make the ride that much more swift an' enjoyable. My name is Jonas Hamilton. Pleased to make yer acquaintance."

Ben and I introduced ourselves and shook hands with Jonas. His grip was strong, his hand roughened by some type of hard labor.

"Let's git on board, gentlemen," the black-whiskered driver bellowed. "We need to git movin' so's we can reach Silverton before nightfall."

Stephen wished us the best of luck once more and shook our hands. Ben stepped up into the stagecoach and I followed him. Jonas was right behind me. Ben took the seat to his immediate left. I sat beside him. Jonas sat across from us. I stared out the window, watching Stephen as he walked across the compound to his quarters. The gates were opened and we drove through them, followed by the soldiers. The driver cracked his whip and cried out to the horses and we were on our way.

The stagecoach jostled and creaked, and seemed to hit every possible rut in the trail. The driver continually berated his horses to increase their speed. I continued to stare out the window, watching the sand, rocks, and cactuses flash by. I turned my head to look at Ben, only to find him staring at me. I smiled, and he returned it immediately. We were finally on the last leg of our journey. I thought once more about how lucky I was (despite everything that had happened to me) that this handsome, virile man beside me had entered my life. Over the past few days I'd become ever more confident that we'd find this Bart Jensen quickly once we reached Silverton. We'd clear Ben's name, and then Ben and I could start planning our life together. I was certain that the pressure of reaching Silverton and finding Bart Jensen was taking a heavy toll on him.

Jonas soon struck up a conversation. He was from Boston, which explained the accent, and had only been in the West a short time. He was indeed a preacher, called to the West to save Christian souls. Jonas asked what had brought us to Fort Benson. I related Ben's and my capture by the band of outlaws, our subsequent capture by the Apaches and, ultimately, our rescue by the soldiers from the fort. The preacher listened raptly, asking several pointed questions about us that became more and more difficult to answer without revealing too much about our relationship. As I was speaking, Jonas had spread his legs apart. The tight cloth of his pants outlined his large ball sac and the fat head of his cock. Holding my gaze with his own, he reached down and tugged gently at his crotch. I could see his dick swell beneath the material. Out of the corner of my eye I could see that Ben was staring at the preacher's crotch as well. Jonas began to slowly knead the thickening bulge at his crotch, his eyes never wavering from mine.

"I here tell it's not uncommon in these parts fer men to relieve certain urges of the flesh with other men." Jonas asked, softly, "Is that true, Jake?"

I stared once more at the lump in his crotch before answering him. It had grown considerably.

"It happens between some men, Jonas."

"Would you an' Ben be some of those men?"

"Why don't you come over here an' find out, preacher man," Ben replied for me.

The preacher smiled, removed his hat, and rose from his seat. He had to hunch over because of the low coach roof. Grabbing one of the roof beams for support, he started toward us, trying to stay on his feet in the swaying stage. Just as he reached us the coach lurched, throwing the preacher to his knees in front of me. His face landed in my crotch.

"Right where I was headed anyway," he said, laughing as he righted himself.

Jonas undid the buttons on my shirt and the undershirt beneath it. He pulled both shirts open, exposing my chest and stomach. He ran his hands over me.

Then, leaning into me, Jonas took my left nipple into his mouth and began sucking the tender piece of flesh. He smelled of soap and spunk. He worked the taut nub briefly, then moved to the right one and gave it the same treatment. Biting it a final time, he then licked from my tits, up my throat, to my lips. He kissed me deeply, then forced his tongue into my mouth and twirled it around my own. The preacher licked the inside of my mouth several times, then withdrew his tongue. He trailed it back down my throat, between my tits, and down to the waistband of my pants. My cock was already stirring. He freed the buttons on my pants and drawers, slid his hand inside, and pulled my dick out through the piss flap.

As he stroked it to full hardness, the fat head emerged from my foreskin. Jonas swirled his tongue over the crown and through the piss slit, lapping up the clear fluid. When it was gone, he licked the knob once more, then encircled it with his lips before slowly sinking down on my hawg. Holding it in his mouth, he sucked noisily on it, then began sawing steadily up and down. Ben leaned over me and started biting and sucking my nipples, picking up where Jonas had left off. I moaned softly and placed my arm around his shoulder. On Jonas's next slide up my pole, he let it plop from his mouth.

"Stand up, Jake," he said, hoarsely.

I stood up in the cramped stagecoach, grabbing the side door for support. Jonas pulled my pants and drawers down around my ankles. Pushing me back down on the seat, he grabbed my basket in his left hand. Pulling it to his mouth, he tongued the fat orbs then took each into his mouth in turn, sucking on them and biting them gently. I placed my hand on the back of Jonas's head and pushed his face into my sac. Jonas sucked my balls for a moment longer, then spit them from his mouth and tongued the entire sac of flesh. He then swallowed my dick once more and resumed his sawing.

"Suck it, preacher," I cried.

When Ben moved to my left nipple, Jonas grabbed the right one between his thumb and forefinger and began pulling and pinching the swollen teat. With his other hand he grabbed my nut sac and began squeezing it. His hot, wet mouth on my cock, and both men working my nipples, had me moaning loudly and squirming on the seat. It wasn't long before I felt the beginning of my explosion.

"I'm gonna blow!" I shouted.

Jonas sawed up to the head of my stiffer and held it in his mouth as he swirled his tongue over it. Ben bit down on my nipple one last time. I gasped and whimpered as I emptied my seed into the preacher's hot, waiting mouth. He swallowed every drop of it. When I was spent, he licked my dick clean, then engulfed it and held it in his mouth as it softened. I leaned back against the front wall of the coach, my chest rising and falling rapidly. The preacher finally released my hawg. He smiled up at me, shuffling on his knees until he was in front of Ben. He undid the buttons on Ben's shirt and undershirt with one hand while he stroked the sizable lump at Ben's crotch with the other. Jonas pulled both shirts open, exposing Ben's hairy chest and stomach.

"Another hairy one," Jonas murmured, as he began nuzzling Ben's left nipple.

Ben sighed and leaned against me. Placing his hand on the back of the preacher's head, he pushed Jonas's face into his tit. Jonas sucked on the nipple as if he was nursing. Moving from the left nipple to the right, he tongued and bit the hardened point of flesh. Finally releasing the nipple, Jonas licked Ben's chest and stomach, then swathed a path down to his crotch. He licked Ben's stiffer through the cloth of his pants. Grabbing the sizable mound, Jonas rubbed and squeezed it several times. Ben began thrusting his hips toward the preacher as Jonas stroked the lump faster and faster.

I put my hand on Ben's neck, turned his face to me, and kissed him full on the mouth. He returned my kiss ardently, his tongue pushing between my lips and probing my mouth. I sucked his tongue briefly, then released it, licked his stubbled chin and throat, and worked my way down to his tits. I bit and sucked the nubs until Ben was thrashing on the seat.

I paused and glanced down at the preacher. He was undoing the buttons on Ben's pants and drawers. Pulling Ben's fat cock out through the piss flap in his drawers, Jonas licked up and down the thick shaft. A generous amount of clear fluid was bubbling from Ben's piss slit. Jonas swirled his tongue over the fat knob. As he ran his tongue through the slit several more times, Ben's moans increased tenfold and he jerked repeatedly beside me. The preacher licked the thick crown, then swallowed Ben's entire prick and began sawing up and down on it. He freed Ben's balls through the piss flap as well, and began kneading them.

My hawg was fully hard again and straining toward the preacher. Ben, noticing my stiffer, spit into his free hand, coated my dick with it, and started stroking me. I continued to bite and suck his nipples as he pumped my cock. Our combined moans and small cries filled the stagecoach. I released Ben's right tit and looked up into his eyes. His desire filled them.

"Stroke me," I whispered.

Ben's hand moved faster on my hawg. I sat back and let him bring me to my second explosion.

"Here it comes, boys," I gasped.

I bucked my hips and yowled as the first blast of spunk shot from my dick and landed on the preacher's cheek. Ben aimed my stiffer at Jonas's face and I sprayed the preacher's nose, forehead, and both cheeks with my juice. Some of it also landed in Ben's crotch hair. Jonas never paused in his bobbing on Ben's pole.

As the last drop hit the preacher's cheek, Ben moaned "I'm gonna shoot." Jonas sawed up and held Ben's knob tightly between his lips. Ben pumped his hips frantically as he emptied into Jonas's mouth, his moans loud and long. The preacher didn't hesitate once as he swallowed every drop of Ben's load. When Ben was spent, he collapsed against me. The preacher looked up at us, my spunk running down his face. He calmly wiped my seed from his face with a finger and ate it. When he was finished, I bent down and kissed him soundly. He rose from his knees, a little shakily, and returned to his seat.

"Well, gentlemen," he said, a smile playing about the corners of his mouth, "you've admirably an' enjoyably confirmed what I've heard 'bout some of the men in these parts. I'm goin' to git a little shuteye now. It's still a few more hours until we reach Silverton."

He laid his head back and closed his eyes. I turned to speak to Ben. He eyes were closed, his chest already rising and falling evenly. I settled back myself and soon drifted off.

When I woke, Ben's hairy ass was staring me in the face. He was standing behind the preacher, his pants bunched at his ankles. He was holding Jonas at the waist and plowing steadily into him. The cheeks of his ass clenched and unclenched on each of his thrusts. Jonas was bent over facing his seat, his pants also around his ankles, his hands clutching the edge of the seat for support. He was yelping like a bitch coyote in heat, and speaking incoherently. I couldn't tell if he was praying or urging Ben to greater efforts.

"Give it to him, Ben," I said as I stood up and, using one of the roof beams to steady myself, stepped behind Ben. With my free hand, I unbuttoned my pants and drawers, pulled out my cock, and stroked it until it was hard. I spit into my hand, spread Ben's ass cheeks, and deposited the saliva directly on his shit hole. I spit again and lathered my dick, placed the head of it against the tiny opening, and pushed firmly against it. Ben pushed back, the outer ring gave way, and I entered him effortlessly. I slid in to the hilt, striking his secret muscle dead center. His chute was hot and tight. Ben moaned and wiggled his ass against me. I began steady in-and-out thrusts, pulling out until just the knob remained inside him, then plunging back in. I soon matched Ben's thrusts into Jonas, while the three of us struggled to stay on our feet inside the swaying stagecoach.

The coach suddenly hit a series of violent bumps, which must have caused the preacher to lose his grip, because the next thing I knew we were stumbling backward, still attached. I struck the edge of the seat behind me and sat down heavily upon it, pulling Ben and Jonas down with me and forcing my dick deep inside Ben. He moaned loudly when the head of my cock slammed into the muscle inside his asshole. We paused to catch our breath, then Jonas grabbed a roof beam in each hand to steady himself and resumed riding Ben's pole. After a moment Ben began moving up and down on my stiffer. We soon had our rhythm going again.

Ben humped up and down on my cock wildly as the preacher did the same on his. I was sure our mingled cries and moans could be heard above the noise of the horses and the stage-coach. All too soon I felt my release building. I drove up into Ben one final time, hollered his name, and clutched him fiercely as I filled his asshole with my seed.

I stayed inside Ben and wrapped my arms around him as the preacher continued to ride him. On Jonas's next plunge I felt Ben's convulsions begin and he cried out repeatedly. When Ben was spent, he lay back against me, pulling Jonas tightly to his chest. All three of us were covered in sweat. The scent of our coupling permeated the stagecoach. The preacher was the first to stir. He sat upright and slid up off Ben's pole. He pulled up his pants and drawers and plopped down on his seat once more. Ben slid up off of my dick, pulled his pants and drawers up as well, and took his seat beside me. I buttoned my drawers and pants without standing and slumped against the side of the stagecoach.

"Thanks again, gentleman, fer yer pleasurin'," Jonas said, grinning from ear to ear. "I take it you two are quite familiar with pleasurin' each other."

"Yes, indeed, Jonas," Ben answered swiftly and decisively. He smiled at me, reached for my hand, and squeezed it hard.

"You two most assuredly make a handsome pair."

So saying, he slumped on his seat and closed his eyes. Soon his snores were reverberating inside the coach. I leaned over to Ben and kissed him several times. He returned my kisses passionately, then, placing his head on my shoulder, he quickly drifted off to sleep. I soon joined him.

I woke just as the stagecoach was pulling into Silverton. The sun had just started to set. The preacher was awake and staring out the window. Ben was still sleeping soundly beside me. I nudged him awake and kissed him. We stared out the coach windows as we headed down the main street.

Silverton was a typical western town. A row of rough-hewn, unpainted clapboard buildings lined each side of the street. As I looked around, I was sure it wouldn't be too difficult to find Bart Jensen in this small town. That is, if he was still here.

Ben and I said good-bye to Jonas, thanked the soldiers for their escort and the drivers for our passage, and went in search of a hotel. We found one a short way down the dusty street. A rickety, weather-worn sign hanging from the second floor proclaimed it to be Shirley's Haven. We pushed through the batwing doors and stepped inside. Several cowboys were sitting around wooden tables in the cool, dim, smoky interior, sipping whiskey or finishing up their evening meal. The barmaid, an older woman whose face had seen better days, eyed us evenly as we approached the bar.

"My name's Shirley, boys. What'll it be?"

"Two whiskeys," I replied.

She grabbed two glasses and a bottle from underneath the bar, filled the glasses, and set them and the bottle in front of us. We downed them and I ordered two more. As she poured them, Ben leaned over the bar, within whispering distance of Shirley.

"I'm lookin' fer a fella by the name of Bart Jensen," he said.

Shirley eyed him suspiciously and made no reply as she set

the bottle of whiskey on the bar.

"I'm an old friend of Bart's," Ben went on to explain. "He told me to look him up the next time I was in Silverton."

"I don't recognize the name, stranger," the old woman finally replied. "What does this Bart Jensen fella look like?"

As Ben described Bart to her, I saw recognition dawn in the old woman's blood-shot eyes. She eyed Ben intently.

"Ya just described a man that comes in here quite frequently. His name is Tom Sullivan, though, not Bart Jensen. He works fer young John Stewart, out on his ranch."

When she'd finished speaking, Shirley left us to tend to another customer. Ben then turned to me; I could see his hands were shaking.

"I think Tom Sullivan is Bart," he blurted out.

I stared back at him, my surprise plainly showing on my face. "What makes ya think that?"

"Well, Shirley said the description I gave her of Bart matches that of Tom Sullivan. Sullivan was an old friend of Bart's. He used to stop by the ranch in Abilene occasionally."

"So," I asked, "what's Tom Sullivan got to do with this?"

He paused and stared at me intently.

"Tom's been dead fer over a year now, Jake. He was killed by a wild bronc at our ranch. I believe Bart is usin' Tom's name, an' that he's workin' at the Stewart ranch."

Before I had a chance to reply, Shirley came back down the bar to where we were standing. Ben asked her for directions to the Stewart ranch. When she had given them to him, we finished our second whiskeys and ordered two more. When Shirley had poured them, I ordered separate rooms for the night, ever mindful of the fact that not all folks in these parts were tolerant of the type of relationship Ben and I had formed. I also ordered for both of us the steak dinner that was advertised for supper, and a bottle of whiskey. I finished my whiskey, placed a few coins on the bar, and grabbed the fresh bottle that Shirley set in front of me. We went and sat at a nearby table. I filled both glasses and sipped mine in silence. Ben drank his in one gulp and refilled his glass. He fidgeted in his chair, his eyes wandering around the room. Not once did he look at me. When our dinner arrived, it was certainly nothing to write home about. The steak was tough and overdone and the baked potato was almost raw, but we ate it anyway, our hunger overriding our distaste. When we finished our meals, I poured another whiskey for myself and Ben. He had refilled his glass three times during dinner. He sat back in his chair and looked me in the eye.

"I want to thank ya again, Jake, fer givin' me the chance to prove to ya that I'm innocent of killin' that ranger. Once I find Tom Sullivan, I'll be free an' clear."

"Don't ya mean once we find Bart Jensen, Ben?"

Ben stared at me a moment before replying.

"It's goin' to be hard enough to get close to Bart on my own, Jake, let alone if'n you're with me. He's not expectin' me to be in Silverton. Most likely he figgers I've already been strung up in Abilene. He'll immediately be suspicious when he sees me. Considerin' the circumstances under which he left, he's goin' to know that I didn' look him up just to be social. As fer you, he can smell the law a mile away, an' he'd run as soon as he saw ya."

I fought to quell my rising anger.

"Don't ya think I have a big stake in this as well, Ben? I left Abilene under orders to track ya down an' haul ya back fer a trial an' most likely a hangin'. Even though ya escaped from me, an' then kidnapped me, just bein' with ya, an' watchin' ya these past few weeks has convinced me that you're no cold-blooded killer."

I paused, my hands trembling.

"I've tried to show ya by my actions how much you've come to mean to me, Ben. But I guess sometimes words are needed. I don't know if this is a good time or not, seein's how a big part of this is still left undone, but I love ya very much, Ben Masters. An' dependin' upon how ya feel towards me, I want ya to be a part of my life from now on."

Tears welled up in the corners of Ben's eyes. My own eyes were suddenly moist.

"I feel the same way 'bout you, Jake," he said, his voice quavering, "but I was afraid to say anythin' to ya until I cleared my name. Besides, there's somethin' I haven't told ya."

My heart pounded in my chest as I waited for him to continue. When he didn't, I gently prodded him with a "Yes, Ben?"

He lowered his eyes to the table once more and spoke in a voice so low that I could barely hear him.

"I haven't had much luck in the love department, Jake. Every time I do fall in love with a man it ends badly."

Ben paused and downed his whiskey before continuing. I immediately poured him another.

"Fer more than five years, Bart Jensen an' I were together like you want us to be together. I loved him very much, even after he started turnin bad.'"

"What do ya mean, 'after he started turnin' bad'?"

Ben's voice was now barely above a whisper when he replied.

"Bart always had big dreams. He wanted to be a successful rancher an' own several hundred head of cattle an' large herds of horses. He wanted to be a respected man in Abilene, an' rub elbows with the cattle an' land barons. He was never happy with the meager livin' we eked out on our small ranch. Me, I was happy with a roof over my head, enough to eat, a good horse beneath me, an' Bart by my side. Bart made some bad investments, hopin' to git rich quick an' easy like. Before long, our money was runnin' pretty thin. An' when any money did come our way, Bart would spend it drinkin' an' gamblin'. He was also becomin' quarrelsome with ev'ryone 'round him, includin' me. He started blamin' ev'ryone else fer his problems. He said no one ever gave him a fair shake. He said I never supported any of his get-rich-quick schemes. Also, when he was drinkin', he'd throw a fit if'n another man even spoke to me. It was gittin' so's I'd spend all of my time at home while Bart was drinkin' an' gamblin' in the saloon.

"One night when he was gone, a group of men came to the house lookin' fer him. I'd never seen any of 'em before, an' I didn' recognize their names when they gave 'em to me. One did the talkin' fer the group. He told me they were backing Bart financially on some big land deal. I told him I didn' know where Bart was or when he'd be back. I knew trouble was brewin'. As soon as they rode off, I saddled my horse an' headed into town. I checked the saloon right off, but Bart wasn't there. The men who had stopped by the ranch were, however. The one I'd spoken to at the house cornered me and identified himself and the other men with him as Texas Rangers. He told me that if'n I knew what was good fer me, I'd tell him Bart's whereabouts. He told me it would go easier on Bart if'n he turned himself in. I told him I had no idea what he was talkin' 'bout. We were still talkin' when Bart came into the saloon. He was drunker than a skunk, an' immediately became completely enraged when he found me talkin' to the ranger. Before I had a chance to explain to him what was goin' on, or warn Bart who the man was, Bart punched the ranger in the mouth, knockin' him down. I stepped between them, but Bart shoved me roughly aside as the ranger got to his feet, jumped Bart an' wrestled him to the floor. I scuffled back to their tangled bodies and was tryin' to pull the ranger off Bart when Bart drew his Colt an' shot him. We both leapt up in shock as the gun fell to the floor between us, then Bart pushed me an' ran out of the saloon. A second ranger went to the first ranger's side, turned him over, an' shouted that he was dead.

"Everyone in the saloon was suddenly millin' 'bout me. Someone shouted that I'd shot the ranger. I panicked an' ran.

When I got back to our ranch, Bart was there, packin' some of his belongin's. I told him 'bout the rangers comin' to the house lookin' fer him earlier in the evenin'. He said it was best that he left. He'd head to Silverton an' lay low for a few months. He asked me to go with him. When I told him that they were blamin' me fer killin' the ranger, I saw no concern fer me in his eyes, just relief fer himself. He said that I was a well-respected man in Abilene, an' that no one would believe that I had killed the ranger. I'd be just fine if'n I stayed in Abilene until I had cleared my name, he claimed. Then I could join him in Silverton an' we'd start a new life. When I realized that Bart was willin' to let me take the blame fer the shootin', leavin' him free an' clear, the last bit of feelin' I had fer him died. As he was headin' toward the door, I grabbed his arm an' told him that he couldn't leave me to be blamed fer the shootin'. He must have hit me with somethin' because that's the last thing I remember until I woke up a short time later. When I ran to the barn, Bart's horse was gone. I knew that the other rangers were probably already on their way to the ranch, lookin' fer me or Bart, or both of us. I packed a few things an' high-tailed it out of there myself. I set out for Silverton to find Bart, knowing that only he could clear my name. That's where you came in."

When Ben finished speaking, he downed his whiskey and finally looked me in the eye. I downed mine in one gulp and refilled both glasses.

"When I talked to the rangers 'bout the shootin', Ben, they were convinced you had done it. Apparently no one saw Bart draw his gun. They did confirm Bart had started the fight. They also told me they had spoken to several folks in the saloon who were familiar with the relationship that you an' Bart had. I've known 'bout it all along. That's another reason why I didn' confess my feelin's fer ya. I wasn't sure how ya felt 'bout Bart."

"I feel nothin' fer him now. Like I told ya, he knocked me out an' left me high an' dry in Abilene. The only reason I'm lookin'

fer him is so's I can clear my name. I have no interest in resumin'
a relationship with him."

I gave an involuntary sigh of relief at Ben's last statement. Ben
smiled at me, grabbed my hand, and reassuringly squeezed it.

"You've been sayin' all along, Ben, that once ya find Bart
you'll be cleared of the killin'. Just how are ya plannin' fer that
to happen? I don't know Bart at all, but from what little you've
told me, he sounds like he's a very uncarin' an' dangerous feller.
I can't imagine him willingly confessin' to the shootin' an' placin'
himself next in line fer a hangin'. An' you're the only witness that
can testify that Bart pulled the trigger. Also, as fer him imper-
sonatin' Tom Sullivan, it would just be yer word against his."

Ben downed his whiskey before replying.

"Believe me, Jake, I don't think fer a moment that Bart will
confess to the murder just to clear my name. At one time he did
love me, but I think that ended a few years back, when his jeal-
ousy took over completely an' he no longer trusted me. An' even
if'n he did still have feelin's fer me, Bart's not the type of man to
sacrifice himself unnecessarily. That was made evident the night
he left Abilene. He cares 'bout himself too much to do that. I
had a vague plan when I left Abilene of forcin' Bart at gunpoint
back there with me to confess to the killin'. I'd have to git the
drop on him first though, or overpower him in some other way,
because he's a lightnin' draw an' has 'bout fifty pounds on me. I'd
have to keep him tied fer the length of the journey, also."

Fifty pounds, I thought to myself. And Ben was not a small
man.

"Once I've made Bart my pris'ner, I'll bring him back here
an' then we can escort him back to Abilene. He's a slippery fella,
an' havin' you by my side will improve our chances of gittin' him
safely back there."

"I can't abide by that, Ben. I want to ride to the Stewart ranch
with ya. As I've said, I have a big stake in this. If'n Bart's as con-
niving as ya say he is, then two of us goin' is better than one. We

can force him to confess as soon as we bring him back here an' present him to the sheriff in this town. That way, we can just let him escort Bart back to Abilene. As far as I'm concerned, the sooner Bart Jensen is out of our lives, the better."

Ben mulled this over in his mind for a moment, his indecision plain on his face.

"I guess you're right. At this point ya do have a big stake in this, an' it makes sense to git Bart out of our lives as quickly as we can."

"Then it's settled. Let's go purchase some supplies, an' see if'n we can hire horses fer the ride to the Stewart ranch."

We left the saloon and walked down the street until we found a dry goods store. Using the money Stephen had given us, we each bought a hat, some rolling tobacco, and extra ammunition for our Spencers and Colts. I added a bottle of whiskey to our purchases.

"We'll hold off on purchasin' any foodstuffs, Ben, until we've turned Bart over to the sheriff an' leave this town fer good."

We carried our purchases back to the saloon and deposited them in our respective rooms on the second floor. An old man had replaced Shirley behind the bar. I asked him for directions to the livery stable. Once there, Ben chose a large chestnut gelding, and I chose a dark-brown one. We also hired saddles and trappings. We told the liveryman we'd be back to get the horses in the morning.

When Ben and I returned to the saloon, I asked the old man behind the bar to bring a bath to each of our rooms. I also ordered another bottle of whiskey.

"I'll have my two boys haul up the tubs an' start fillin' 'em, gents," he replied. "I'll give ya a holler when they're ready."

He yelled two boy's names as he disappeared into the room behind the bar. Ben and I sat at a table and had several more glasses of whiskey while we waited for our baths. We didn't speak. When the old man called that our baths were ready, we climbed the wooden stairs to our rooms. Mine was the first one on the right; Ben's was across the hall and down one. I paused at the door to my room and turned toward Ben. He stopped and faced me. We stared into each other's eyes for several moments.

"Would ya stay with me tonight?" I asked, my voice overflowing with emotion.

"I'd like that, Jake. Right now, though, I want to be by myself fer a bit. I'm goin' to take a nice long bath. I'll join ya in a little while."

He stepped to me, put his arms around me, and kissed me deeply. When he finally pushed away, he whispered "I love you" and crossed the hall to his room. I watched as he opened the door and stepped inside.

I entered my room and quickly undressed. Grabbing the bottle of whiskey, I stepped into the tub and slowly sank beneath the scalding-hot water. I felt like getting good and drunk. I soaked in the tub until the water was cold and my skin had turned to gooseflesh. I'd managed to almost finish off the bottle of whiskey and was definitely feeling its effects. I got out of the tub and slowly dried off. I sat on the bed and was taking the last pull from the bottle when there was a soft knock on my door.

"Come in."

The door opened and Ben slipped into the room. He was wearing just a towel tied snugly around his waist. His thick cock was clearly outlined beneath it. Stopping a few feet from the end of the bed, Ben simply stood there, staring at me. Reaching down slowly he undid the towel and let it fall to the floor.

I simply sat on the bed, taking in the sight of Ben's naked body as if this was the first time I'd seen it. Maybe, I thought to myself, because of our newly expressed feelings for each other it could be considered the first time. Ben stepped to the end of the bed. His eyes were filled with lust as his gaze traveled over my body. I held his eyes with my own for a moment, then let my gaze wander over his body, from his whiskered cheeks and throat to his well-muscled chest and the swells of his tits. His nipples were hard, poking through the forest of reddish-brown hair that surrounded them. I continued down to his hairy stomach and, from there, to the v that tapered to his crotch. His dick hung limply over his heavy ball sac, the head still wrapped in the foreskin. Inside the sac his right nut hung lower than the left.

Ben began strumming his right nipple with his fingers. He then trailed them lightly over his chest and stomach, before gliding back up to his tit. With his left hand he began working his left nipple as well. His eyes were tightly shut, his head tilted slightly back. His hawg swelled and grew, the head sliding free of its protective skin. I shifted slightly on the bed to face him. The bed creaked loudly. Ben opened his eyes, grabbed his stiffer, and started stroking it.

I began running my hands over my chest and stomach, delighting in the feel of the thick hair growing there. I circled back up to my nipples, twisting and pulling them until small cries escaped from between my lips. My cock had quickly filled with blood and was standing at attention. Ben continued to stroke his dick while he watched me play with my tits. He grabbed his nut pouch with his left hand and repeatedly squeezed the twin globes encased there. I watched his hand glide back and forth on his pole, sliding the skin back over the large knob on each stroke. With his left hand, he alternated between squeezing his balls and twisting his nipples.

I swung my legs onto the bed and lay back against the pillow. Spreading my legs wide, I wet two of my fingers and started probing the hair-covered region below my ball sac. I lifted my legs slightly so Ben could see where my fingers were headed. He watched me intently. When I reached the tiny opening I pushed against it until both fingers slipped inside my channel. I held Ben's gaze as I pulled my fingers out of my asshole, stuck them in my mouth, sucked on them fiercely, then plunged them back in my ass. Ben grunted his appreciation and increased the speed of his strokes.

Ben's nipples were soon red and puffy from the treatment he'd been giving them. He stuck two fingers in his mouth, turned around and bent over, giving me a full view of his hairy ass. Spreading his ass cheeks apart with his left hand, he pushed against his brown spot with the same two fingers. The puckered opening relaxed, and both digits slipped inside his shit hole. My arousal increased tenfold, and I quickly reached the point of explosion. Hearing that my grunts and groans had reached a fever pitch, Ben pulled his fingers out of his hole, swung back around, and resumed pumping his hawg.

My balls rolled up tight against the base of my cock. I heaved on the bed, shouting Ben's name as the first white glob flew from the slit in the head of my dick. I held my hand under the fat knob and caught the heavy flow. When I'd wrung the last drop from the swollen pisshole, I brought my hand to my mouth. Making sure that Ben was watching me, I opened my mouth, tilted my hand, and let the substantial pile slide in. As I swallowed audibly Ben's hand moved still faster on his pole.

On Ben's next stroke, he gritted his teeth and cupped his hand below his cock head as I had done to mine. His body bucked and jerked as his hand filled with his thick cream. When he was spent, he licked the huge puddle from his hand, then licked his lips. He eyed me intently as he walked around to the side of the bed, climbed onto it, and sprawled on top of me. Seeking my lips with his own, he kissed me several times. I eagerly returned his kisses. Sliding his tongue between my lips, he probed the inside of my mouth. I could taste his spunk on his tongue.

Ben twirled his tongue around mine a final time, then withdrew it and began covering my face with kisses. He kissed me once more on the mouth, then began licking my throat. The feel of his tongue on the stubbled skin there sent chills up and down my spine. From there he tongued a path through my chest hair to my right tit. Ben took the tender nipple in his mouth and bit down on it until I cried out. He immediately released the tiny nub and bathed it with his tongue. Moving to my left nipple, he bit and tongued it as well. Reaching behind him, I grabbed the cheeks of his ass and roughly kneaded them. Ben released my left nipple and began swabbing the hairs on my stomach. He stopped briefly to flick his tongue in and out of my navel several times, then continued down to my crotch. Once there, he bathed my crotch hair with his tongue, then licked my cock from crown to base before working my balls. He licked and sucked each one, then tongued the areas where my legs joined my crotch. Returning to my sac, he licked beneath it as far as he could toward my back door. Never quite reaching it, he tongued the inside of each thigh, then both legs. When he had finished, he was squatting at my feet at the end of the bed. He ran his tongue between each toe, then sucked them into his mouth one by one and nibbled on them until I was moaning uncontrollably.

Sliding off the foot of the bed, Ben grabbed me by my ankles and turned me onto my stomach as easily as if he was flipping flapjacks. As he licked the bottoms of my feet, I fought hard to control my laughter. He then tongued his way back up each leg, over my ass cheeks, and over my entire back, ending up at the back of my neck. He then frog-leaped back down to my ass. Spreading the cheeks apart, Ben licked along the hairy crack, gliding right around the tiny, puckered opening. He also worked on the sensitive area where the crack ended and my ball sac began. When he moved back up to my bunghole, he stuck the tip of his tongue into it as far as he could and held it there. Ben then pulled his tongue out of my asshole and replaced it with the head of his dick. He pushed hard just once and the knob slipped through, and his shaft slid deep into my channel. He began plowing into me fiercely and steadily, obviously intent this time only on satisfying his own animal lust. I rose up on my hands and knees to give him greater leverage for his thrusts. His hawg was hot and thick inside my corn hole. The noise his balls made as they slapped against my ass and our individual grunts and moans filled the room. On Ben's next plunge, he wrapped his arms around my midsection and rested his weight full upon my back as he continued to drive into me. We were coupling like two dogs in the street. Ben thrust into me twice more, then cried out as his eruption began. His seed flooded my hole. When he was spent, I collapsed onto the bed with him still on top of me. He stayed inside me until his dick grew soft, then pulled out, the head making a small sucking noise as my asshole released it.

Ben rolled off me and lay beside me. I turned onto my side to face him. He got up and went to the wooden bucket in the corner. I watched his stream of bright-yellow piss as it flowed into the bucket. Ben's pissing triggered my own need, and when he returned to the bed I got up and relieved myself. When I lay back down beside him, he placed his hand on my right cheek and slowly ran his fingers across it. He slid closer, his whiskey breath hitting me in the face, his lips seeking mine. He kissed me long and deep, then climbed on top of me again. I wrapped my arms around him, and we soon drifted off to sleep.

When I woke, the room was in near darkness, the oil lamps having used up most of their fuel. Ben was now lying next to me, his face at my crotch. He was slowly sawing up and down on my stiffer. When he realized I was awake, he rolled onto me, his bag of balls landing heavily on my nose. I opened wide and his cock slid down my throat. I could taste his spunk as well as my asshole on the thick shaft. Ben began plunging his dick into my mouth as he resumed his bobbing on my hawg. I gripped his ass cheeks to control his thrusts, lest he choke me with his massive hawg. After several plunges I withdrew my right hand, wet a finger, and slid it into his back door; Ben did the same to mine. His mouth was hot and wet as it slid up and down on my pole. His finger plunged steadily in and out of my chute. Before long I was ready to blow.

I moaned as the first drop shot from my stiffer, the moan muffled by Ben's pole. Ben swallowed all of my seed, released my cock, propped himself up on his hands, and started rapidly thrusting into my mouth. He hollered my name when the first blast of his spunk shot forth, hitting the back of my throat. I quickly swallowed his cream, trying not to gag on the heavy flow. When he was done shooting, Ben swung around so that we were face to face once more. He kissed me long and hard and then, cradling me in his beefy, hairy arms, we drifted off once more.

When I woke up the second time, sunlight was streaming through the curtains at the window next to my bed. Ben was gone. I suddenly had a bad feeling and, dressing quickly, I went across the hall to his room. I knocked on the door but there was no answer. I opened it and stepped inside. The room was empty. A piece of paper was laying on the pillow. I walked to the bed and snatched it up, filled with an uncertain dread. It was a note from Ben.

CHAPTER TWELVE

I quickly read Ben's message.

Dear Jake,

I'm sorry for going after Bart on my own, after we agreed last night to go together. I feel that my chances of capturing him will be better if you're not with me. I've come such a long way, and I don't want to mess things up now. By the time you read this note I will be at the Stewart ranch. And with a little bit of luck I will have found Bart and forced him, either at gunpoint or hog-tied and placed behind my saddle, to return to Silverton with me. I'll be back with him as soon as I can, Jake, and we'll be able to start our life together. Please don't try to follow me.

Love,
Ben

I folded the note and shoved it in my shirt pocket. I ran to my room, grabbed my gear, and took the stairs to the saloon two at a time. Shirley was busy serving breakfast to a couple of men at one of the tables. I waited impatiently at the bar and, when she returned, I asked her if she'd seen Ben leave early this morning. She hadn't. I asked her for directions to the Stewart ranch a second time. When she'd given them to me, I thanked her and ran from the saloon and down the street to the livery. I asked the liveryman if Ben had been in to get his horse, and he informed me that Ben had been there well over two hours ago. Damn, I thought to myself. He had a big head start on me. I quickly saddled the gelding and rode out of town.

I gave my horse his head, and we fairly flew down the dusty road. I knew immediately that he was a runner, and I knew I'd make good time to the ranch. When I came to the first fork in the road Shirley had told me of, I bore left. After riding for several miles, I came to a small bridge that spanned a sluggish, muddy stream. I galloped across it without slowing, rounded a bend in the road, and came to the second fork. I rode to the right this time, and within a few miles I came to a large, open gate. It was flanked on both sides by rough-hewn posts at least ten feet high. An identical post was laid across the tops of these two, forming a giant doorway in the middle of the road. Hanging from the top post was a hand-carved sign that read STEWART. Shirley had said that once I reached the gate it was only a short ride until I reached the Stewart's main house, and before long a house became visible in the distance. As I rode up to it, several barking dogs swarmed around me. An old man was sitting on the front porch in a weathered rocking chair. He eyed me suspiciously, but gave no greeting. I dismounted and tipped my hat to him.

"Mornin', mister. My name's Jake Slater. I'm lookin' fer John Stewart."

The man stared at me blankly and made no reply.

"Who ya lookin' fer, mister?"

I turned around and found myself facing a young man, ruggedly built.

"Don't mind ol' pappy there," the man said. "He ain't spoken since a bull kicked him in the head three months ago. He's old John Stewart, an' I'm his son, young John."

John offered his hand and I clasped it in mine. His grip was strong and firm, his hand callused from hard work. His eyes were sky blue, his cheeks and throat covered in blond stubble. A large tuft of blond hair burst above the top button of his dark-blue homespun shirt. His cheeks, as well as his lips, were chapped from the wind and sun. His broad shoulders and wide, brawny chest were clearly outlined beneath his shirt. His denims were worn and hugged his thick thighs and legs. The bulge at his crotch was considerable. His boots were scuffed and covered in dust.

"Pleased to meet ya, John. My name's Jake Slater. I'm lookin' fer a feller by the name of Ben Masters. He rode out to yer ranch early this mornin', lookin' fer a friend of his that's workin' here." I quickly described Ben to him.

John looked me over from head to toe before replying. I didn't miss when his gaze lingered at my crotch.

"Well, a fella that looked just like that an' was askin' fer Tom Sullivan did ride this way a few hours ago. I told him the same thing I'll tell you. Tom is stayin' up at the line cabin fer a few days with one of the other hands, roundin' up some strays. I can ride up there with ya if'n you'd like."

"Actually, I'd prefer to go alone. I'd be much obliged, however, if you'd give me directions to the cabin."

"Suit yerself."

I listened carefully as John gave me directions. I repeated them back to him, because I couldn't afford to get lost when this hand was so close to being played out. I thanked him, swung up onto the gelding, turned it around, and was just ready to put heels to it when John hollered for me to hold up.

"I just remembered somethin'. You're the second fella this mornin' that was lookin' fer Ben. Shortly after he went on to the cabin, another stranger rode up to the house. Said he was a friend of Ben's from Abilene. Said his name was Smith. Joseph Smith."

A cold hand seemed to grip my heart. Ben had never mentioned that name to me during the time I'd known him. Why would a friend of Ben's from Abilene be looking for him in Silverton. Was it another ranger, also sent out to bring Ben to justice? I knew I had to find Ben fast. I thanked John again and rode off in the direction he'd indicated. My heart was now hammering in my chest, and my stomach was twisted up in knots. My lawman's intuition told me something bad was brewing. Something real bad. What if this stranger got to Ben before I did? If it was another Texas Ranger, would he shoot Ben on sight, or haul him back to Abilene for hanging?

I soon spotted the stand of pine trees at which I was to head north. After a few more miles, I reached the rugged, rock-strewn hills that signaled the final approach to the cabin. When I'd crested the largest of these hills, I halted. About a hundred feet from the bottom of the hill stood the cabin. Smoke curled lazily from its chimney into the still morning air. Two horses stood in a corral to the right. There was no movement outside the cabin and, from the little I could see of its interior through the front windows, no movement inside either. I scanned the area once more, then decided upon a course of action: I'd circle north around the cabin and come in behind it.

My plan quickly proved to be a bad one. After riding only a short distance, I came to a deep, impassable ravine. I was forced to ride around it for several miles before I found a spot that I could traverse. By the time I arrived at the back of the cabin, a good hour had to have passed. There were still only the two horses in the corral, and no movement that I could see outside or within the building. There were no windows on this side, which allowed me to boldly ride right up to the rear of it. I dismounted and crept around to the front. Both front windows were open. I crouched below the nearest one. Noises were coming from within, but it wasn't conversation. Emboldened by my urgent need to find Ben, I raised my head and looked inside.

What I saw made my heart ache, but it also filled me with a cold rage. A large fieldstone fireplace took up the entire back wall of the cabin. A rough-hewn table stood in the center. A bed was against the wall to the left of the table. On the bed was Ben, on his hands and knees, facing me. He was naked and being plowed from behind by a hairy, well-built man.

Had Ben tricked me all along, using me to lead him safely back to his lover, Bart Jensen?

Feeling like a complete fool, I stood up, drew my Colts, stepped quickly to the front door and kicked it in. Surprised looks appeared on the faces of Ben and the handsome stranger. The stranger immediately pulled out of Ben and made a heroic dash for the Colt that was laying on the table. Ben simply stared at me, his mouth agape. I covered the stranger with both pistols. My rage was a fire within me, and I fought the urge to kill the man on the spot, without waiting for an explanation.

"Don't try it, Bart," I growled. "I'll kill ya right where ya stand."

The man paused in midstride, a puzzled look on his face. He started to speak, but I cut him short.

"Get back on the bed, an' don't make no sudden moves neither."

The man moved to the bed and sat on the edge of it. Ben found his voice at last.

"Jake, wait a minute, please don't shoot. Jake, listen to me. This man isn't Bart Jensen. Bart's not here. He's out ridin' the line. I'm waitin' fer him to return."

I looked at Ben, uncertain whether I should believe him or not.

"Shut up," I growled.

"I'm tellin' ya the truth, Jake. I meant what I told ya 'bout Bart an' me back in Silverton. I would never be with him like this again."

I eyed Ben silently then holstered my guns.

"What's yer name, fella."

He stared at me for a moment, the fear still plain on his face.

"Douglas, mister. Douglas Harris. I work fer young John Stewart. Tom Sullivan an' I have been up here fer the past few days roundin' up strays. As I told Ben, I've never heard of this Bart Jensen fella. Tom's out huntin' right now, but he should be back soon."

"He is back," said a deep, gravelly voice, full of anger.

I whirled to my left, reaching again for my Colts as I did so. But I paused midway when I saw that I was already covered by a tall, rugged man standing in the doorway of the cabin. He held a Colt in each hand: one pointed at me, the other at Ben and Douglas. He was dressed all in black, his clothes dusty and rumpled. His eyes were a dark blue, his hair as black as night. The beginnings of a beard and mustache covered his cheeks, chin and throat. Although sinister-looking, he was also very pleasing to the eye.

"Bart!" Ben cried.

So, I thought to myself, after all this time and all these miles, this is the infamous Bart Jensen.

"Drop yer guns on the floor, lawman. An' no tricks neither, or I'll put a bullet in ya. I already killed one lawman down in Abilene an' I'm not afraid to kill another."

Ben had been right. Bart had immediately recognized me as the law. I hesitated for a moment, then slid my Colts from their holsters and dropped them on the floor. Bart turned his attention to Ben and Douglas.

"Howdy, Ben. You're lookin' good. Fancy findin' you here. I see you've sampled Douglas's many charms. Still runnin' 'round on me after all this time, eh?"

"The day ya rode out of Abilene, Bart, an' left me to take the blame fer you shootin' the ranger was the day our relationship ended. But even when we was together, Bart, I never even looked at another man."

"You're a goddamned liar, Ben."

Before any of us realized Bart's intention, he shot Douglas in the chest. Douglas fell off the bed and onto the floor with a loud thud. As Bart swung the muzzle of his pistol toward Ben, I grabbed one of my Colts from the floor and shot Bart twice. He pulled the trigger on one of his pistols on reflex, and I saw Ben fall back onto the bed. Bart then turned to me, an incredu-

lous look on his face, and I shot him once more. He dropped
his guns and crumpled to the floor. All of this happened in the
space of a few seconds. I went to Ben, fearing the worst. He
was laying on his back, blood staining the bed. Upon examining
him, I was relieved to see that the bullet had only creased his
arm. There was a lot of blood, but the wound wasn't fatal. Ben
opened his eyes.

"Are ya okay, Jake?"

"I'm fine."

"What about Douglas? Is he dead?"

I got up from the bed and knelt by the naked man on the
floor. The bullet had taken Douglas directly in the heart. His
sightless eyes pointed toward the ceiling. I closed them and
walked over to Bart. I could tell at a glance that Ben's ex-lover
was dead as well. I returned to the bed and sat beside Ben.

"Yes, Ben, I'm afraid Douglas is dead. Bart is also. I'm sorry, I
had no choice but to shoot him. He was goin' to kill ya."

Ben was silent for a moment, then struggled to sit up, wincing from the wound in his arm as he did so. He looked down at
Douglas and then over at Bart.

"Thanks, Jake, fer savin' my life. It's quite clear that Bart
intended to kill me. But now that he's dead, there's no one to
prove that I didn' shoot the ranger."

"Didn' ya hear Bart say that he'd already killed a lawman
in Abilene, an' wouldn't hesitate to shoot me? No one back in
Abilene knows that you an' I are together now, Ben. If'n I tell
the law back there that Bart confessed to the killin', who's not
goin' to believe me?"

Ben looked up into my face, renewed hope showing on his
own. I eased him back on the bed, tore a section of the sheet
from it, and wrapped it around Ben's arm to stanch the flow of
blood.

"We need to git ya dressed, Ben, an' take ya back to Silverton
so's a proper doc can look at yer arm."

I helped Ben with his pants and shirt, mindful of his injured arm, and eased him up off the bed onto his feet. I was just tugging on his boots when a cold, hard voice spoke from behind me for the second time that day.

"Well look at this, will ya. It's Jake Slater an' his pris'ner, Ben Masters. I've been waitin' fer you boys fer quite a while now."

I stood up and turned around, and my heart froze in my chest. Sheriff Rawlins was standing in the doorway of the cabin, a pistol in each hand. They were pointed at Ben and me. Rawlins's hatred was plain to read on his face. I felt Ben's body stiffen against me.

"Now move away from him, nice an' easy like, Slater."

I stepped away from Ben. Rawlins's cold, hard eyes followed me.

"I warned ya, Slater, if'n ya didn' untie me in that cell I'd git even with ya. My deputy was not the first one to find me. The circuit judge happened to ride into town shortly after you left. Of course, my office was the first place he stopped. An' ya know what he found. When word got 'round 'bout what had happened to me, I quickly became the laughin' stock of the whole town. It got so's I couldn't show my face in public, so I left one night without tellin' anyone. I've been in Silverton fer several weeks now, waitin' fer either one of ya to show up. I saw ya come in on the stage, but I needed to wait until a more private reunion could be arranged. I saw Ben ride out this mornin', an' followed him. I was pretty sure, Slater, that you'd eventually show up. An' ya didn' disappoint me. After I'm done with ya, Slater, I'm takin' Ben back to Abilene fer hangin'."

"Ya can't do that, Rawlins," I cried. "Ben is innocent. Bart Jensen is the one that done the shootin'. He confessed to it right before I was forced to kill him."

"I know, Slater. I was outside an' heard the whole conversation. But Bart's dead, an' you will be shortly. That will only leave Ben, an' who's goin' to take his word fer it?"

I felt the bullet tear into my right side almost at the same time that I heard the shot. A curious warmth spread through my side, and a sudden wave of dizziness coursed through my body. I heard Ben yell, and then heard another shot. Both sounded far away. The same warmth was suddenly in my left side as well. I felt myself slowly falling to the floor. My brain warned my body to brace itself for the impact, but when I landed I didn't feel a thing. From where I lay, I could see Sheriff Rawlins standing next to Ben. He had a hold of Ben's arm, and the muzzle of his Colt was pressed to Ben's head. They walked over and stood looking down at me. Ben was crying.

"I swore I'd git even with ya, Slater. As ya slowly die, think of Ben on his way to Abilene to be hanged. An' don't think I won't partake of his ample bounty repeatedly before we get there, either."

He laughed, and the last thing I saw was him pushing Ben out the cabin door.

· · ·

I heard voices around me, but I didn't know whose they were nor could I make out any words. I tried to open my eyes, but for some reason I couldn't. My whole body was one big ache. I felt a hot liquid pass through my lips and burn its way down my stomach. Then silence descended upon me once more.

When next I heard voices, I was able to open my eyes. The ache in my body had dulled somewhat. I looked around, not recognizing my surroundings. I was definitely no longer in the cabin. I was in a bedroom, laying on a huge four-poster bed, propped up on numerous large, soft pillows. Tall windows on three sides of me let in late-morning sunshine. A chair stood in the corner to my immediate right, my clothes neatly folded upon it. When I turned my head to the left I saw an old man and an old woman. They were turned sideways to me, talking in hushed tones. On a table next to the bed was a tray with a teapot, a cup, and a bowl on it.

I tried to call out to the pair, but was only able to make a hoarse croaking noise. It got their attention, though.

"Doc Thompson, he's awake," the woman said.

The two of them came instantly to my bedside.

"How are ya feelin', Mr. Slater? Fer awhile there we thought we was gonna lose ya."

I tried to speak, but was unable to form the words. How had this stranger known my name, I thought to myself.

"Go git John," the man ordered the woman.

She turned and hurriedly left the room. Go get John, he'd said. John who? Where was I? I must have drifted off, because the next time I opened my eyes the room was empty. I tried to recall what had happened, and it came back to me little by little. Sheriff Rawlins had shown up at the line cabin. He'd shot me twice, and left for Abilene with Ben. Remembering proved too much for me, though, and I drifted off again.

When I woke again, young John Stewart was sitting in a chair beside my bed. He smiled at me when he saw my eyes were open.

"Hello, Jake. Do ya know where ya are?"

I at last found my voice. "You're young John Stewart," I murmured, "so I must be at yer ranch."

"That's right, Jake. I got worried when I saw that stranger and the man you were lookin' for coming ridin' back through without ya, so I rode up to the cabin and found Douglas dead and you near death. So I brought ya back here and you've been in an' out of consciousness since then. Doc said both bullets passed clean through ya, but we still wasn't sure if'n ya was goin' to live."

"Where's Ben? I've got to find Ben," I cried, weakly.

I struggled to sit up, but waves of dizziness and nausea swept over me. John pushed me gently back against the pillows.

"Ya need to rest an' git yer strength back, Jake, before ya go lookin' fer Ben."

I tried to reply, but a heavy tiredness suddenly overcame me. I closed my eyes once more.

As the days passed I came to more and more frequently, and for longer periods of time. I knew days were passing by the three meals that were brought to me daily. These consisted mainly of breads and soups. At first the woman, whose name I soon learned was Millie, brought the meals, but then John started bringing a few, and soon replaced Millie altogether. Doc Thompson made frequent visits as well. He was impressed with my recovery and proclaimed I'd be back to my old self in a few more days. I discovered that my sides were both heavily bandaged where Rawlins had shot me. These bandages were changed daily, at first by Millie, and then John. When John brought my meals, he'd make small talk about the ranch. I soon found myself looking forward to his visits.

One morning, I had just woken up and was thinking about Ben when John entered the room with my breakfast.

"The doc says ya should be able to eat somethin' more solid, so I had Millie make ya bacon, eggs, and biscuits."

He set the tray down on the bed, and I sat up somewhat stiffly and made short work of the breakfast. As usual, John talked about the ranch while I ate. When I'd finished eating, he quietly asked what had happened up at the cabin. I'd been dreading this question for days. I settled back and told John the whole story, right from the beginning. For some reason I knew it was okay to tell him about Ben and me. He asked a few questions, but wasn't too surprised by my tale.

"Well, Jake, we'll git ya better as soon as possible so's ya can find Ben an' git on with yer life. Now, let's git those bandages changed."

He took the tray off the bed and set it on the table. He pulled back my covers and was greeted by my morning stiffer. He stared at it for a moment, then quickly cut off the old bandages and expertly replaced them with new ones. When he was done, he stood looking down at me. My cock was still fully hard.

"I can take care of that fer ya too, Jake, if'n you'd like."

"That would be right kind of ya, John."

He went to the door and locked it, then climbed onto the bed and grabbed my dick. His hand was rough, yet warm. He ran his thumb through the slit in the fat head, gathering up my clear fluid, and sucked it from his thumb. He then bent over my hawg. When I felt his hot breath on the crown, I almost blew my load. John swirled his tongue over the knob, then ran the tip of it through the piss slit once more, gathering up the fresh fluid bubbling there. He engulfed the head, sucked on it briefly, then released it and licked down the thick shaft to my ball sac. He tongued the entire sac, then took both of my nuts in his mouth and sucked on them gently.

I moaned and squirmed on the bed, wincing at the slight ache in my sides. John trailed his tongue back up the shaft, sucked briefly on the head of my dick again, then slowly sank down on my pole. His mouth was hot and wet. He began sawing up and down on my tool slowly, so as not to hurt my sides. At the same time he squeezed my bag of balls in his left hand. All too soon my eruption began. John must have known it was approaching when my balls pulled out of his grasp and rolled up tight to the base of my cock. He immediately sawed up to the crown and held it in his mouth. I cried out as the first drop of my spunk spurted into his mouth. More blobs followed, and he swallowed every one of them. When I was spent, he released the head of my stiffer and licked my entire dick clean. When he was finished, he kissed me on the mouth, then stood up and grabbed the tray from the table. He paused at the door and turned to face me, a smile playing about the corners of his mouth.

"I'll be back with yer lunch in a few hours. If'n yer, uh, problem reoccurs, I can take care of it again fer ya."

"I'm sure it will, John, an' I'd be much obliged."

He smiled, unlocked the door, and closed it behind him.

I settled back against the pillows, my thoughts immediately turning to Ben. It had been over a week since the shooting in the cabin. What was happening with Ben and Sheriff Rawlins? They wouldn't reach Abilene for at least a month, even if they were riding hard. However, they could have taken the train. That would cut off about two weeks' worth of traveling. But based on what Rawlins had said about bedding Ben along the way, I was betting Rawlins would be riding in order to draw out Ben's misery. Was Ben even still alive? I had to believe that he was, and that somehow he'd gotten away from Rawlins and was making his way back to me right now. I was filled with a new determination to heal quickly and leave the Stewart ranch in search of Ben. I wouldn't rest until I was reunited with the man I loved.

THE ADVENTURES OF JAKE AND BEN

WILL CONTINUE